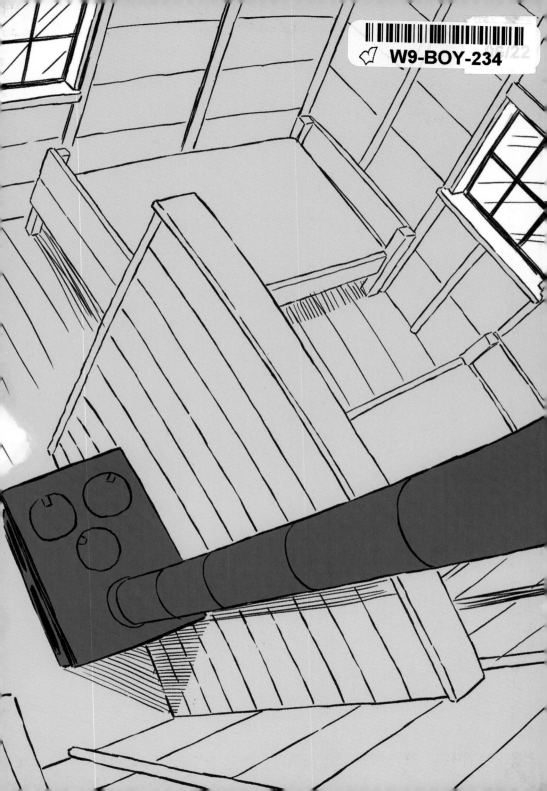

STEALING
HOME

J. Torres
David Namisato

Kids Can Press

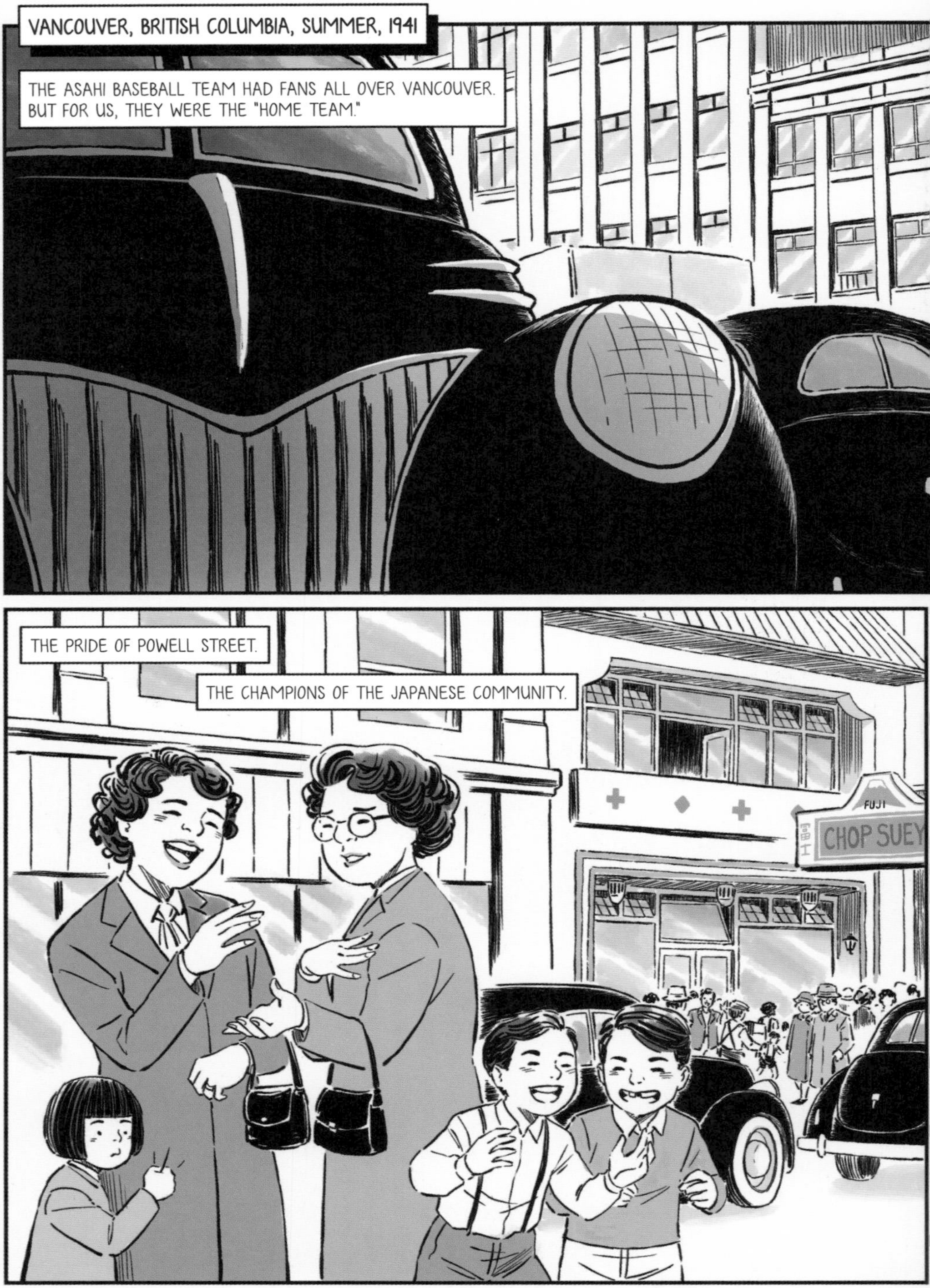
VANCOUVER, BRITISH COLUMBIA, SUMMER, 1941
THE ASAHI BASEBALL TEAM HAD FANS ALL OVER VANCOUVER. BUT FOR US, THEY WERE THE "HOME TEAM."
THE PRIDE OF POWELL STREET.
THE CHAMPIONS OF THE JAPANESE COMMUNITY.
FUJI
富士
CHOP SUEY

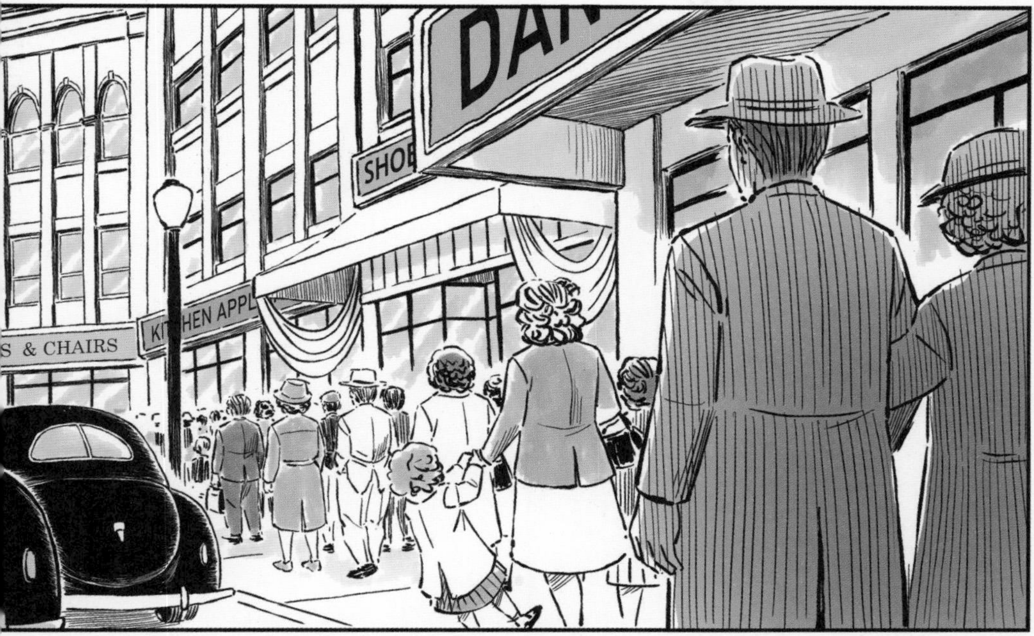
DAN
SHOE
KITCHEN APPL
S & CHAIRS

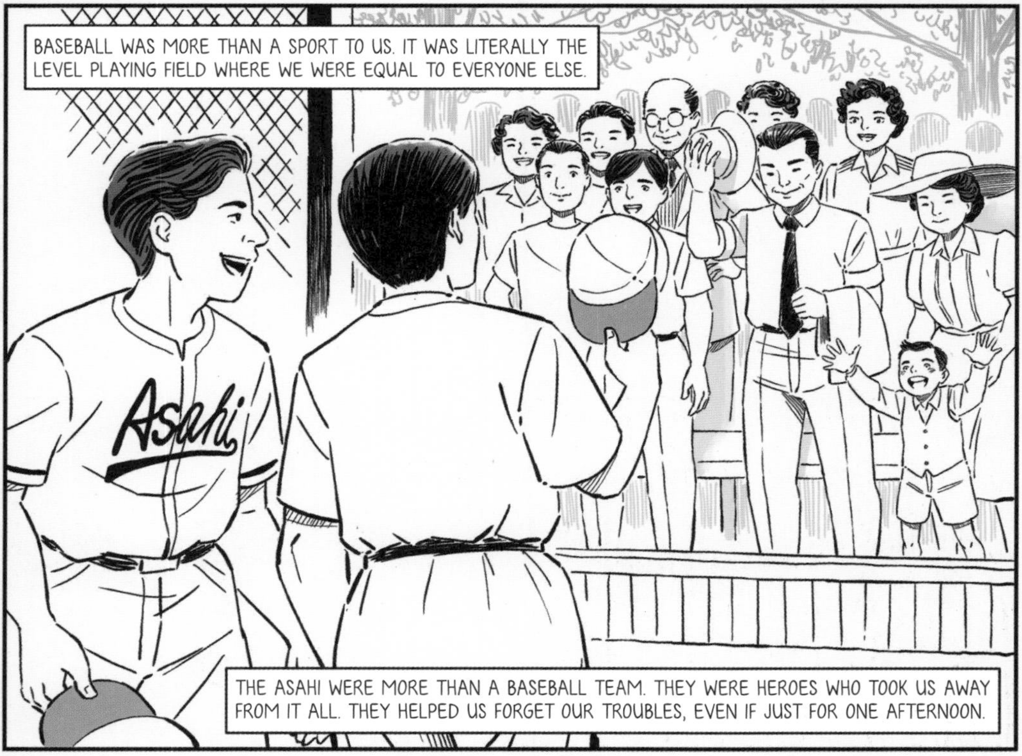
BASEBALL WAS MORE THAN A SPORT TO US. IT WAS LITERALLY THE LEVEL PLAYING FIELD WHERE WE WERE EQUAL TO EVERYONE ELSE.
Asahi
THE ASAHI WERE MORE THAN A BASEBALL TEAM. THEY WERE HEROES WHO TOOK US AWAY FROM IT ALL. THEY HELPED US FORGET OUR TROUBLES, EVEN IF JUST FOR ONE AFTERNOON.

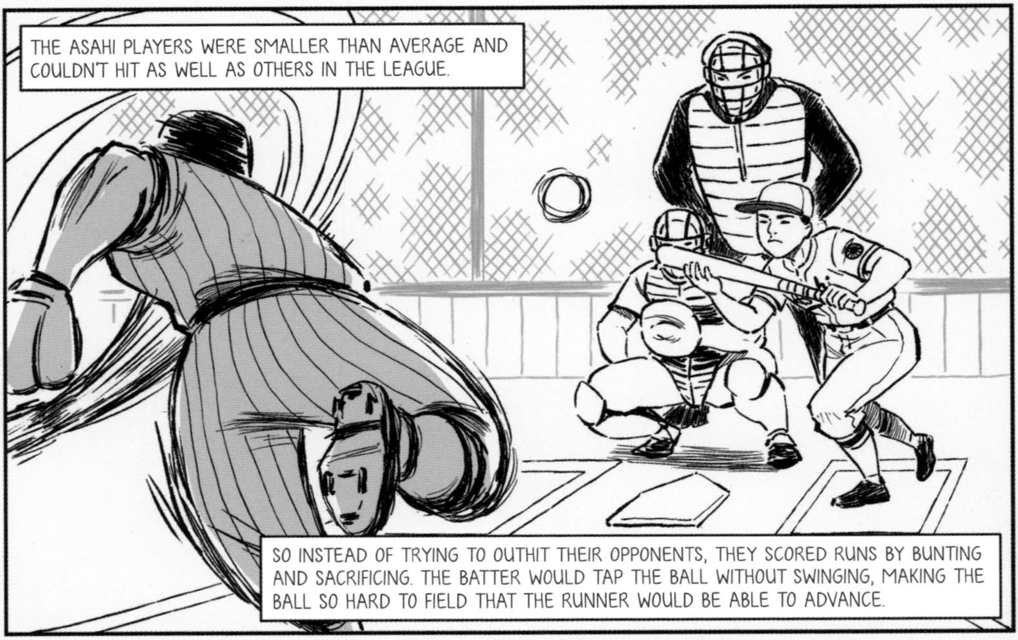
THE ASAHI PLAYERS WERE SMALLER THAN AVERAGE AND COULDN'T HIT AS WELL AS OTHERS IN THE LEAGUE.
SO INSTEAD OF TRYING TO OUTHIT THEIR OPPONENTS, THEY SCORED RUNS BY BUNTING AND SACRIFICING. THE BATTER WOULD TAP THE BALL WITHOUT SWINGING, MAKING THE BALL SO HARD TO FIELD THAT THE RUNNER WOULD BE ABLE TO ADVANCE.

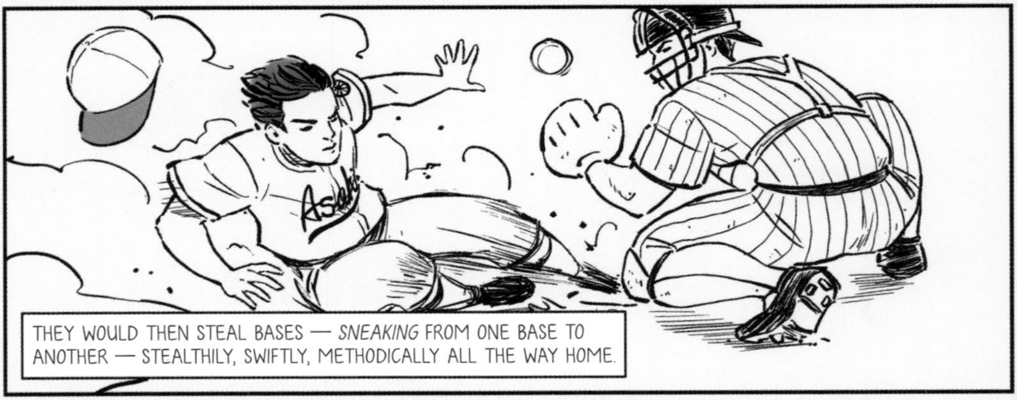
Asahi
THEY WOULD THEN STEAL BASES — *SNEAKING* FROM ONE BASE TO ANOTHER — STEALTHILY, SWIFTLY, METHODICALLY ALL THE WAY HOME.

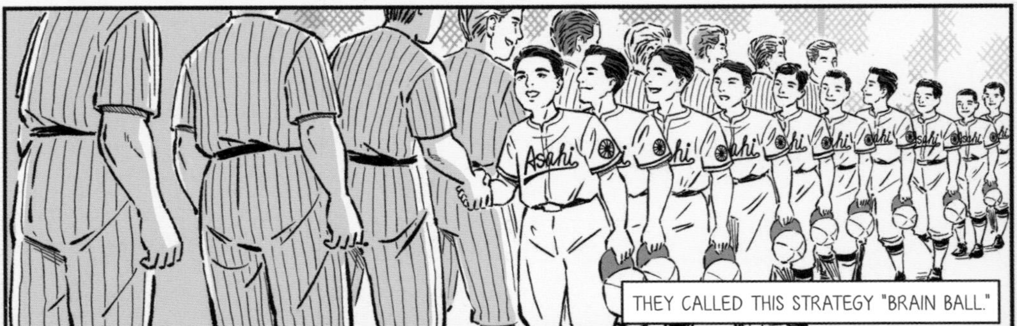
Asahi
THEY CALLED THIS STRATEGY "BRAIN BALL."

IN WHAT WOULD BE THEIR LAST SEASON EVER, THE ASAHI WERE KNOCKED OUT DURING THE SEMIFINALS.

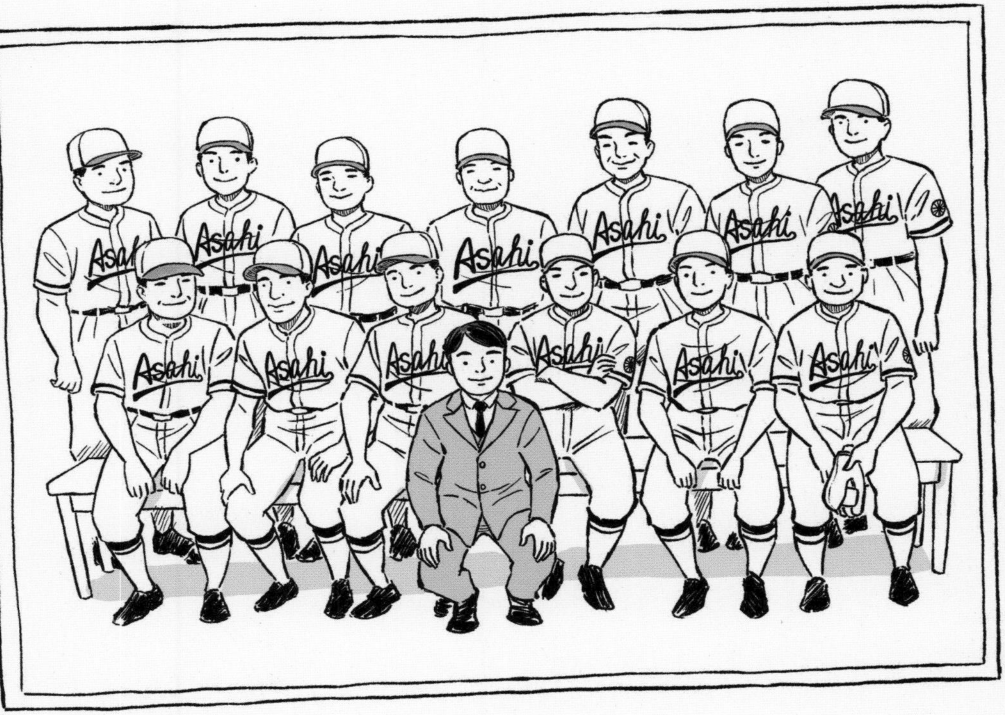
Asahi

IT WAS A SHOCK TO THEIR FANS AND A SURPRISE TO THE TEAM THAT HAD DOMINATED THE LEAGUE AND WERE THE DEFENDING CHAMPIONS.

MY FATHER CALLED IT "A BAD OMEN."

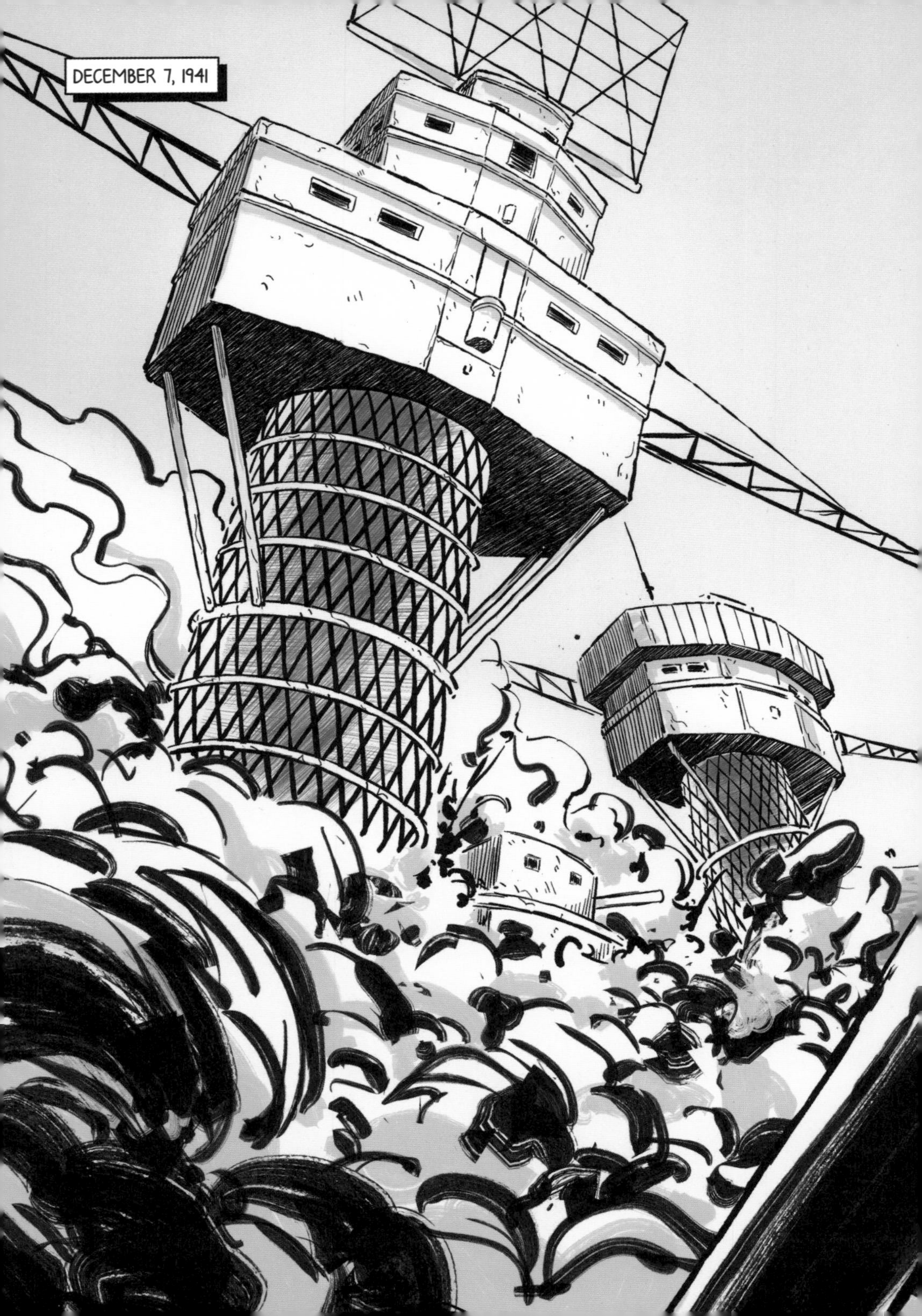
DECEMBER 7, 1941

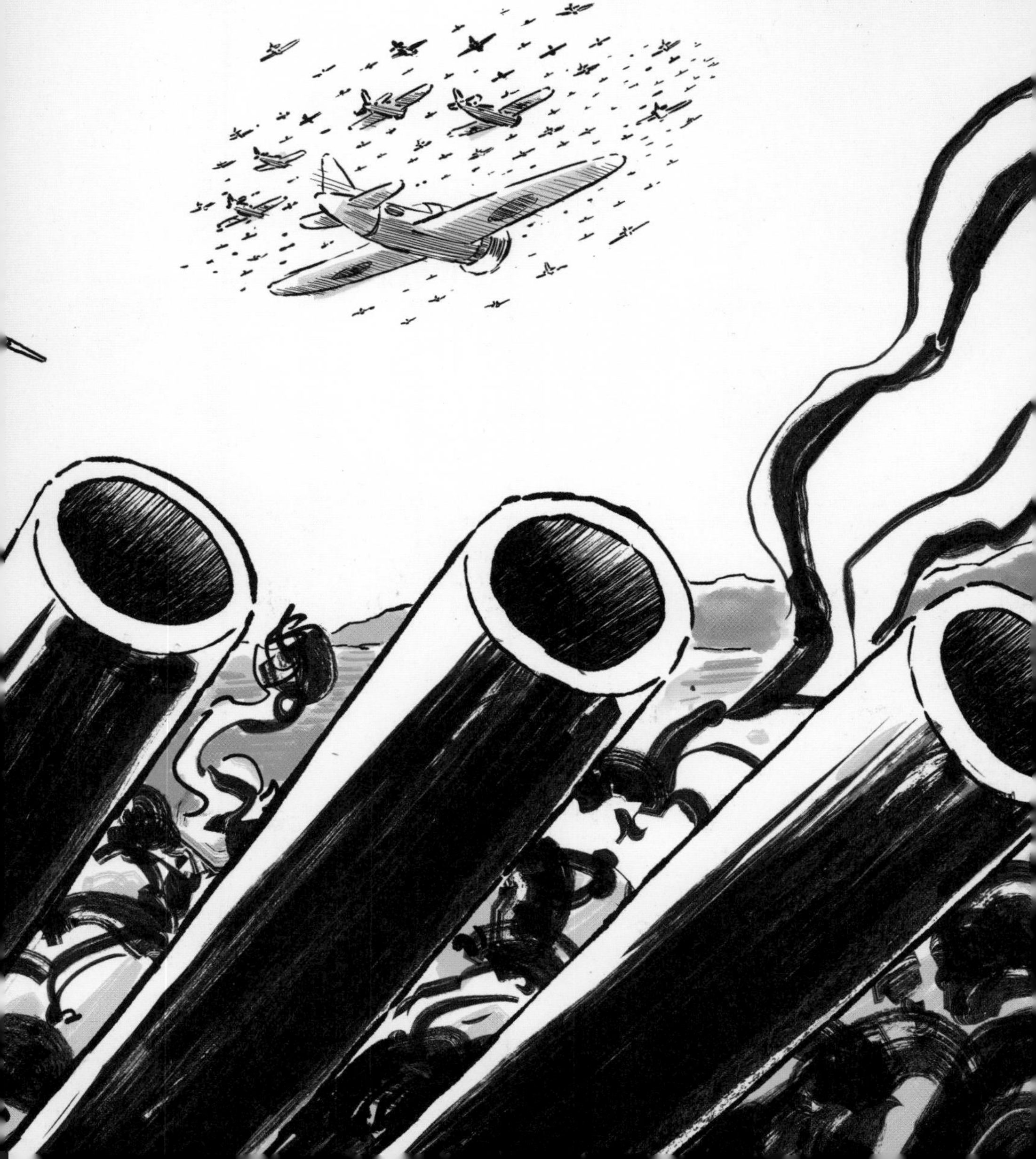

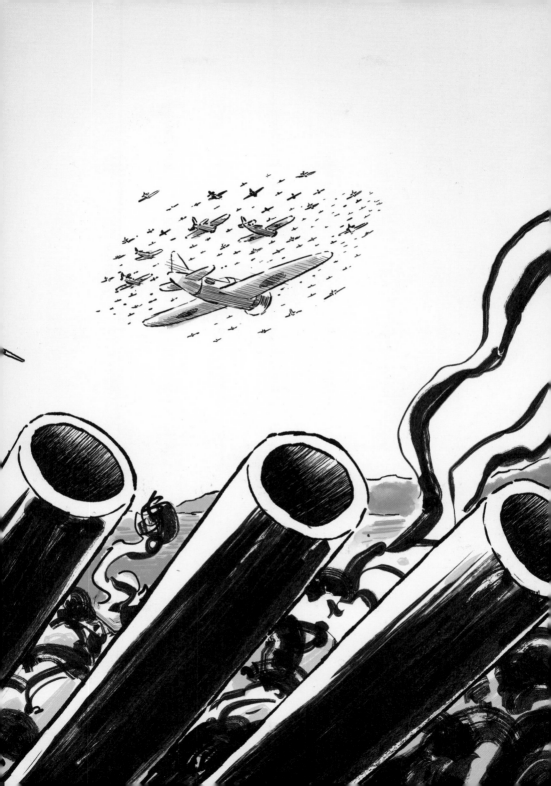

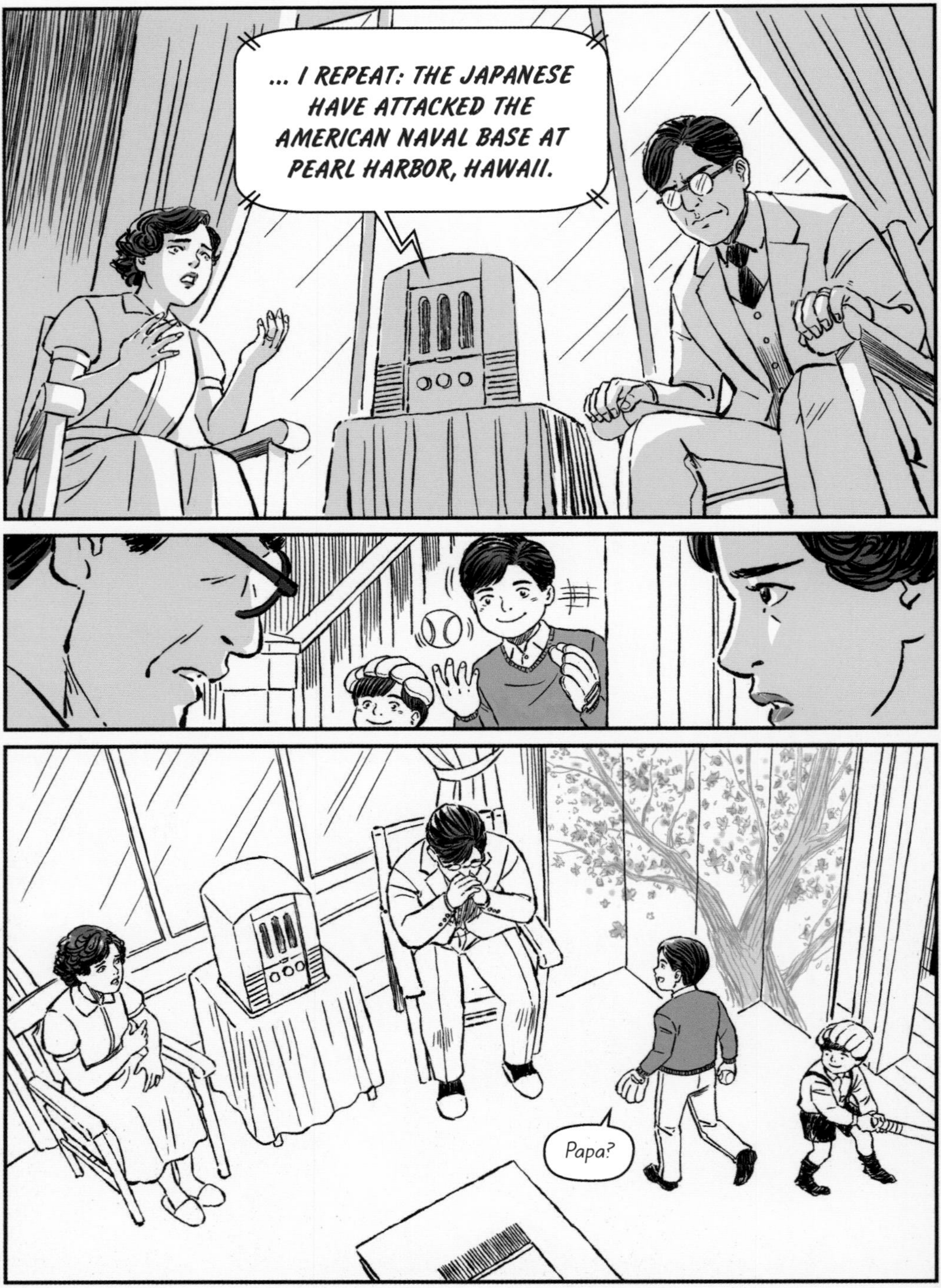
... I REPEAT: THE JAPANESE HAVE ATTACKED THE AMERICAN NAVAL BASE AT PEARL HARBOR, HAWAII.
Papa?

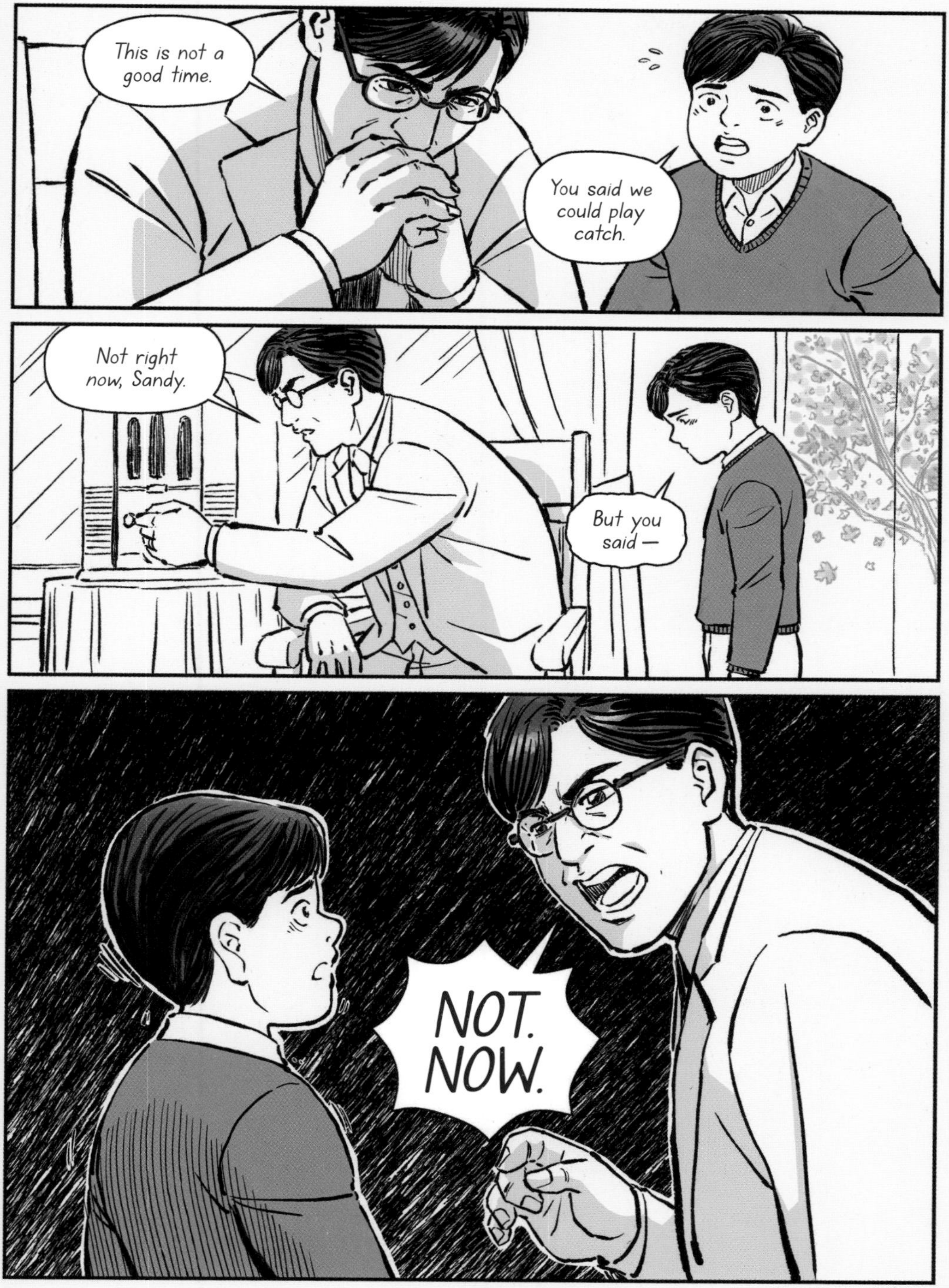
This is not a good time.
You said we could play catch.
Not right now, Sandy.
But you said —
NOT. NOW.

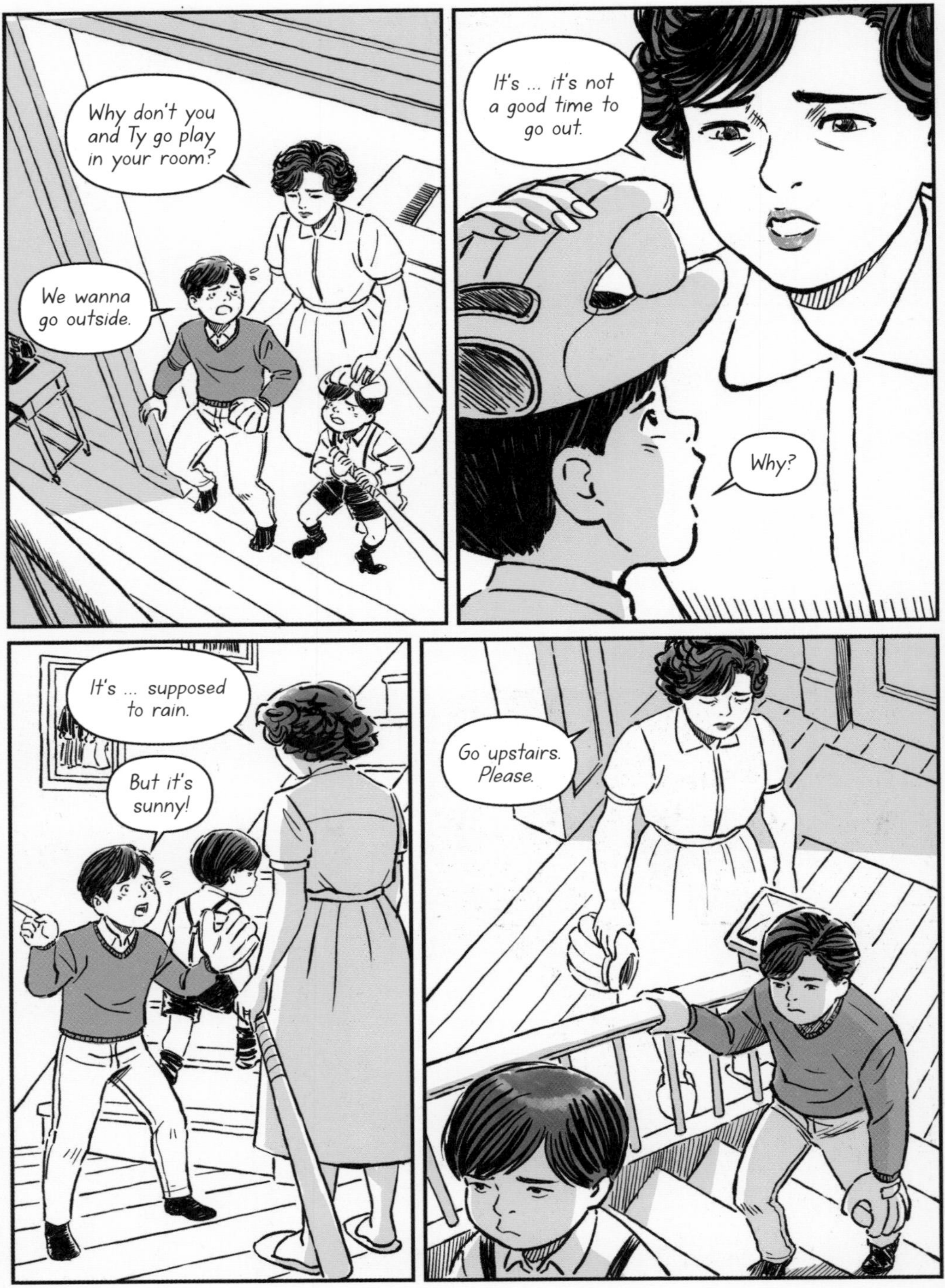
Why don't you and Ty go play in your room?
We wanna go outside.
It's ... it's not a good time to go out.
Why?
It's ... supposed to rain.
But it's sunny!
Go upstairs. Please.

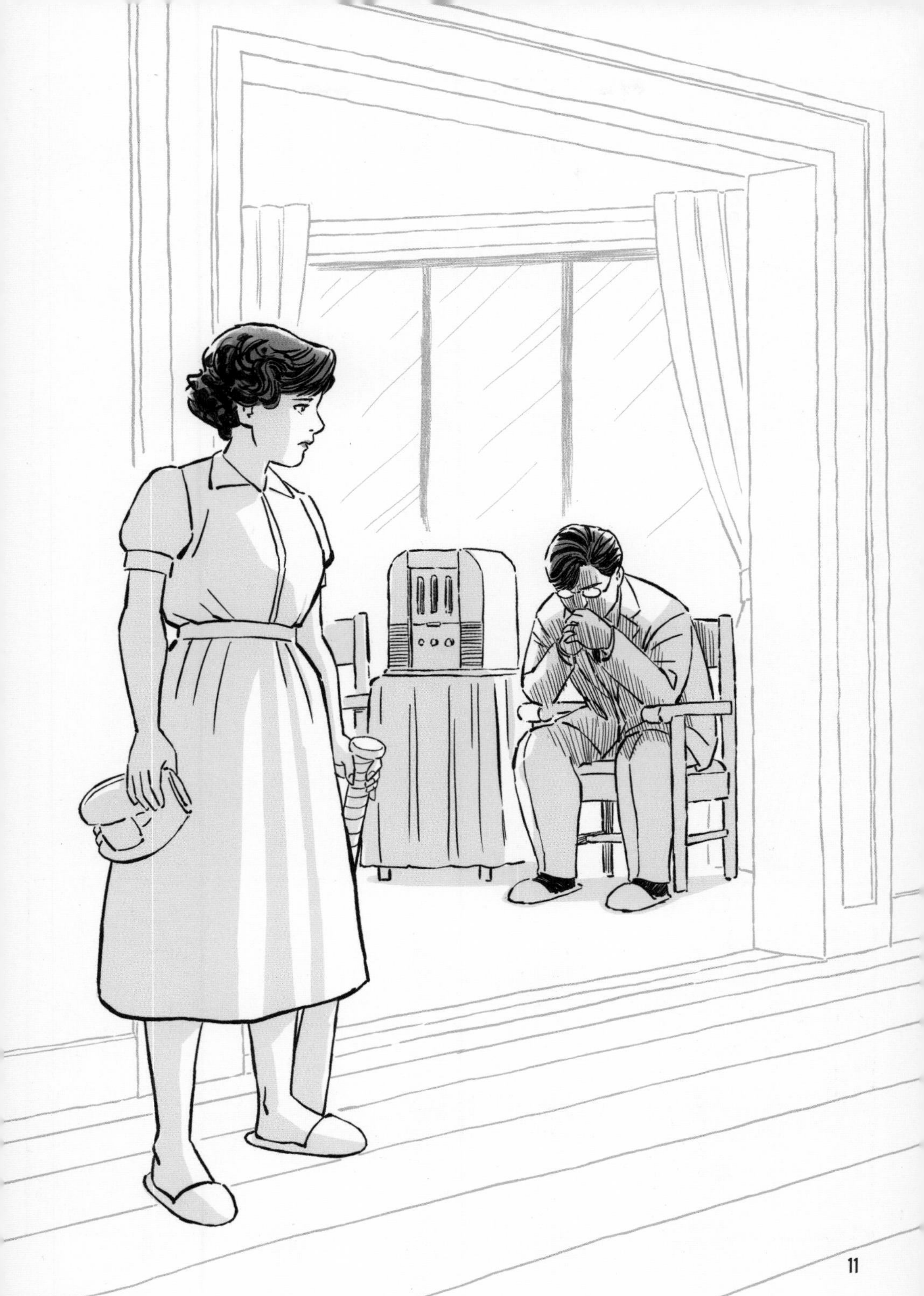

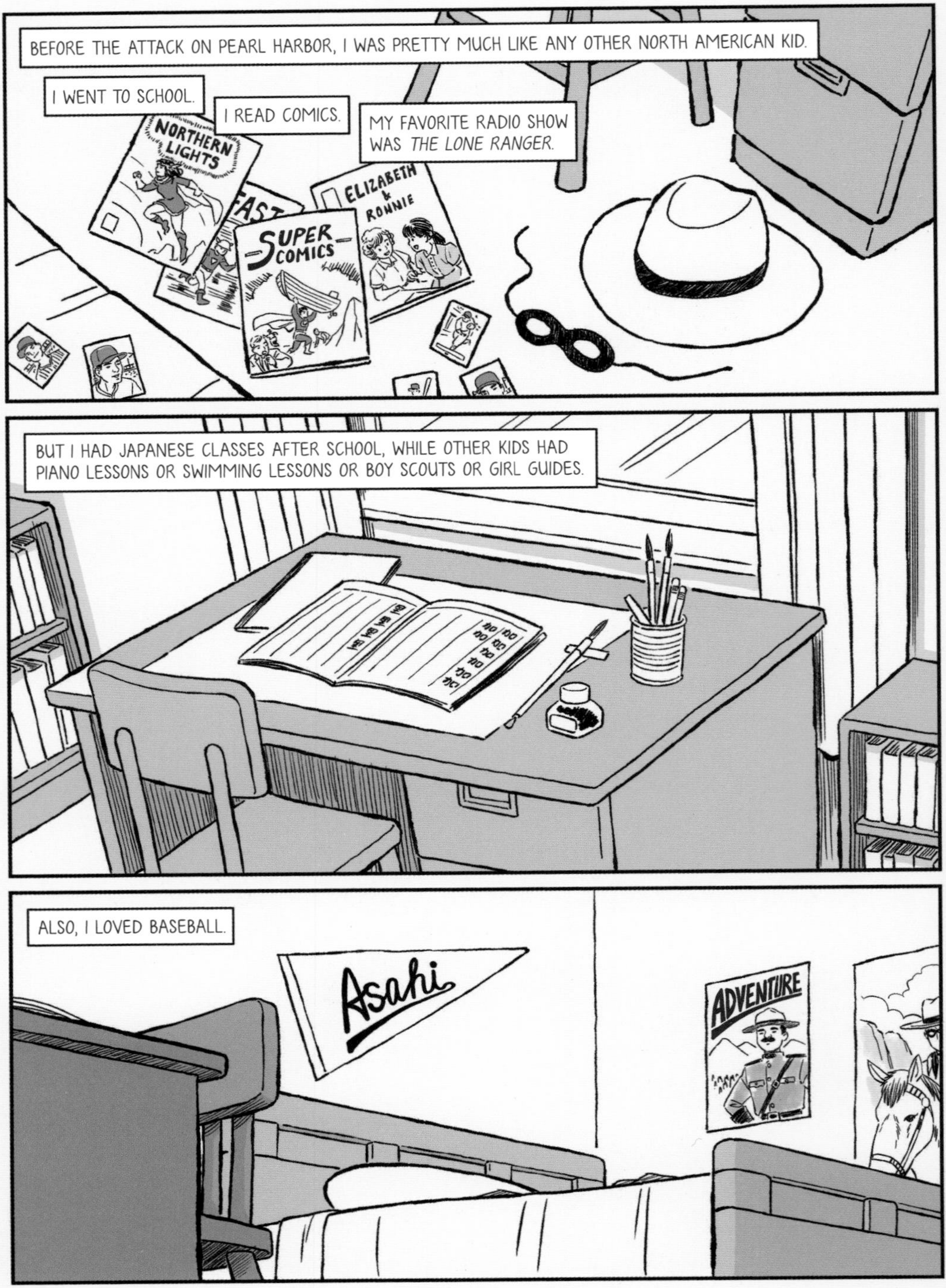
BEFORE THE ATTACK ON PEARL HARBOR, I WAS PRETTY MUCH LIKE ANY OTHER NORTH AMERICAN KID.
I WENT TO SCHOOL.
I READ COMICS.
MY FAVORITE RADIO SHOW WAS *THE LONE RANGER*.
NORTHERN LIGHTS
FAST
SUPER COMICS
ELIZABETH & RONNIE
BUT I HAD JAPANESE CLASSES AFTER SCHOOL, WHILE OTHER KIDS HAD PIANO LESSONS OR SWIMMING LESSONS OR BOY SCOUTS OR GIRL GUIDES.
ALSO, I LOVED BASEBALL.
Asahi
ADVENTURE

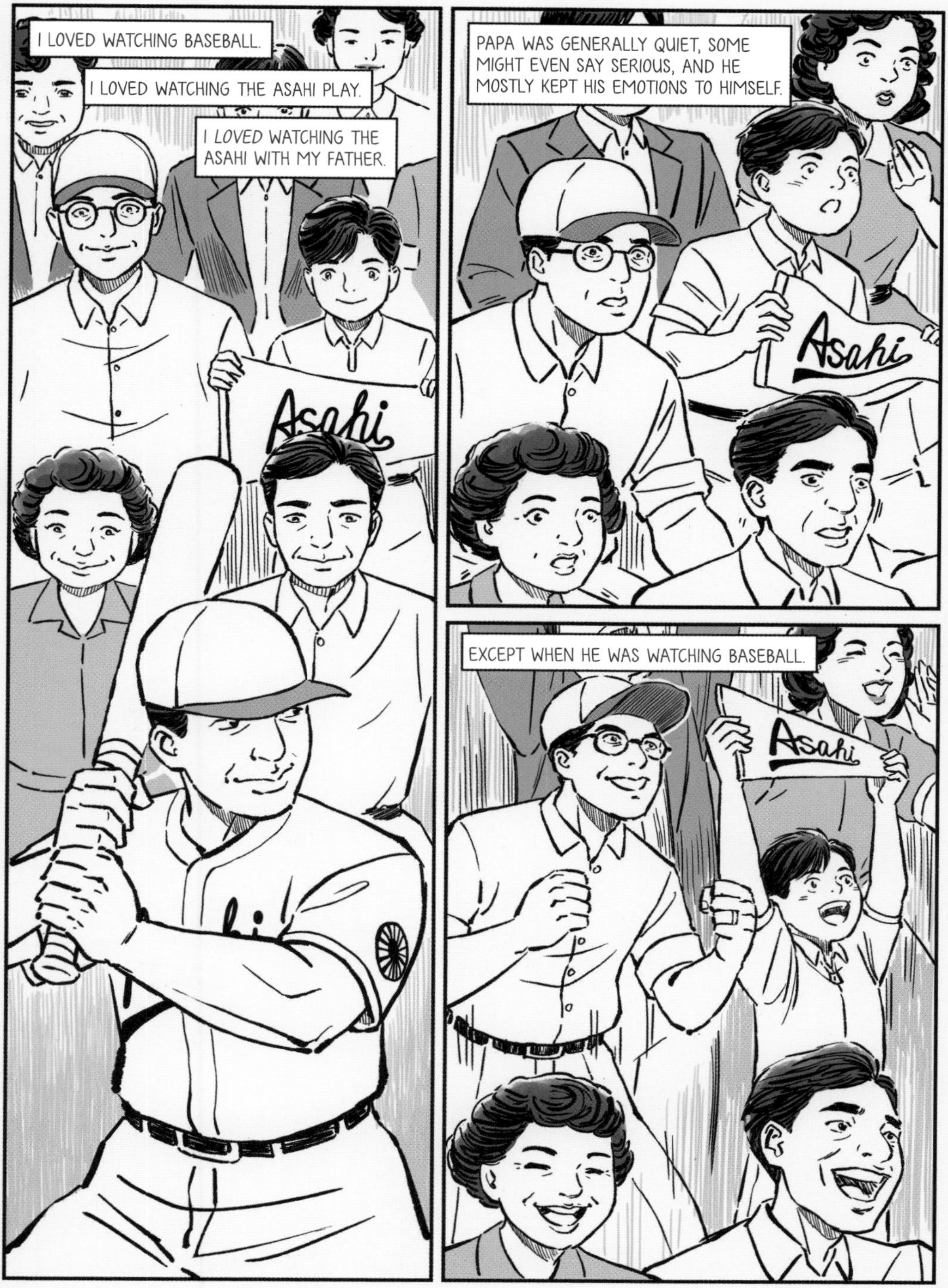
I LOVED WATCHING BASEBALL.
I LOVED WATCHING THE ASAHI PLAY.
I *LOVED* WATCHING THE ASAHI WITH MY FATHER.
Asahi
PAPA WAS GENERALLY QUIET, SOME MIGHT EVEN SAY SERIOUS, AND HE MOSTLY KEPT HIS EMOTIONS TO HIMSELF.
Asahi
EXCEPT WHEN HE WAS WATCHING BASEBALL.
Asahi

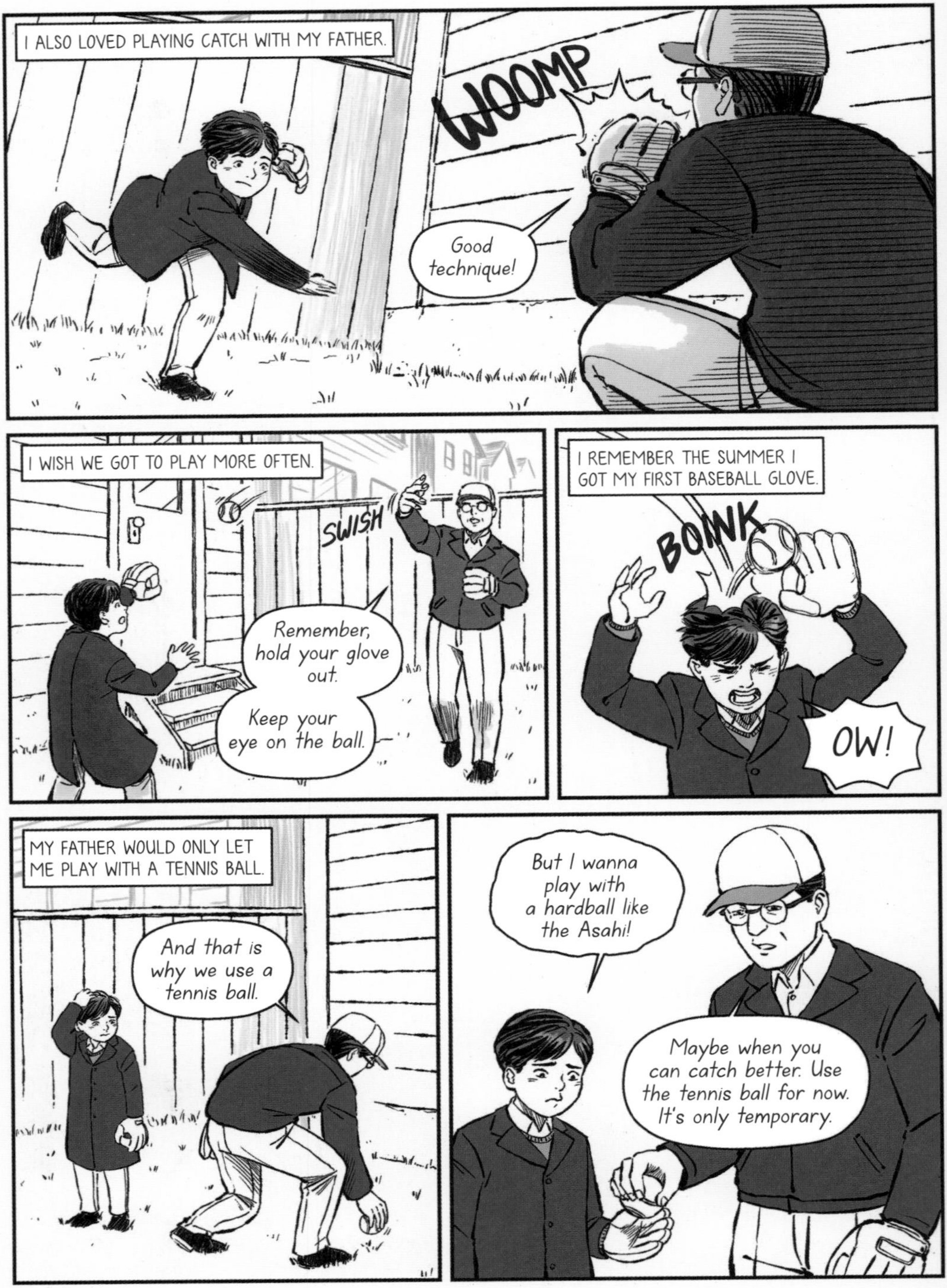
I ALSO LOVED PLAYING CATCH WITH MY FATHER.
WOOMP
Good technique!
I WISH WE GOT TO PLAY MORE OFTEN.
SWISH
Remember, hold your glove out.
Keep your eye on the ball.
I REMEMBER THE SUMMER I GOT MY FIRST BASEBALL GLOVE.
BOINK
OW!
MY FATHER WOULD ONLY LET ME PLAY WITH A TENNIS BALL.
And that is why we use a tennis ball.
But I wanna play with a hardball like the Asahi!
Maybe when you can catch better. Use the tennis ball for now. It's only temporary.

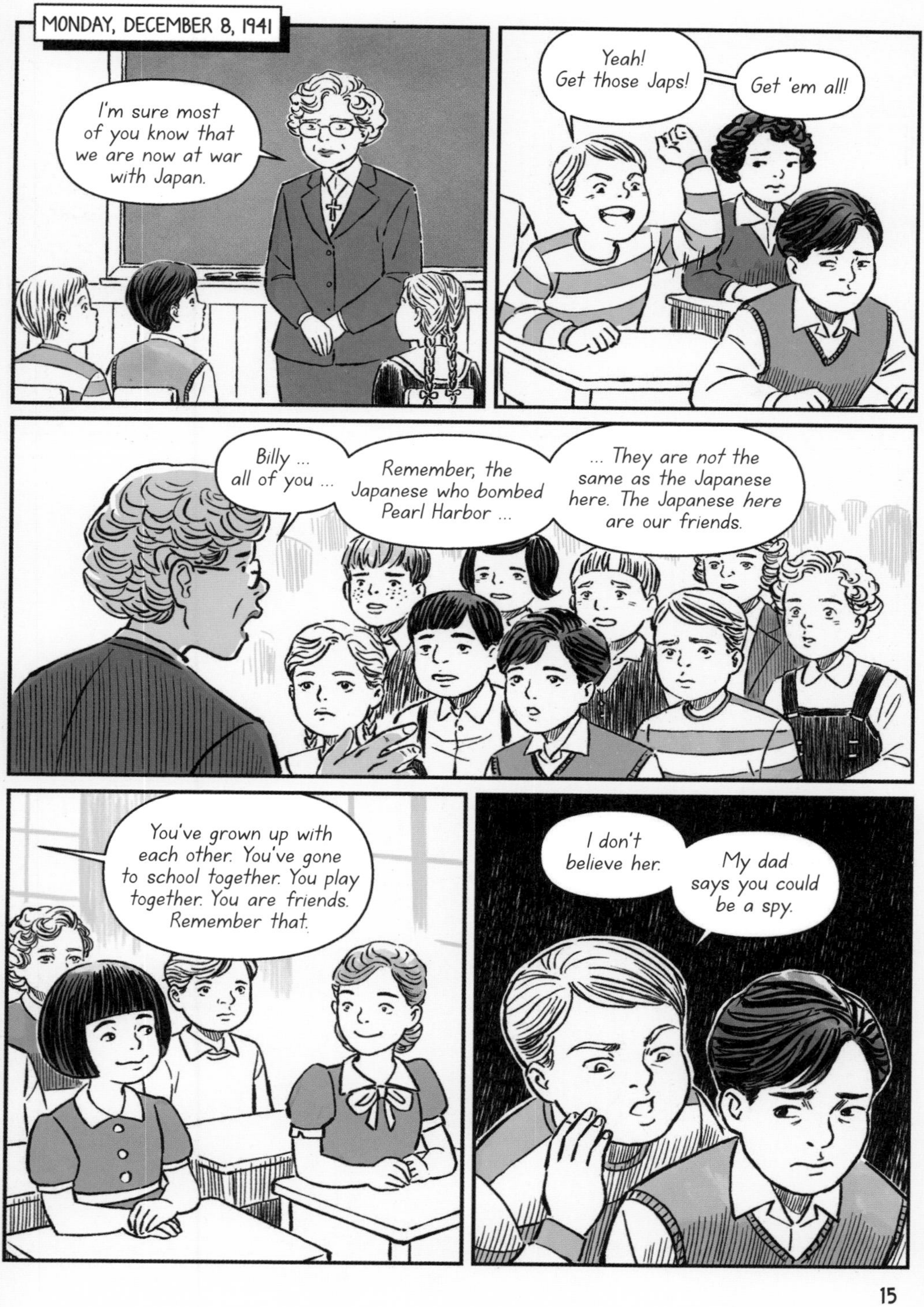
MONDAY, DECEMBER 8, 1941
I'm sure most of you know that we are now at war with Japan.
Yeah! Get those Japs!
Get 'em all!
Billy ... all of you ...
Remember, the Japanese who bombed Pearl Harbor ...
... They are not the same as the Japanese here. The Japanese here are our friends.
You've grown up with each other. You've gone to school together. You play together. You are friends. Remember that.
I don't believe her.
My dad says you could be a spy.

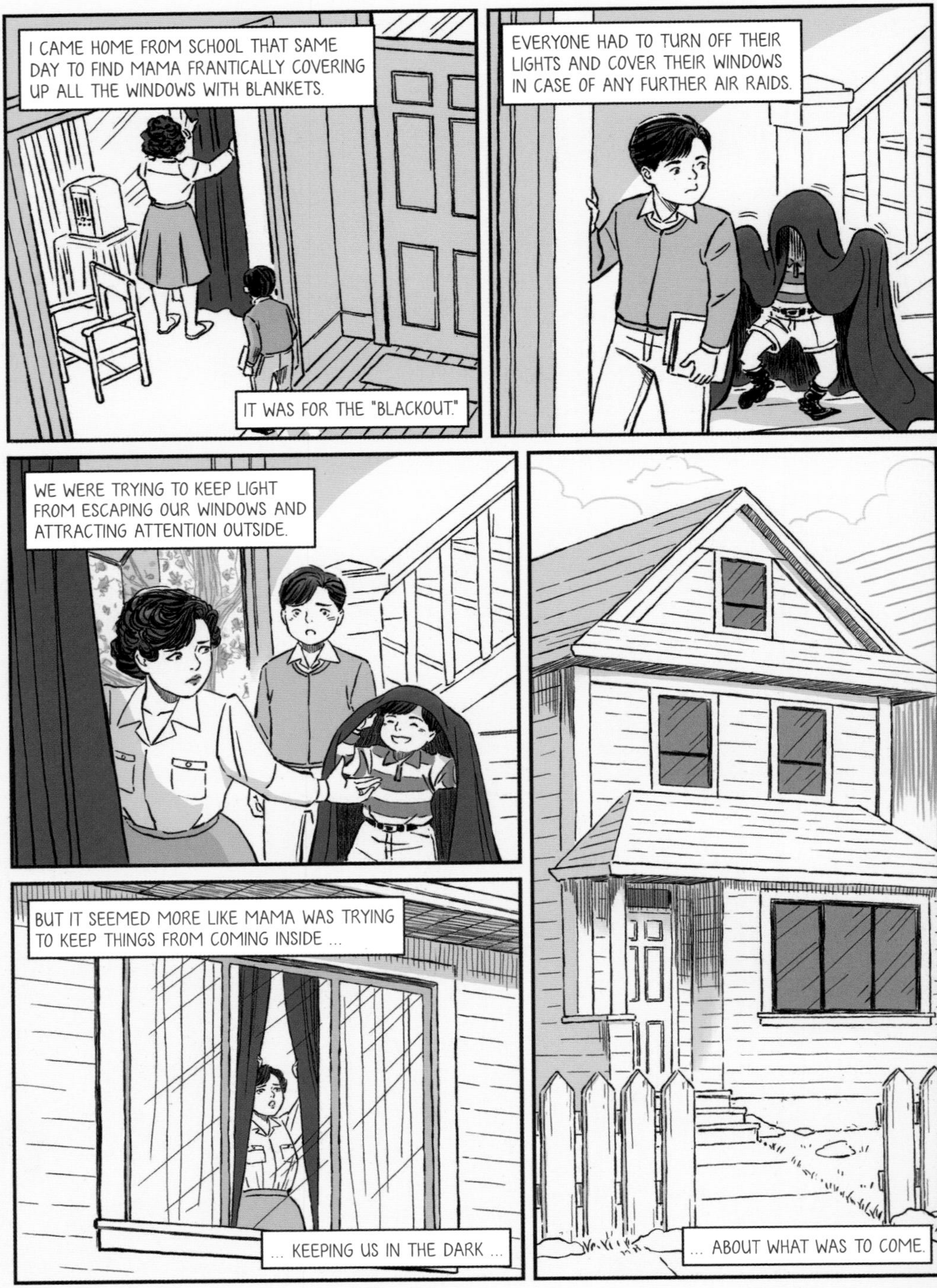
I CAME HOME FROM SCHOOL THAT SAME DAY TO FIND MAMA FRANTICALLY COVERING UP ALL THE WINDOWS WITH BLANKETS.
IT WAS FOR THE "BLACKOUT."
EVERYONE HAD TO TURN OFF THEIR LIGHTS AND COVER THEIR WINDOWS IN CASE OF ANY FURTHER AIR RAIDS.
WE WERE TRYING TO KEEP LIGHT FROM ESCAPING OUR WINDOWS AND ATTRACTING ATTENTION OUTSIDE.
BUT IT SEEMED MORE LIKE MAMA WAS TRYING TO KEEP THINGS FROM COMING INSIDE ...
... KEEPING US IN THE DARK ...
... ABOUT WHAT WAS TO COME.

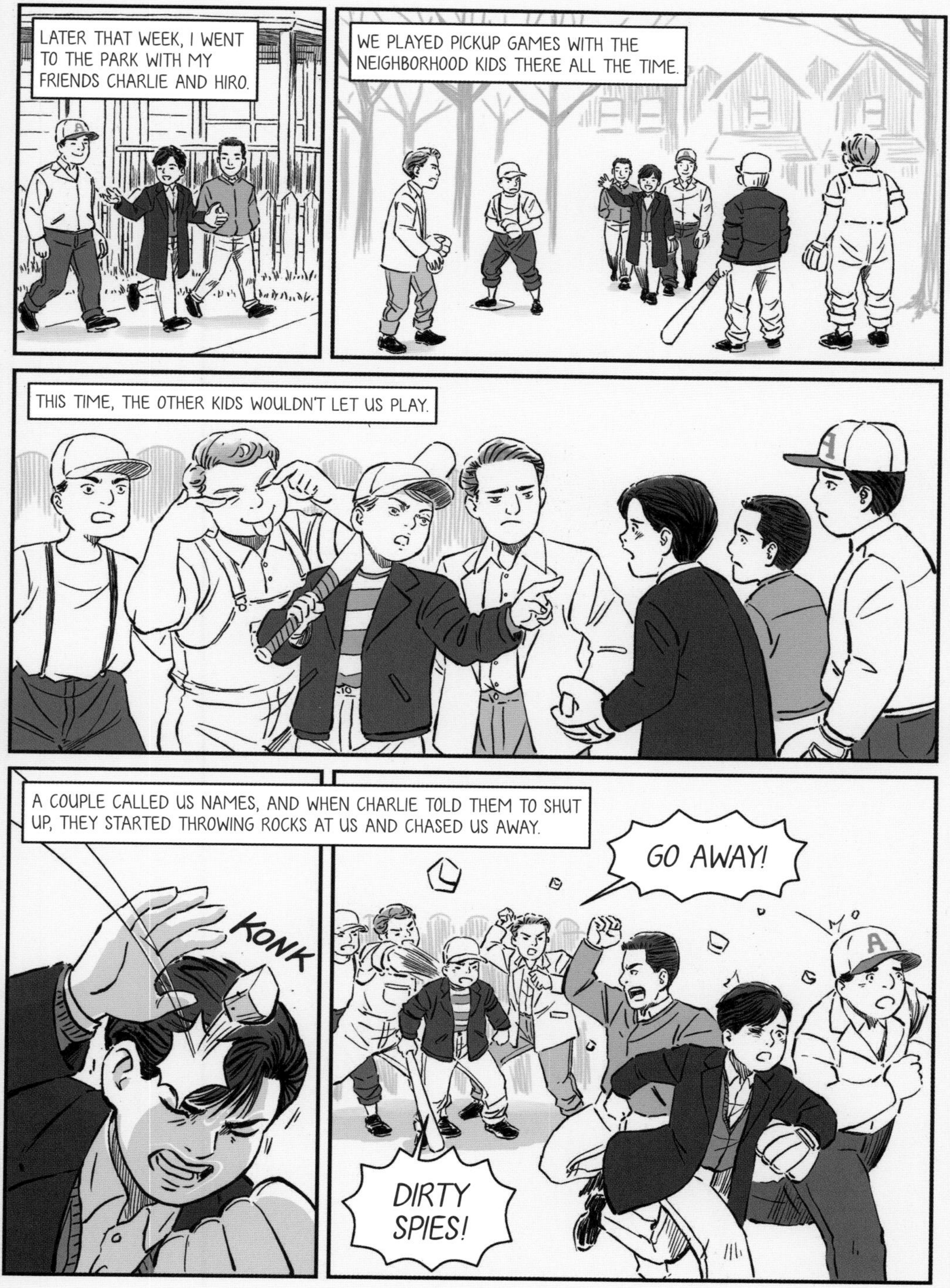
LATER THAT WEEK, I WENT TO THE PARK WITH MY FRIENDS CHARLIE AND HIRO.
WE PLAYED PICKUP GAMES WITH THE NEIGHBORHOOD KIDS THERE ALL THE TIME.
THIS TIME, THE OTHER KIDS WOULDN'T LET US PLAY.
A COUPLE CALLED US NAMES, AND WHEN CHARLIE TOLD THEM TO SHUT UP, THEY STARTED THROWING ROCKS AT US AND CHASED US AWAY.
KONK
GO AWAY!
DIRTY SPIES!

MY FATHER WAS A DOCTOR. HE HAD A PRACTICE ON POWELL STREET. THAT'S WHY EVERYONE CALLED HIM "SAITO-SENSEI."

J. SAITO

Family Doctor

HE WAS BORN HERE, BUT HE WENT TO SCHOOL IN JAPAN.

SENSEI MEANING "TEACHER," WHICH IS A TERM OF RESPECT.

AT THAT TIME, ASIANS WEREN'T ALLOWED TO GO TO MEDICAL SCHOOL IN VANCOUVER.

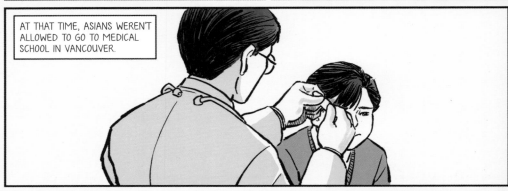

EVEN AFTER HE RETURNED FROM JAPAN, HE WAS ONLY ALLOWED TO WORK IN "ORIENTAL HOSPITALS."

SO HE OPENED HIS OWN PRACTICE ON POWELL STREET, TREATING MOSTLY JAPANESE PATIENTS.

Just stay away from those boys. No baseball for now.

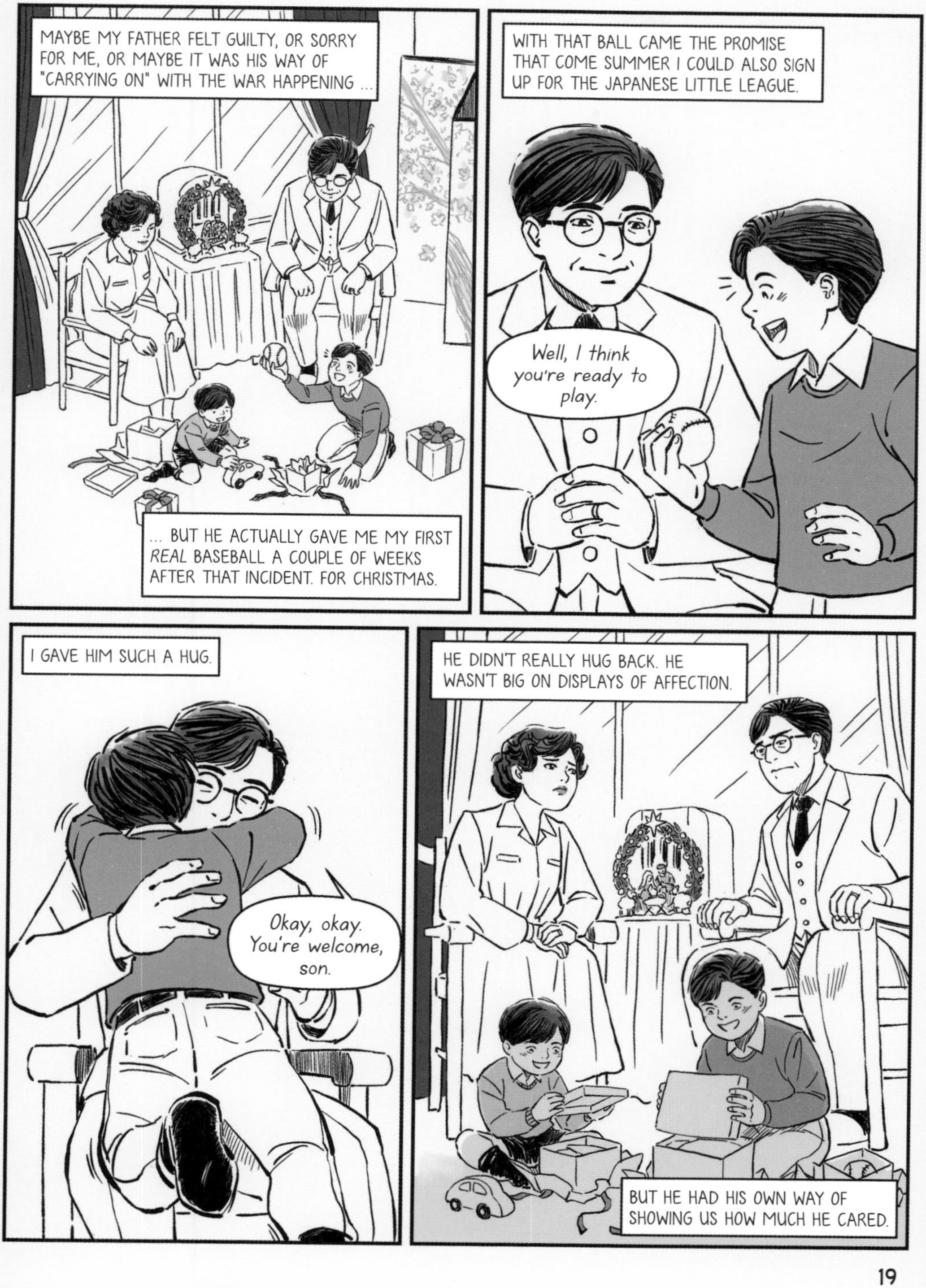
MAYBE MY FATHER FELT GUILTY, OR SORRY FOR ME, OR MAYBE IT WAS HIS WAY OF "CARRYING ON" WITH THE WAR HAPPENING ...
... BUT HE ACTUALLY GAVE ME MY FIRST *REAL* BASEBALL A COUPLE OF WEEKS AFTER THAT INCIDENT. FOR CHRISTMAS.
WITH THAT BALL CAME THE PROMISE THAT COME SUMMER I COULD ALSO SIGN UP FOR THE JAPANESE LITTLE LEAGUE.
Well, I think you're ready to play.
I GAVE HIM SUCH A HUG.
Okay, okay. You're welcome, son.
HE DIDN'T REALLY HUG BACK. HE WASN'T BIG ON DISPLAYS OF AFFECTION.
BUT HE HAD HIS OWN WAY OF SHOWING US HOW MUCH HE CARED.

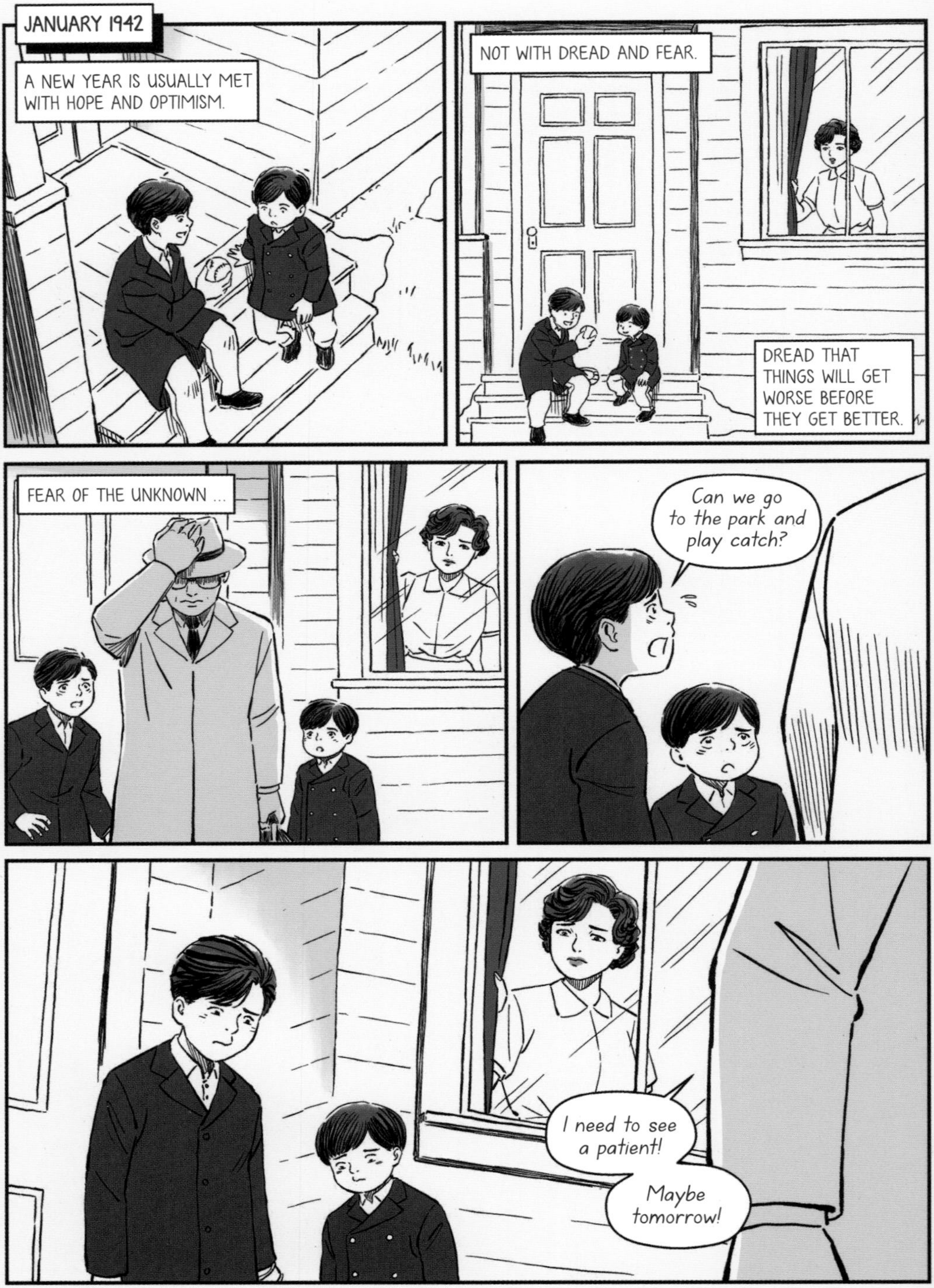
JANUARY 1942
A NEW YEAR IS USUALLY MET WITH HOPE AND OPTIMISM.
NOT WITH DREAD AND FEAR.
DREAD THAT THINGS WILL GET WORSE BEFORE THEY GET BETTER.
FEAR OF THE UNKNOWN ...
Can we go to the park and play catch?
I need to see a patient!
Maybe tomorrow!

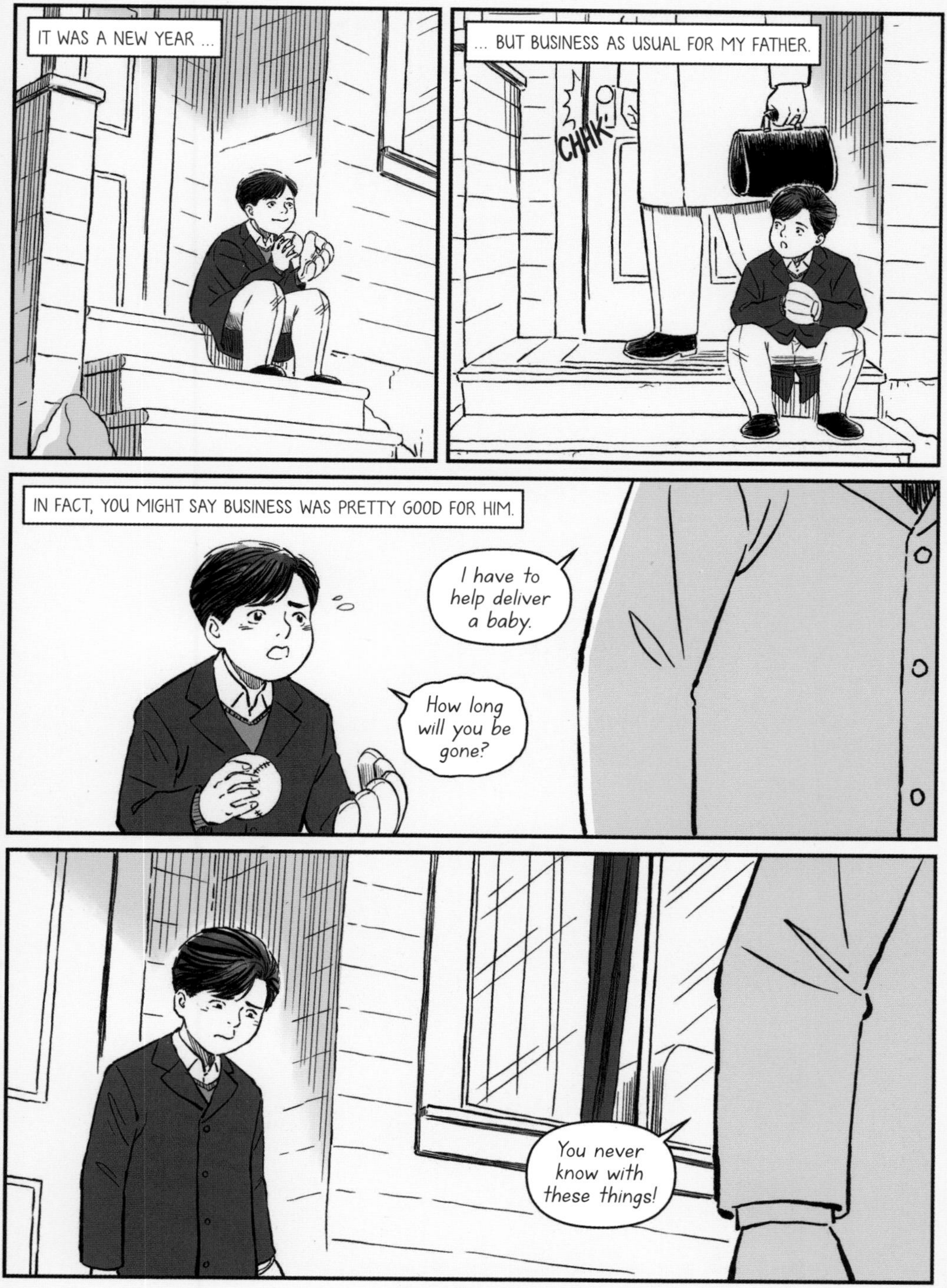
IT WAS A NEW YEAR ...
... BUT BUSINESS AS USUAL FOR MY FATHER.
CHHK
IN FACT, YOU MIGHT SAY BUSINESS WAS PRETTY GOOD FOR HIM.
I have to help deliver a baby.
How long will you be gone?
You never know with these things!

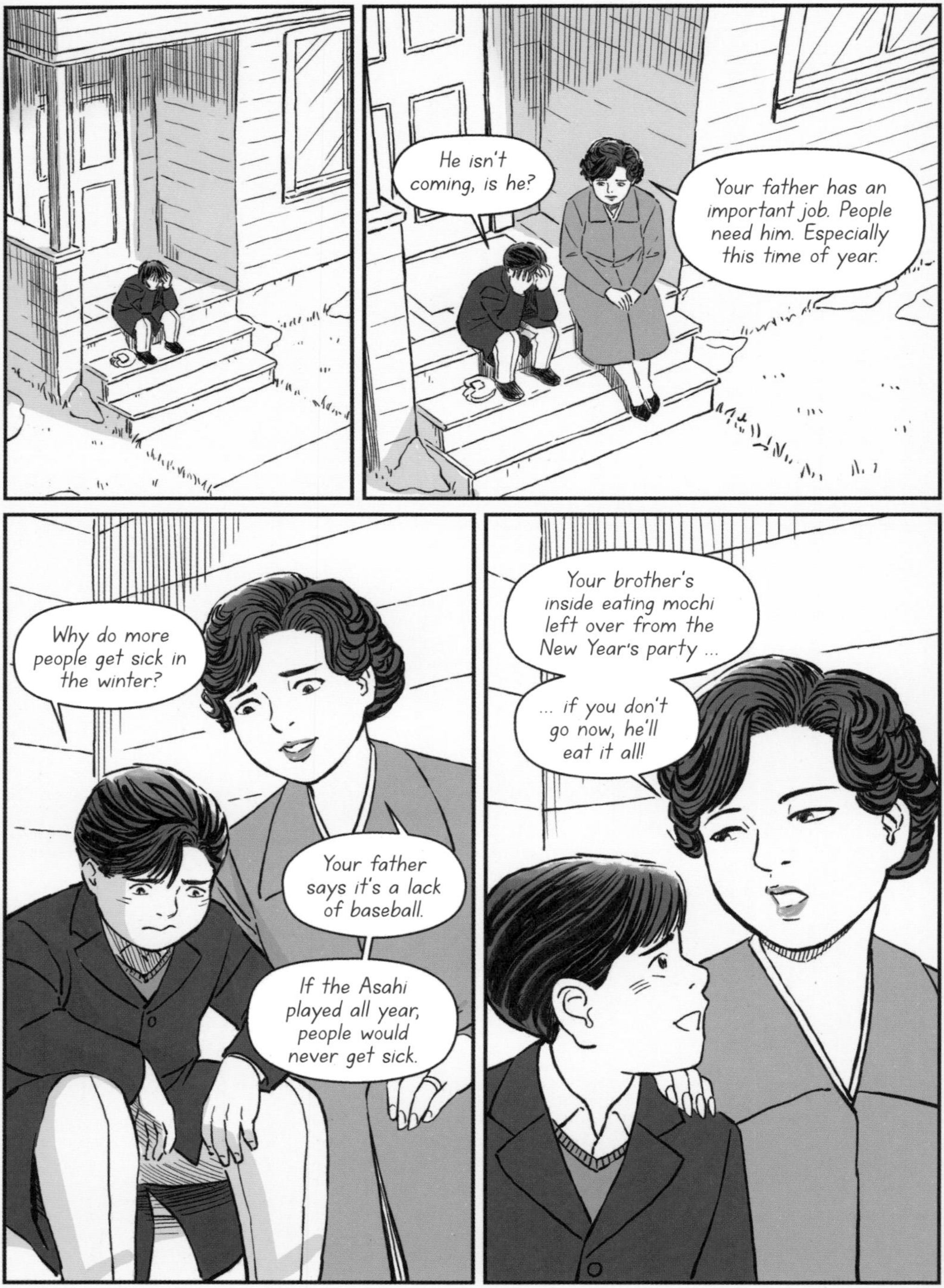
He isn't coming, is he?
Your father has an important job. People need him. Especially this time of year.
Why do more people get sick in the winter?
Your father says it's a lack of baseball.
If the Asahi played all year, people would never get sick.
Your brother's inside eating mochi left over from the New Year's party ...
... if you don't go now, he'll eat it all!

FEBRUARY

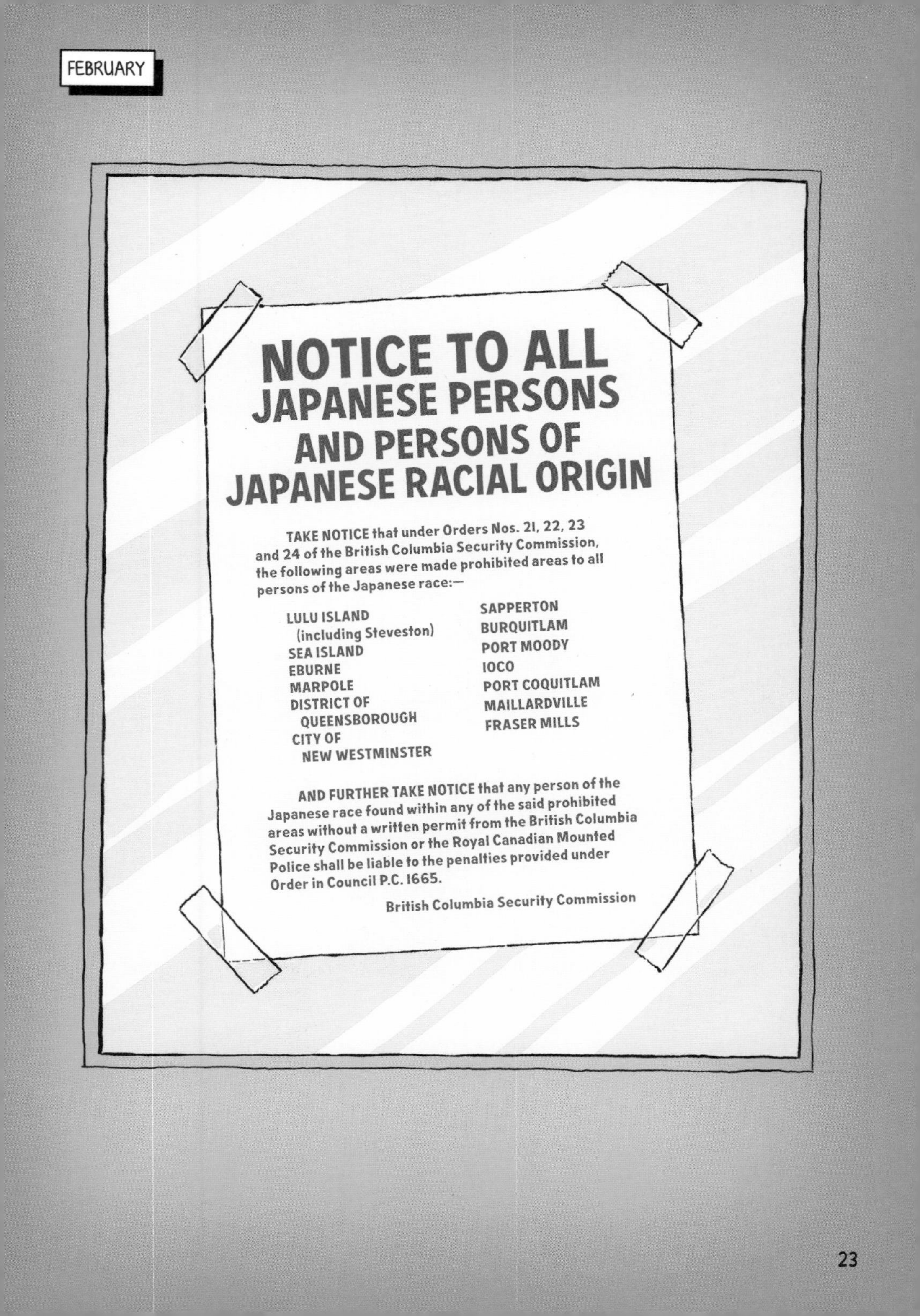
NOTICE TO ALL
JAPANESE PERSONS
AND PERSONS OF
JAPANESE RACIAL ORIGIN
TAKE NOTICE that under Orders Nos. 21, 22, 23 and 24 of the British Columbia Security Commission, the following areas were made prohibited areas to all persons of the Japanese race:—
LULU ISLAND (including Steveston)
SEA ISLAND
EBURNE
MARPOLE
DISTRICT OF QUEENSBOROUGH
CITY OF NEW WESTMINSTER
SAPPERTON
BURQUITLAM
PORT MOODY
IOCO
PORT COQUITLAM
MAILLARDVILLE
FRASER MILLS
AND FURTHER TAKE NOTICE that any person of the Japanese race found within any of the said prohibited areas without a written permit from the British Columbia Security Commission or the Royal Canadian Mounted Police shall be liable to the penalties provided under Order in Council P.C. 1665.
British Columbia Security Commission

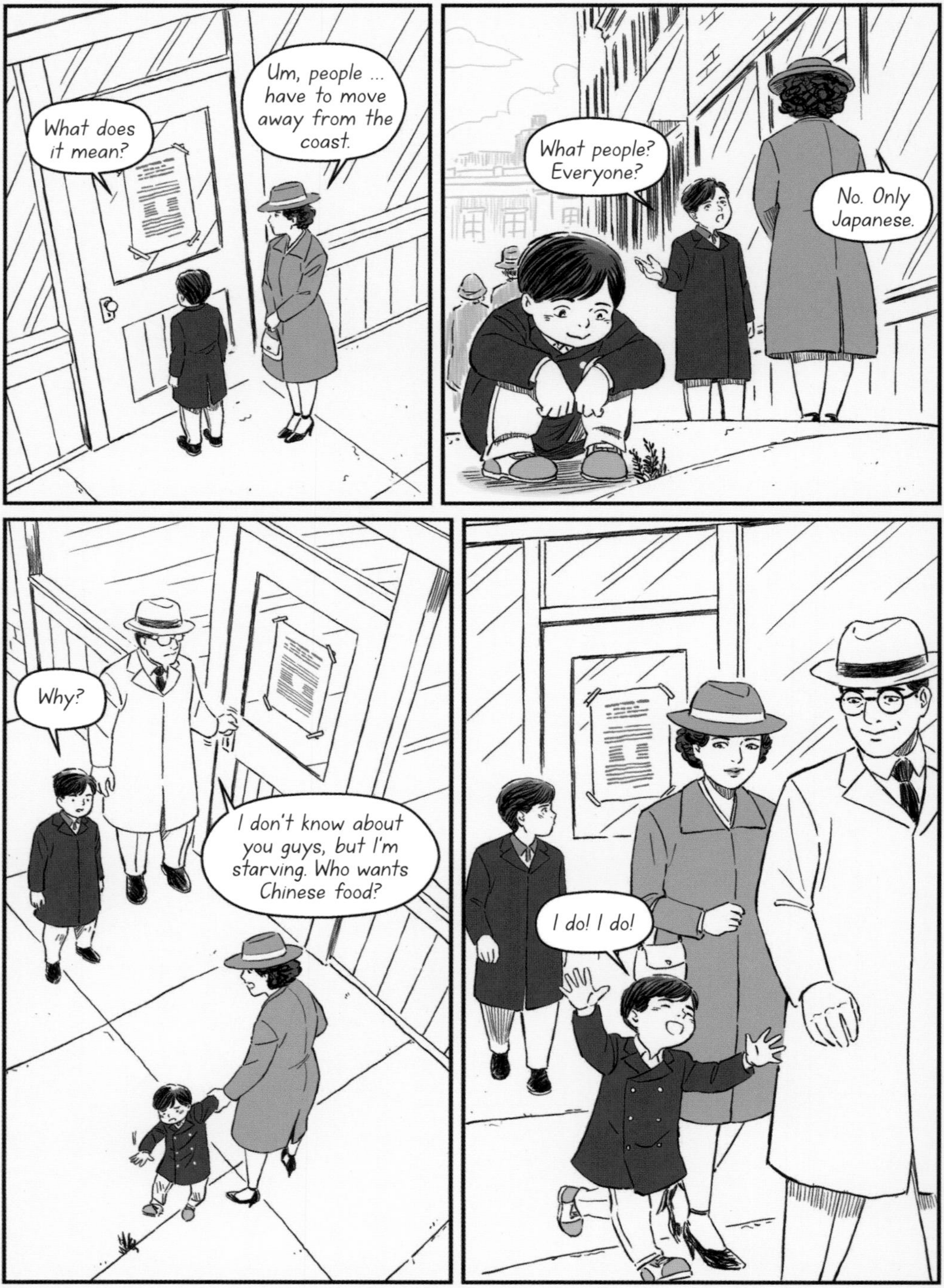
What does it mean?
Um, people ... have to move away from the coast.
What people? Everyone?
No. Only Japanese.
Why?
I don't know about you guys, but I'm starving. Who wants Chinese food?
I do! I do!

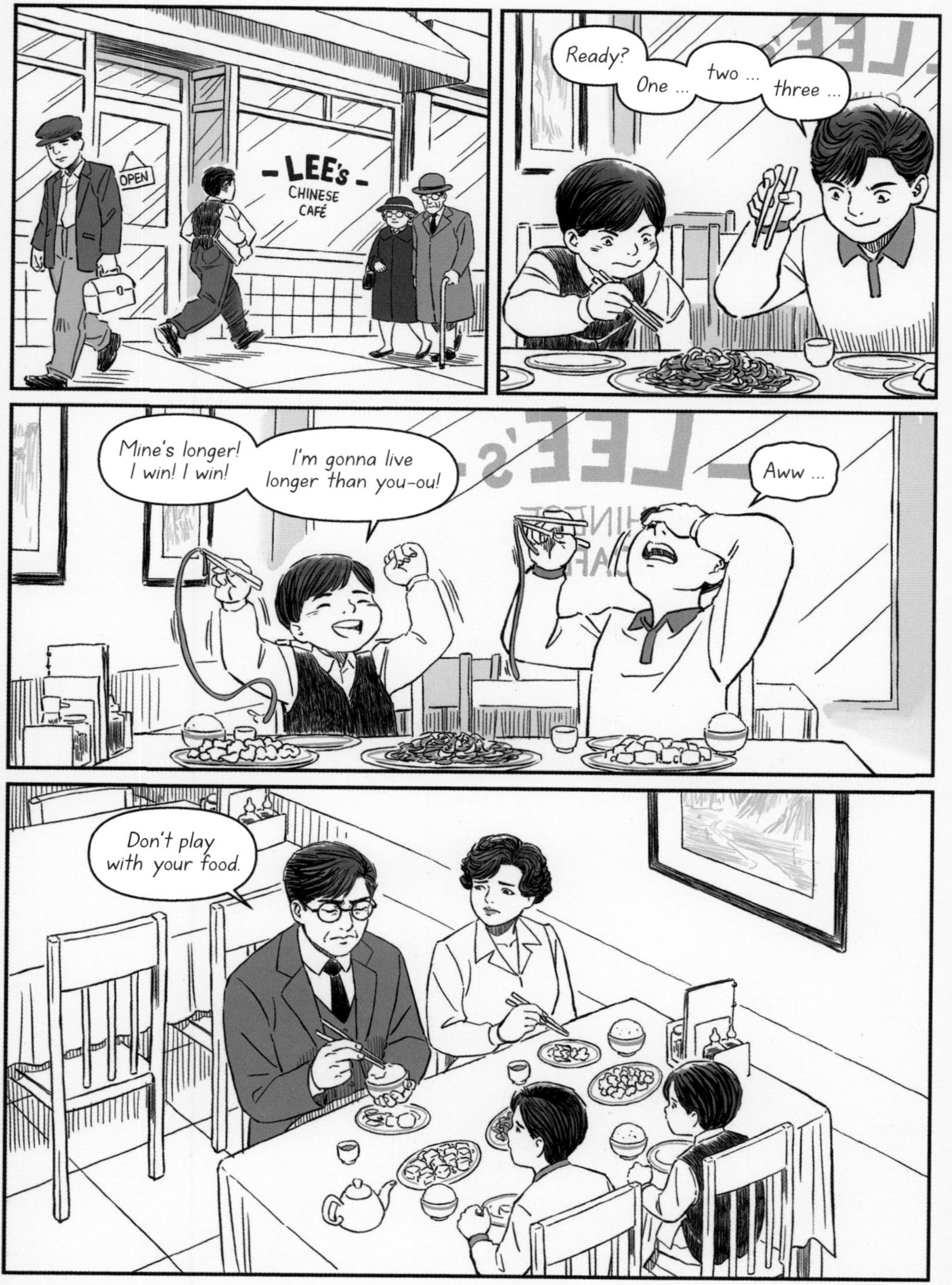
OPEN
- LEE's -
CHINESE
CAFÉ
Ready?
One ...
two ...
three ...
Mine's longer! I win! I win!
I'm gonna live longer than you-ou!
Aww ...
Don't play with your food.

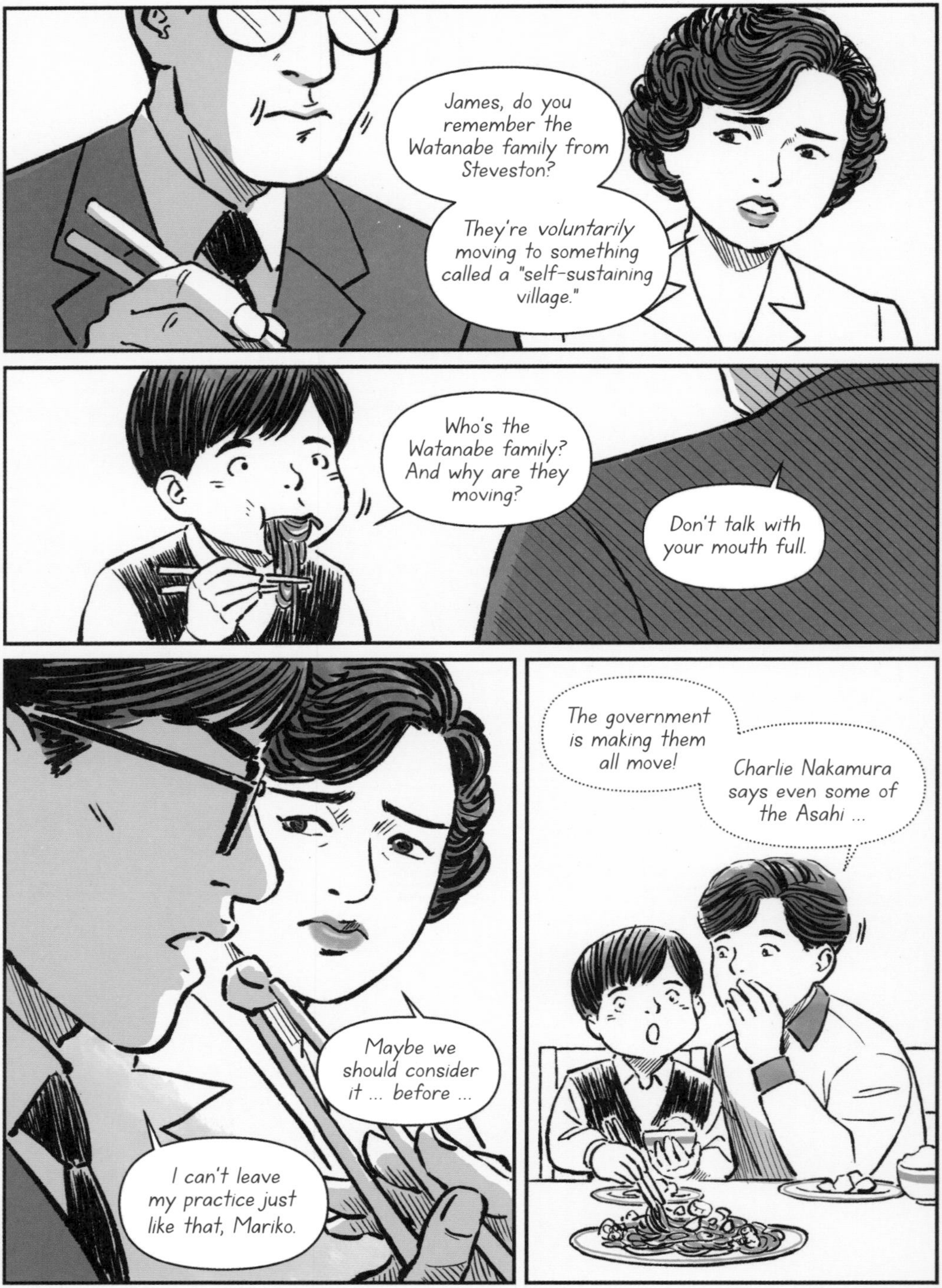
James, do you remember the Watanabe family from Steveston?
They're voluntarily moving to something called a "self-sustaining village."
Who's the Watanabe family? And why are they moving?
Don't talk with your mouth full.
Maybe we should consider it ... before ...
I can't leave my practice just like that, Mariko.
The government is making them all move!
Charlie Nakamura says even some of the Asahi ...

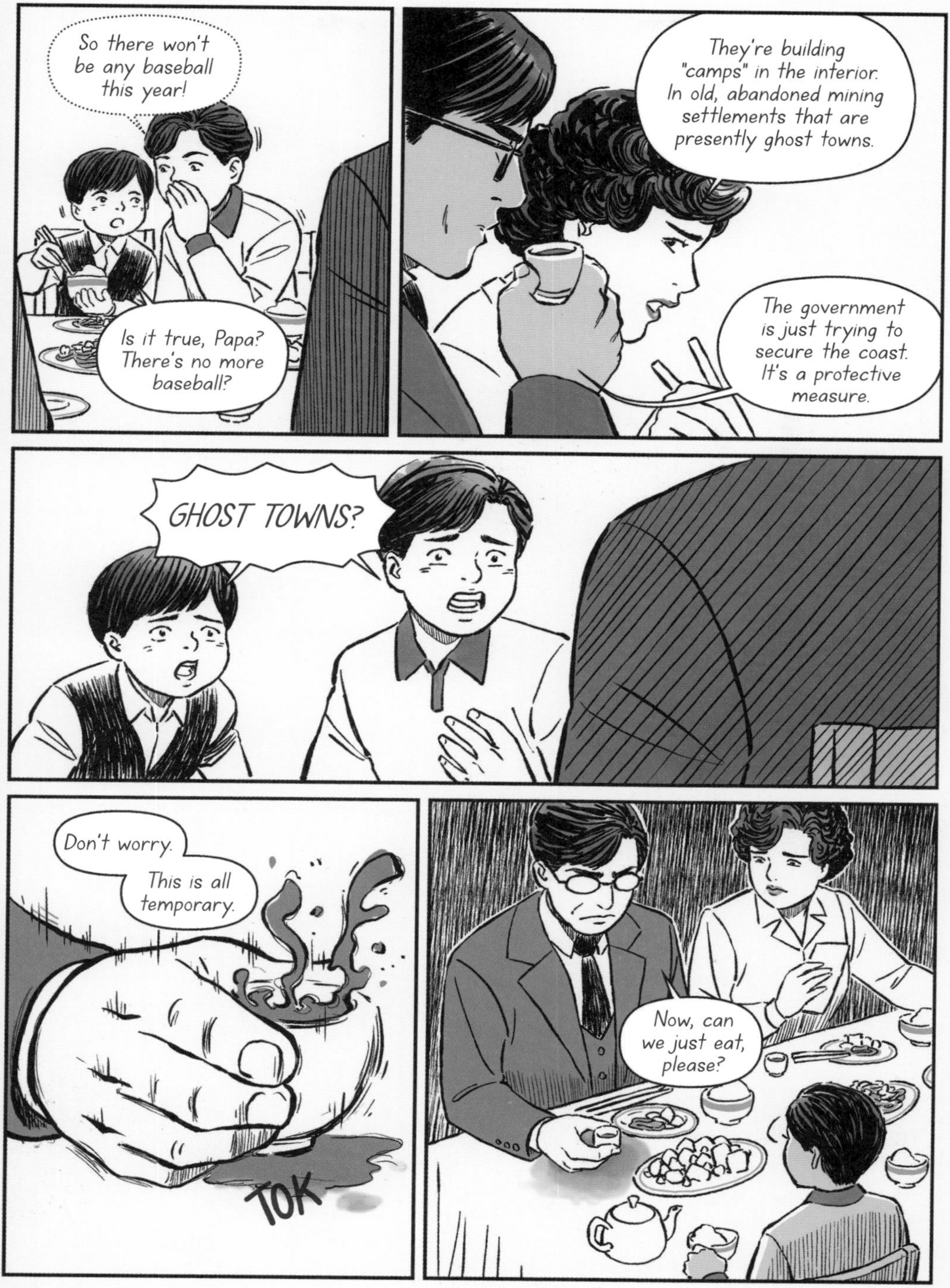
So there won't be any baseball this year!
Is it true, Papa? There's no more baseball?
They're building "camps" in the interior. In old, abandoned mining settlements that are presently ghost towns.
The government is just trying to secure the coast. It's a protective measure.
GHOST TOWNS?
Don't worry.
This is all temporary.
TOK
Now, can we just eat, please?

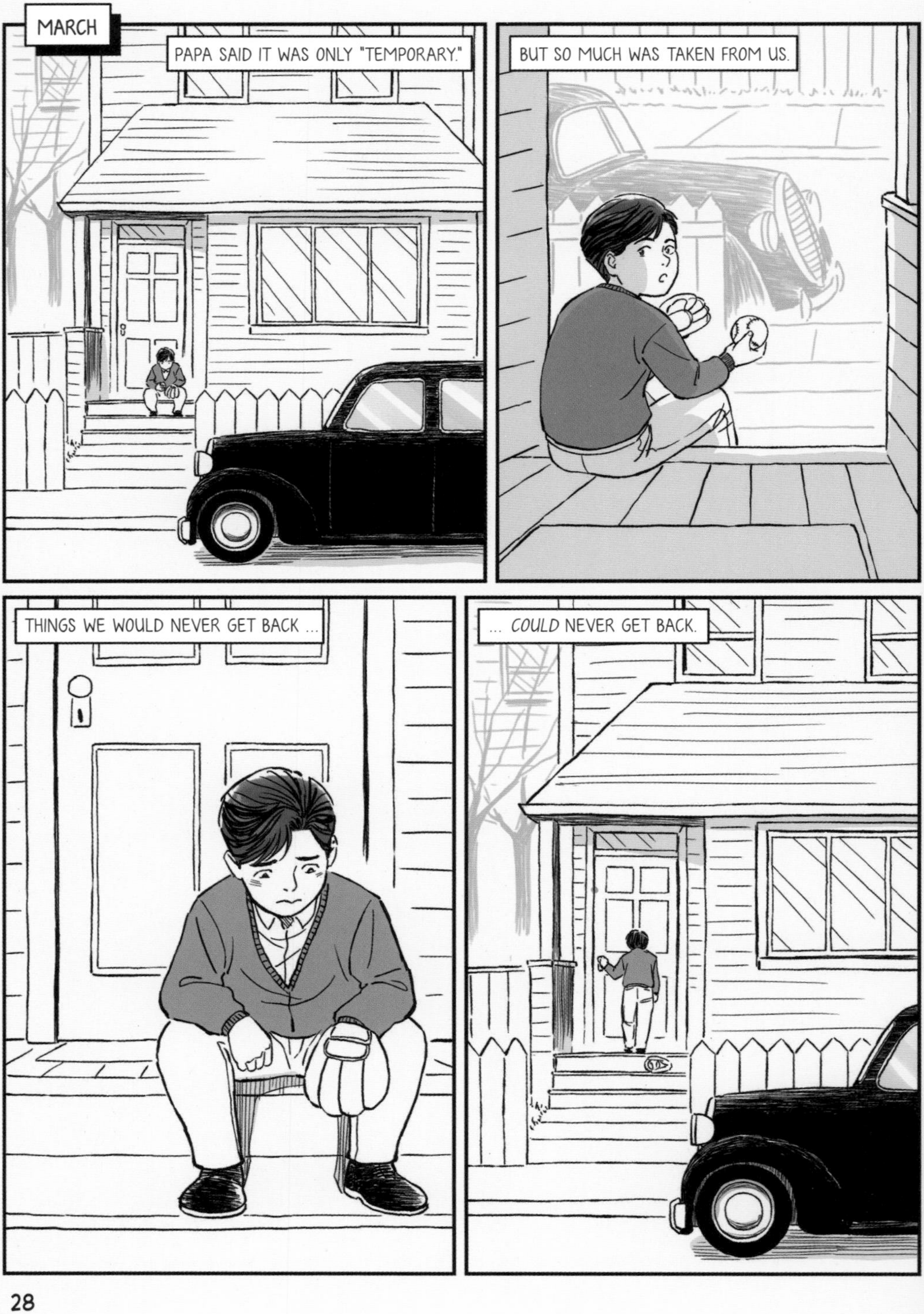
MARCH
PAPA SAID IT WAS ONLY "TEMPORARY."
BUT SO MUCH WAS TAKEN FROM US.
THINGS WE WOULD NEVER GET BACK ...
... COULD NEVER GET BACK.

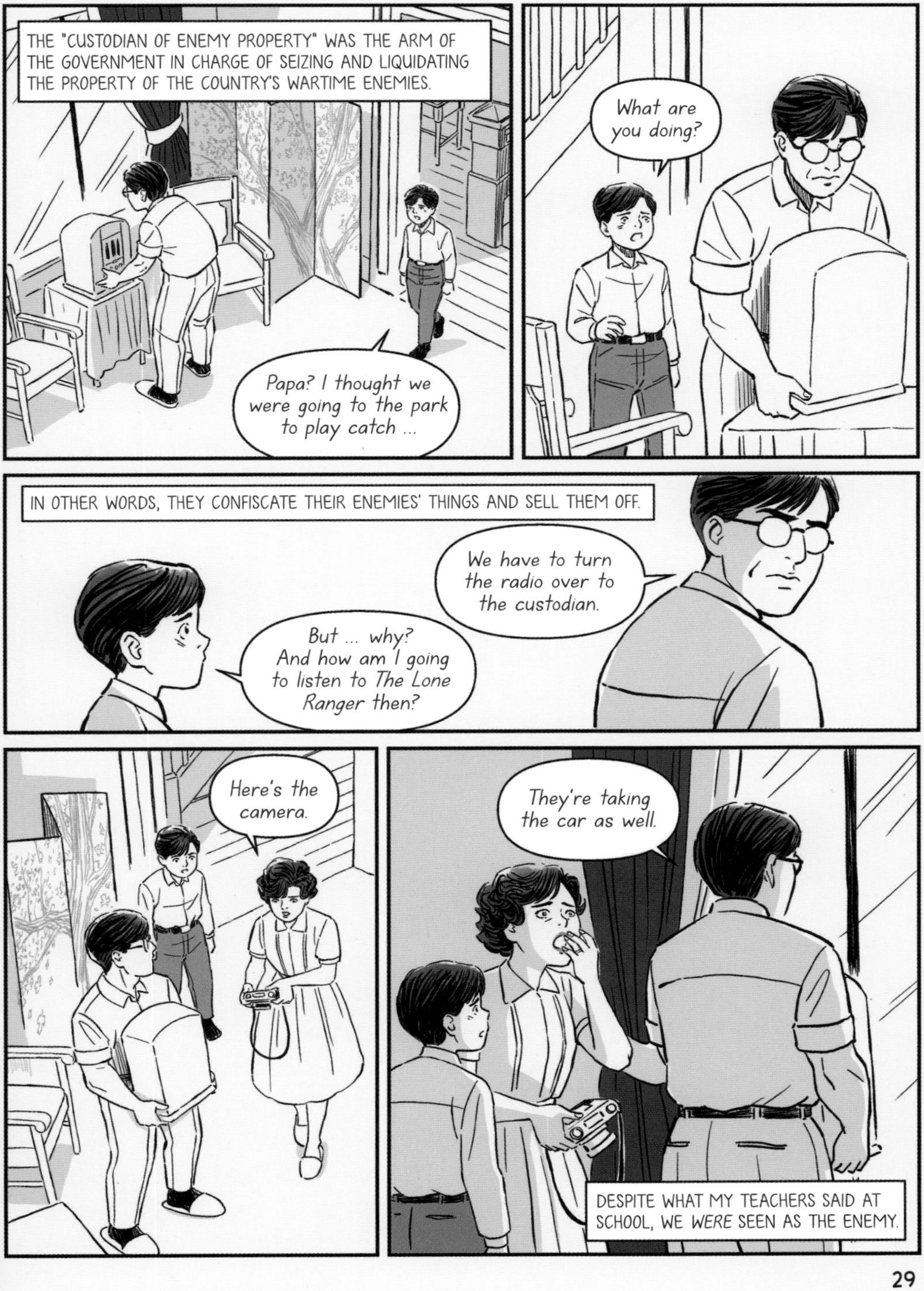
THE "CUSTODIAN OF ENEMY PROPERTY" WAS THE ARM OF THE GOVERNMENT IN CHARGE OF SEIZING AND LIQUIDATING THE PROPERTY OF THE COUNTRY'S WARTIME ENEMIES.
Papa? I thought we were going to the park to play catch ...
What are you doing?
IN OTHER WORDS, THEY CONFISCATE THEIR ENEMIES' THINGS AND SELL THEM OFF.
We have to turn the radio over to the custodian.
But ... why? And how am I going to listen to *The Lone Ranger* then?
Here's the camera.
They're taking the car as well.
DESPITE WHAT MY TEACHERS SAID AT SCHOOL, WE *WERE* SEEN AS THE ENEMY.

WITHOUT THE CAR, IT WAS HARDER FOR MY FATHER TO DO HIS JOB.

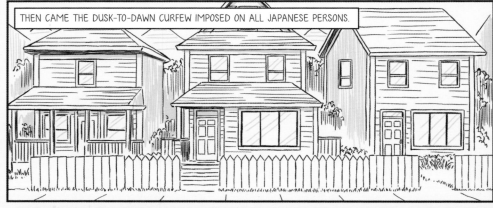

THEN CAME THE DUSK-TO-DAWN CURFEW IMPOSED ON ALL JAPANESE PERSONS.

BACK THEN, DOCTORS STILL MADE HOUSE CALLS. THE CURFEW MADE IT DIFFICULT FOR MY FATHER TO HELP ANYONE AFTER DARK. BUT HE KEPT TRYING.

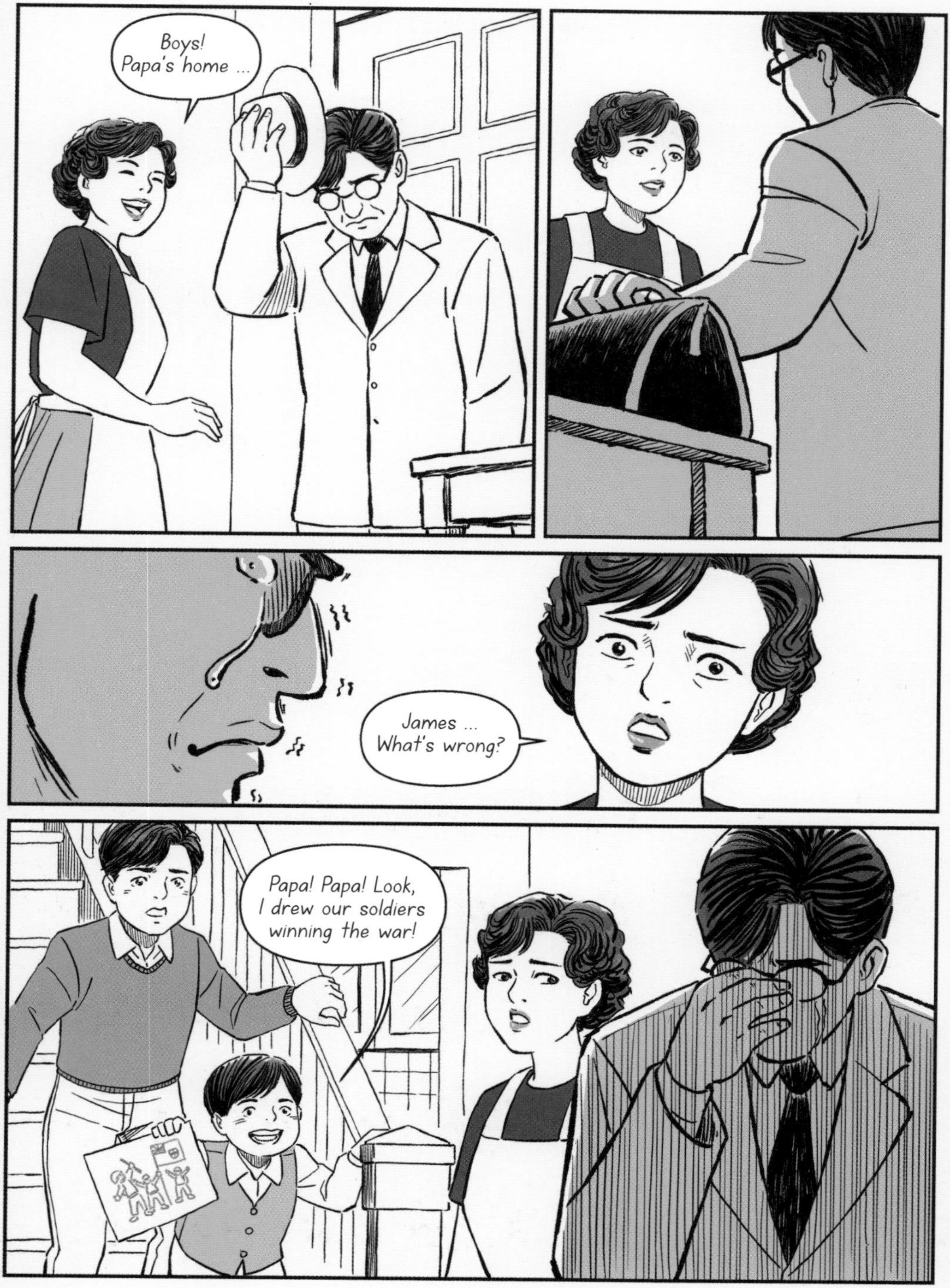
Boys!
Papa's home ...
James ...
What's wrong?
Papa! Papa! Look, I drew our soldiers winning the war!

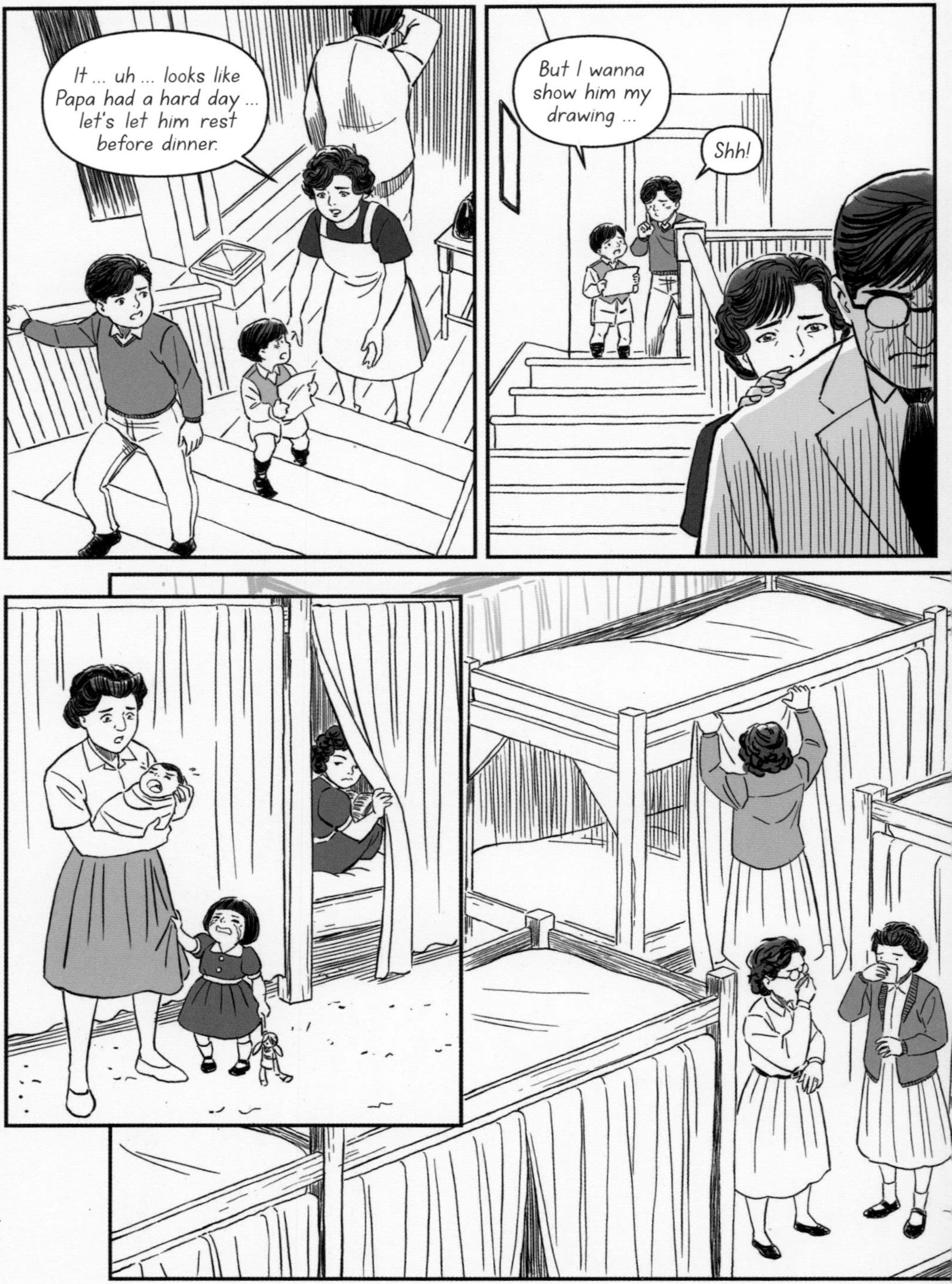
It ... uh ... looks like Papa had a hard day ... let's let him rest before dinner.
But I wanna show him my drawing ...
Shh!

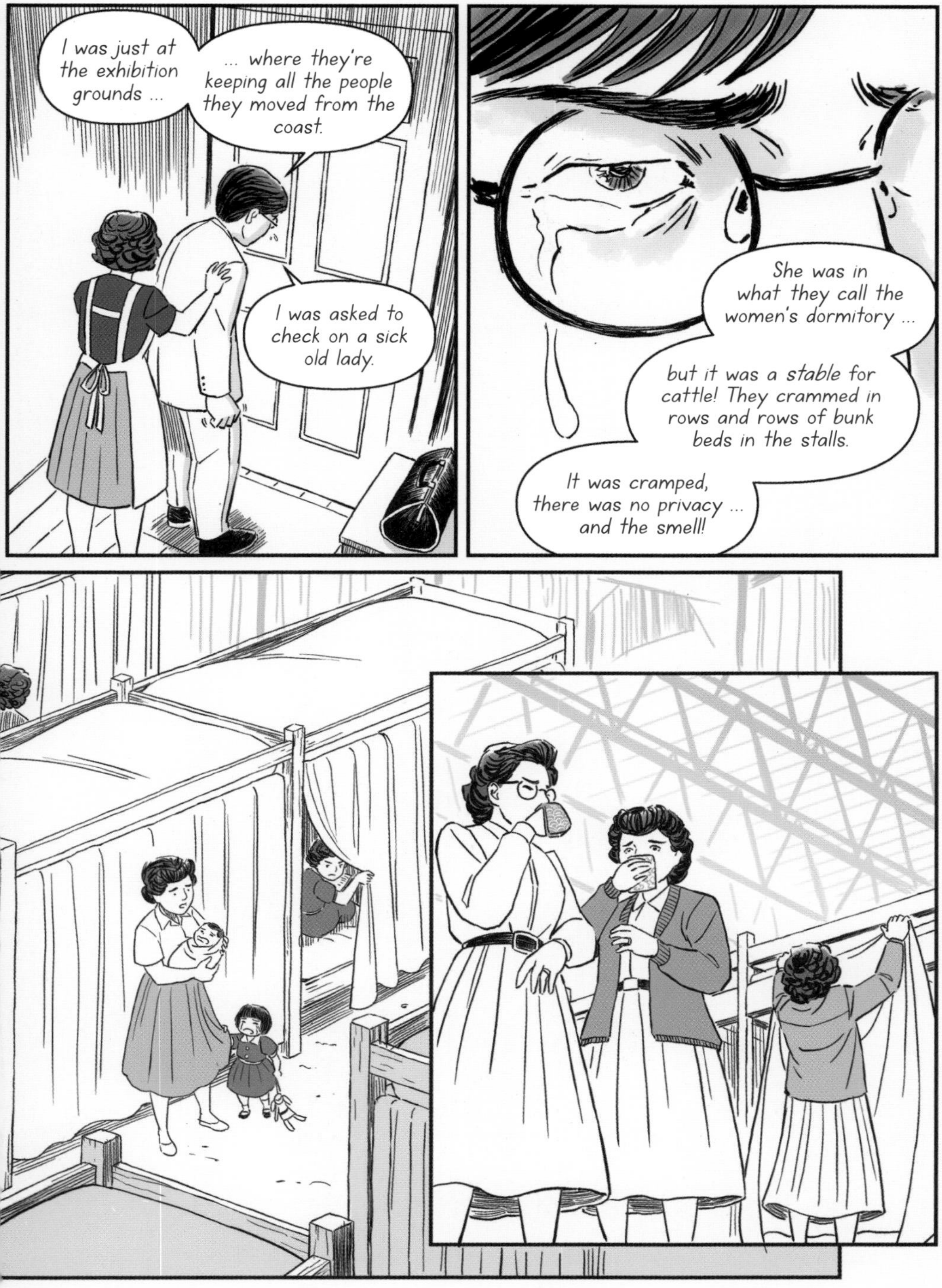
I was just at the exhibition grounds ...
... where they're keeping all the people they moved from the coast.
I was asked to check on a sick old lady.
She was in what they call the women's dormitory ...
but it was a *stable* for cattle! They crammed in rows and rows of bunk beds in the stalls.
It was cramped, there was no privacy ... and the smell!

They said it was only temporary, that everyone would be moved to the camps once they were built ...

But ... all those people ... and the children!

I like that Papa comes home early now ...

Shh!

But why does he sound so sad?

THE STRESS AND STRAIN MADE MY FATHER ACT IN WAYS WE'D NEVER SEEN BEFORE. EVEN MY MOTHER WAS DIFFERENT NOW ...

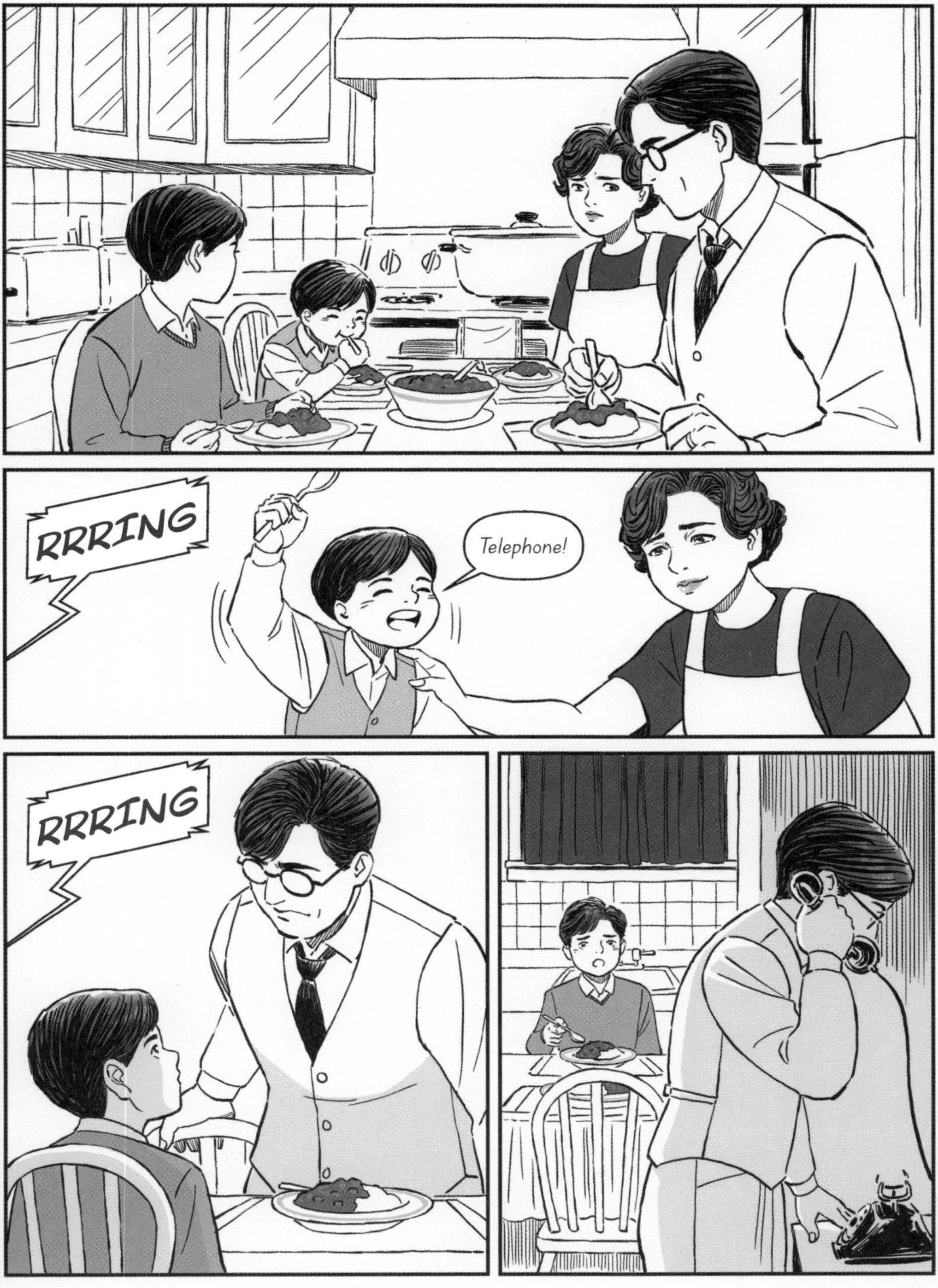
RRRING
Telephone!
RRRING

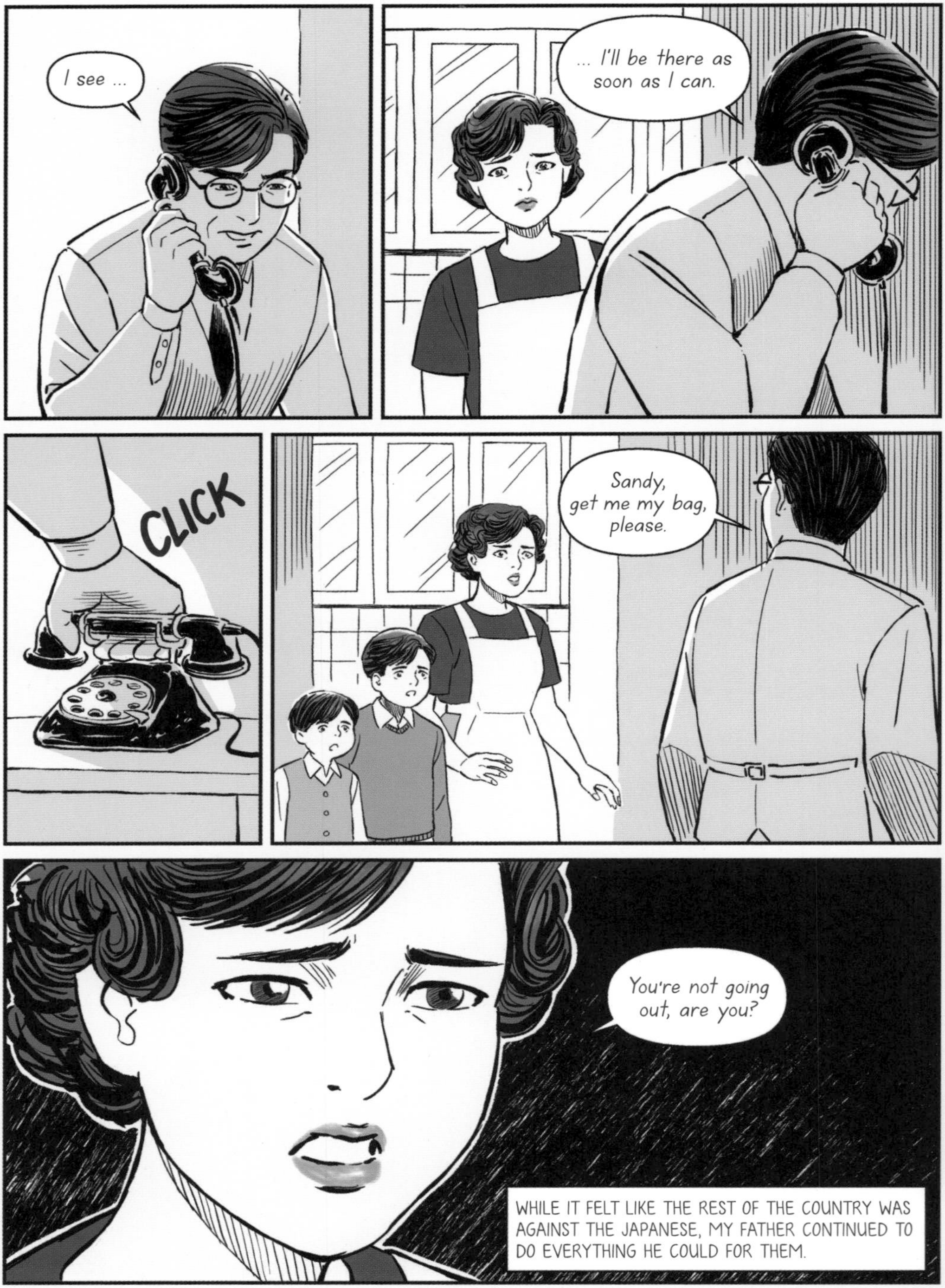
I see ...
... I'll be there as soon as I can.
CLICK
Sandy, get me my bag, please.
You're not going out, are you?
WHILE IT FELT LIKE THE REST OF THE COUNTRY WAS AGAINST THE JAPANESE, MY FATHER CONTINUED TO DO EVERYTHING HE COULD FOR THEM.

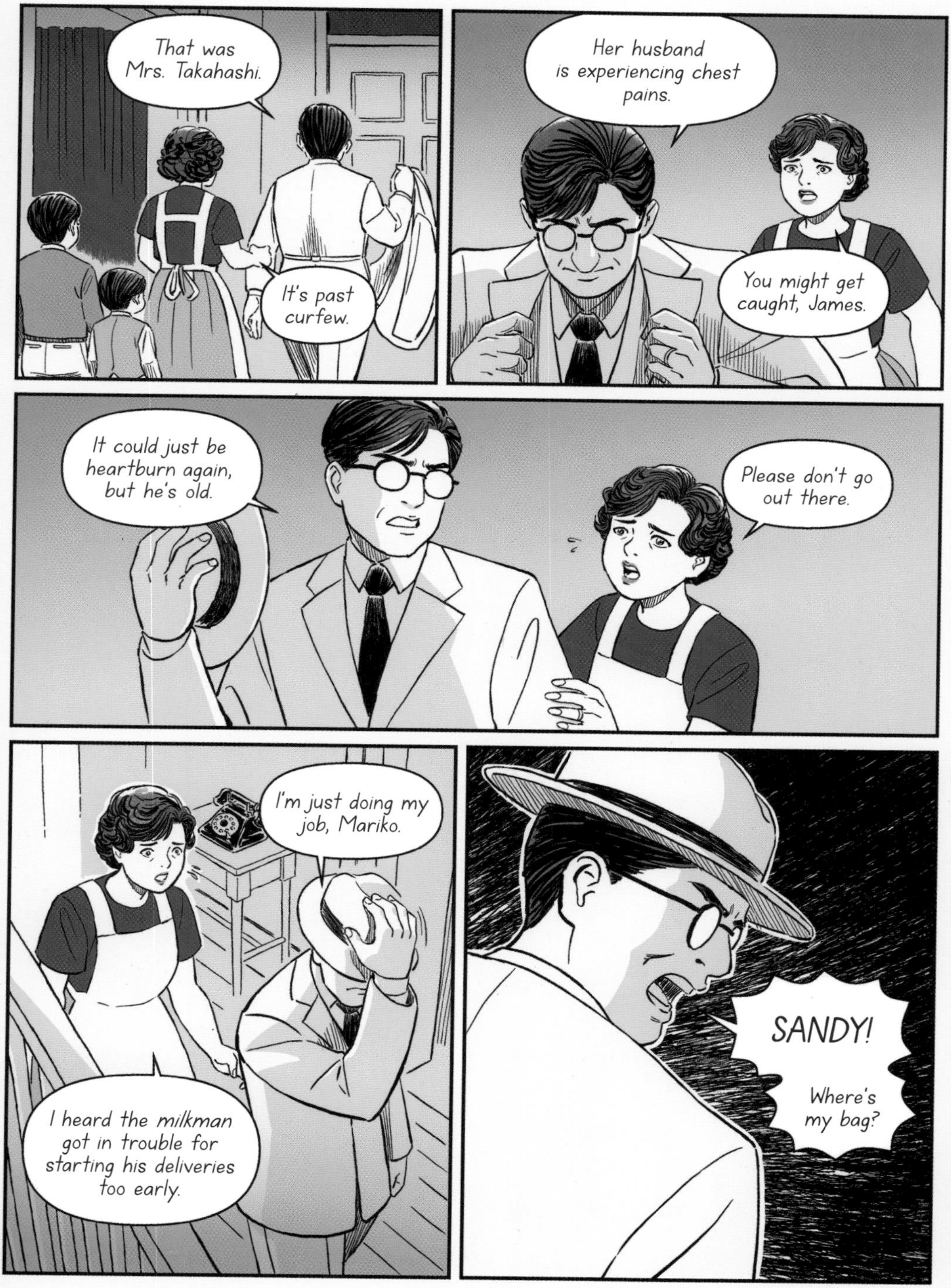
That was Mrs. Takahashi.
It's past curfew.
Her husband is experiencing chest pains.
You might get caught, James.
It could just be heartburn again, but he's old.
Please don't go out there.
I'm just doing my job, Mariko.
I heard the milkman got in trouble for starting his deliveries too early.
SANDY!
Where's my bag?

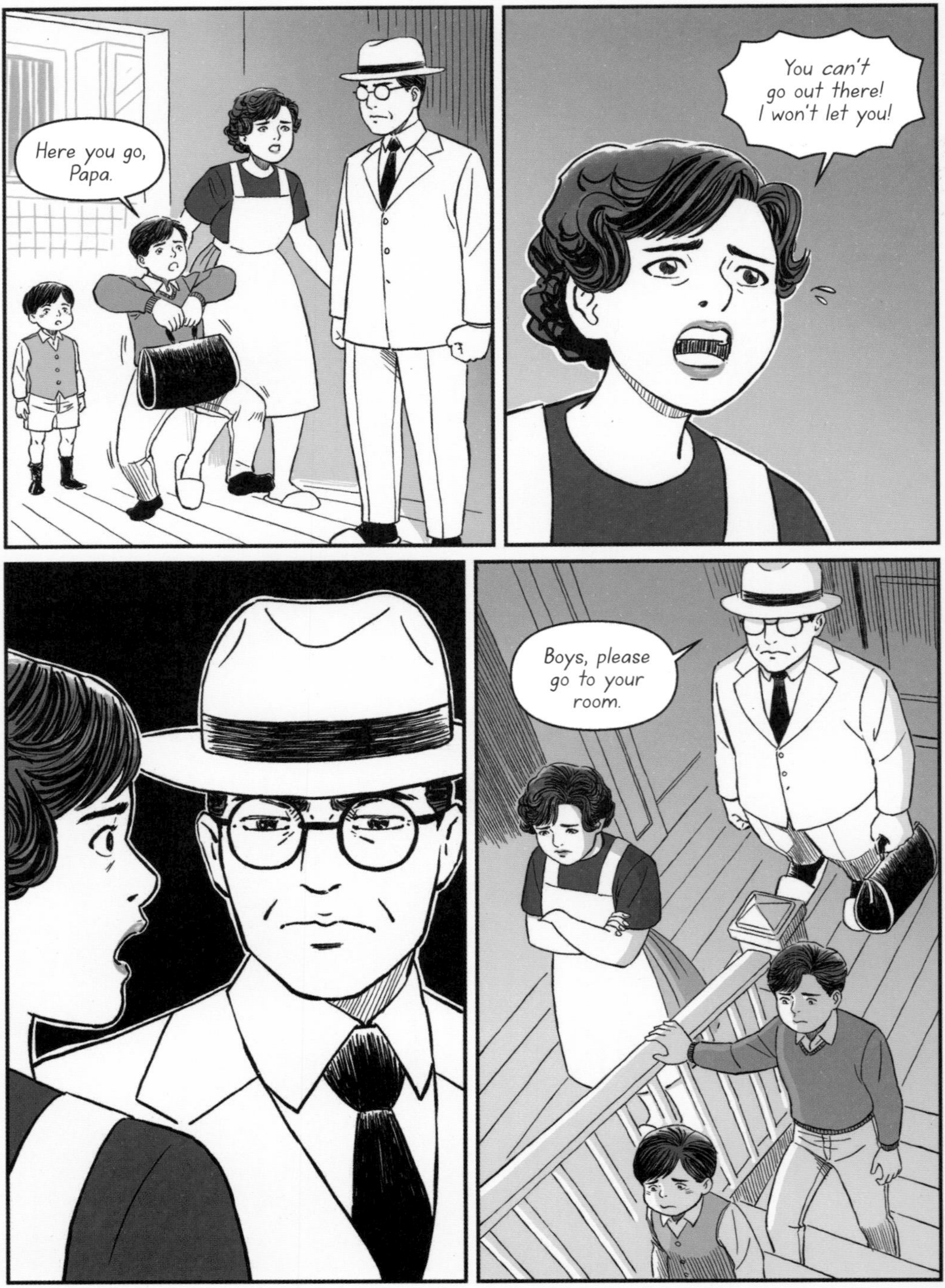
Here you go, Papa.
You can't go out there! I won't let you!
Boys, please go to your room.

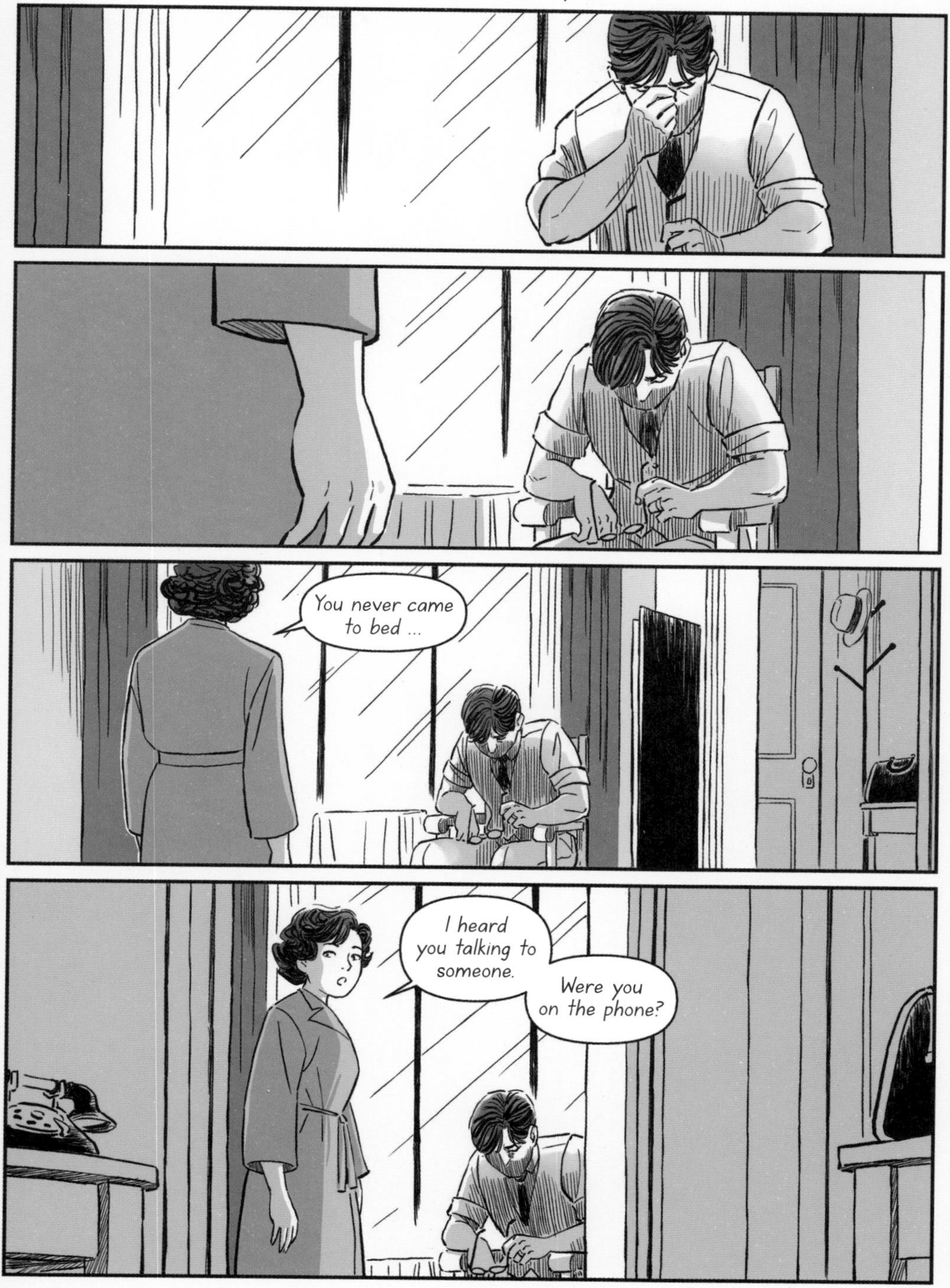
You never came to bed ...
I heard you talking to someone.
Were you on the phone?

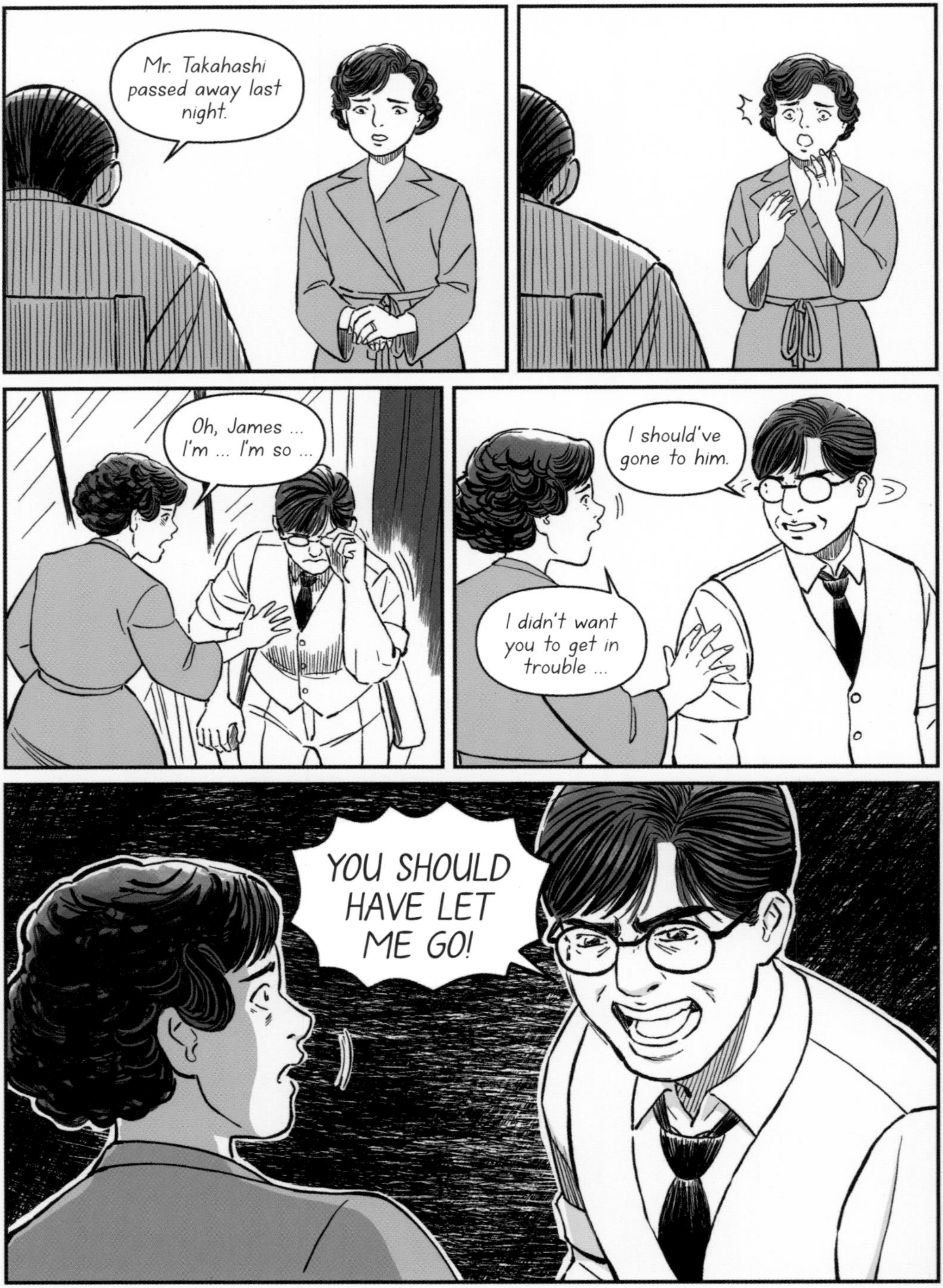
Mr. Takahashi passed away last night.
Oh, James ... I'm ... I'm so ...
I should've gone to him.
I didn't want you to get in trouble ...
YOU SHOULD HAVE LET ME GO!

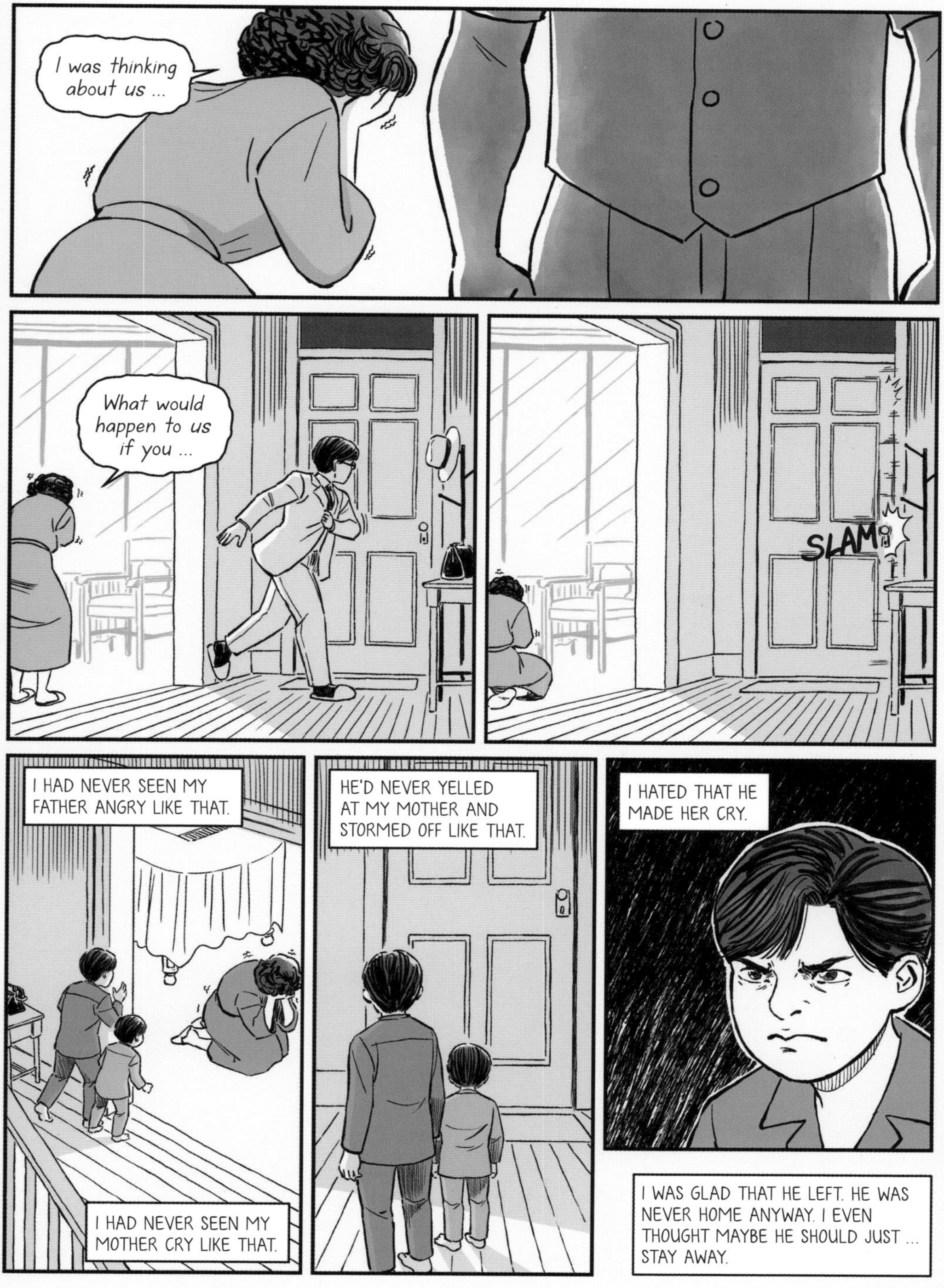
I was thinking about us ...
What would happen to us if you ...
SLAM
I HAD NEVER SEEN MY FATHER ANGRY LIKE THAT.
I HAD NEVER SEEN MY MOTHER CRY LIKE THAT.
HE'D NEVER YELLED AT MY MOTHER AND STORMED OFF LIKE THAT.
I HATED THAT HE MADE HER CRY.
I WAS GLAD THAT HE LEFT. HE WAS NEVER HOME ANYWAY. I EVEN THOUGHT MAYBE HE SHOULD JUST ... STAY AWAY.

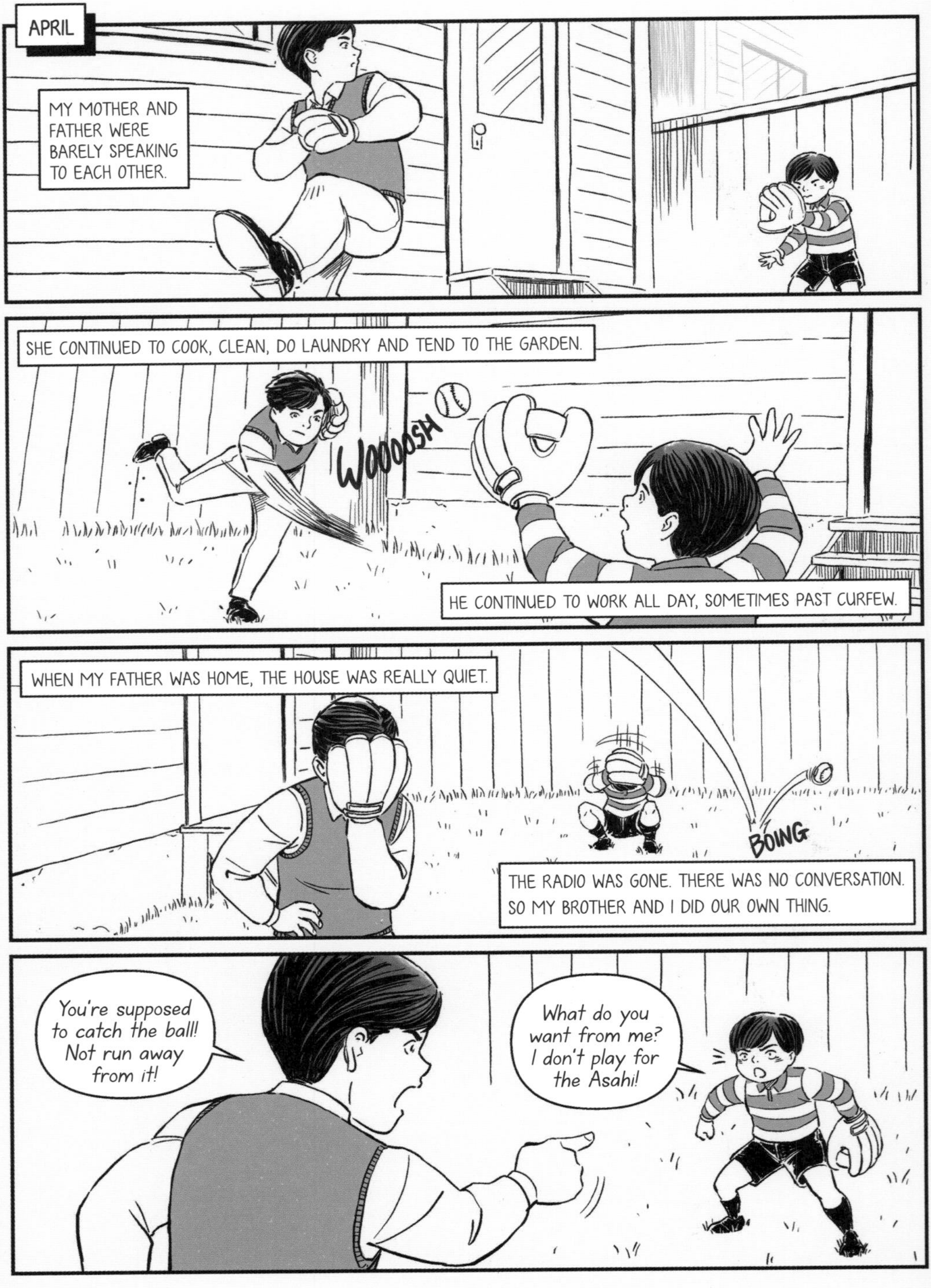
APRIL
MY MOTHER AND FATHER WERE BARELY SPEAKING TO EACH OTHER.
SHE CONTINUED TO COOK, CLEAN, DO LAUNDRY AND TEND TO THE GARDEN.
WOOOOSH
HE CONTINUED TO WORK ALL DAY, SOMETIMES PAST CURFEW.
WHEN MY FATHER WAS HOME, THE HOUSE WAS REALLY QUIET.
BOING
THE RADIO WAS GONE. THERE WAS NO CONVERSATION. SO MY BROTHER AND I DID OUR OWN THING.
You're supposed to catch the ball! Not run away from it!
What do you want from me? I don't play for the Asahi!

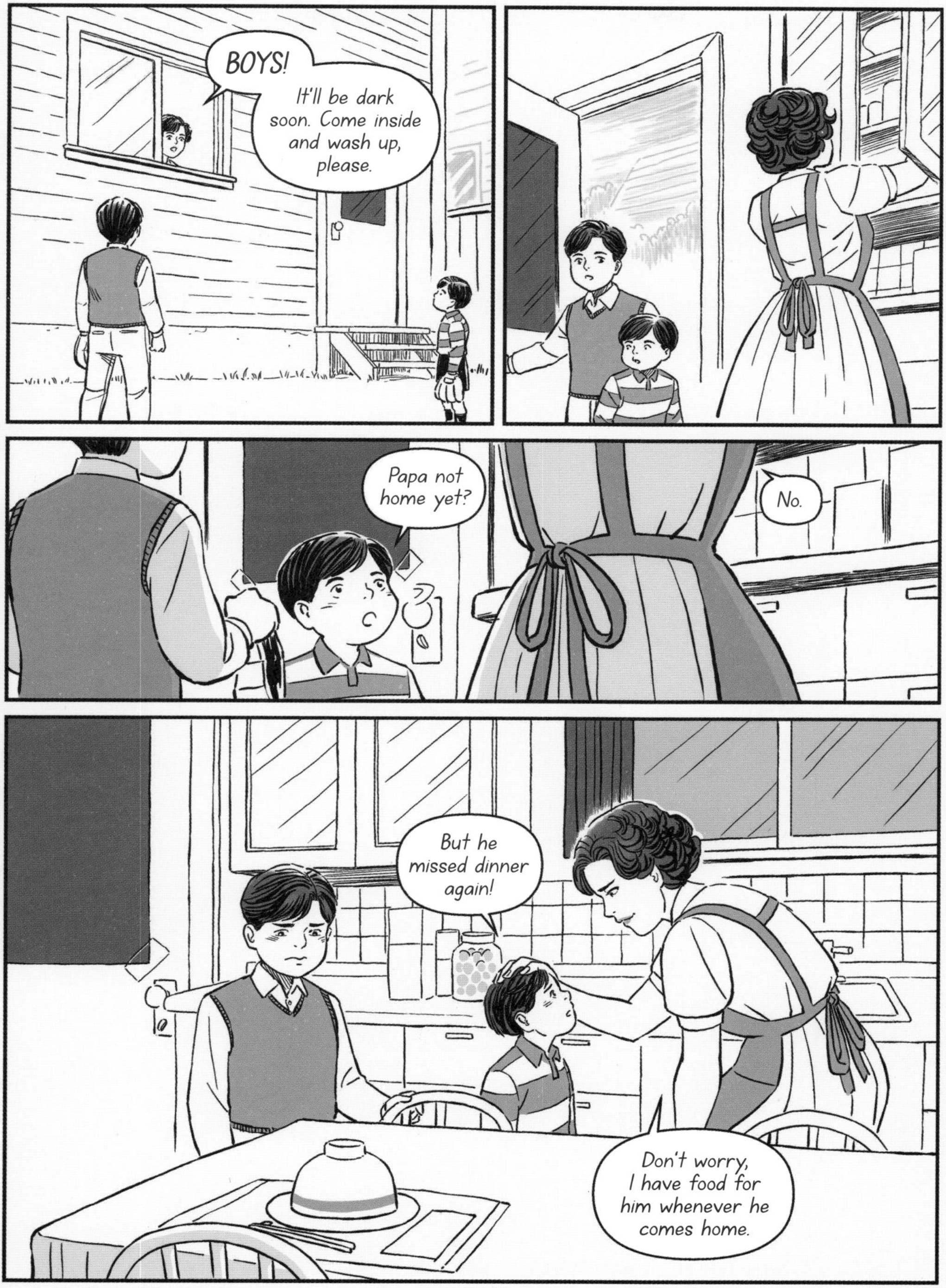
BOYS!
It'll be dark soon. Come inside and wash up, please.
Papa not home yet?
No.
But he missed dinner again!
Don't worry, I have food for him whenever he comes home.

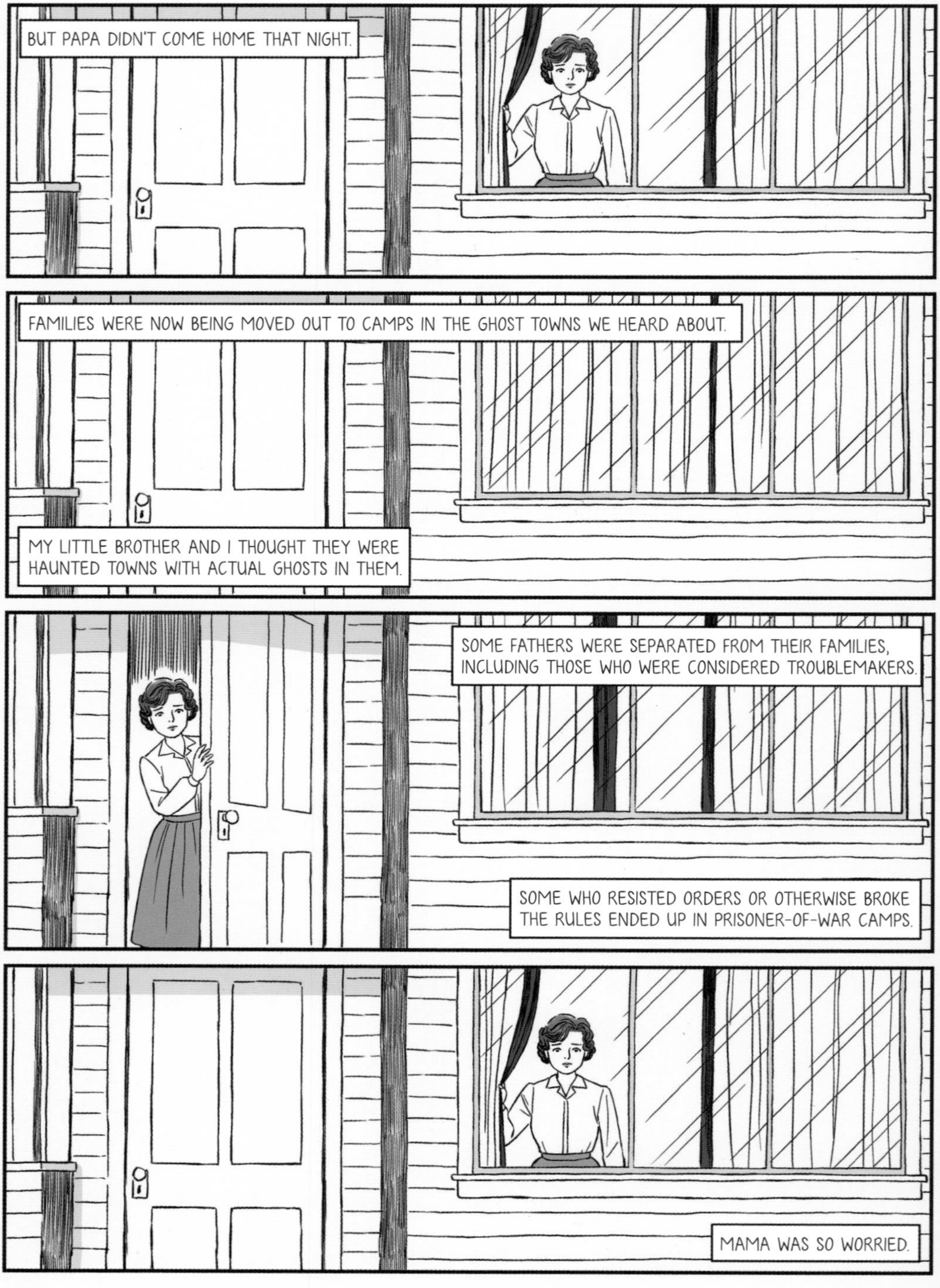
BUT PAPA DIDN'T COME HOME THAT NIGHT.
FAMILIES WERE NOW BEING MOVED OUT TO CAMPS IN THE GHOST TOWNS WE HEARD ABOUT.
MY LITTLE BROTHER AND I THOUGHT THEY WERE HAUNTED TOWNS WITH ACTUAL GHOSTS IN THEM.
SOME FATHERS WERE SEPARATED FROM THEIR FAMILIES, INCLUDING THOSE WHO WERE CONSIDERED TROUBLEMAKERS.
SOME WHO RESISTED ORDERS OR OTHERWISE BROKE THE RULES ENDED UP IN PRISONER-OF-WAR CAMPS.
MAMA WAS SO WORRIED.

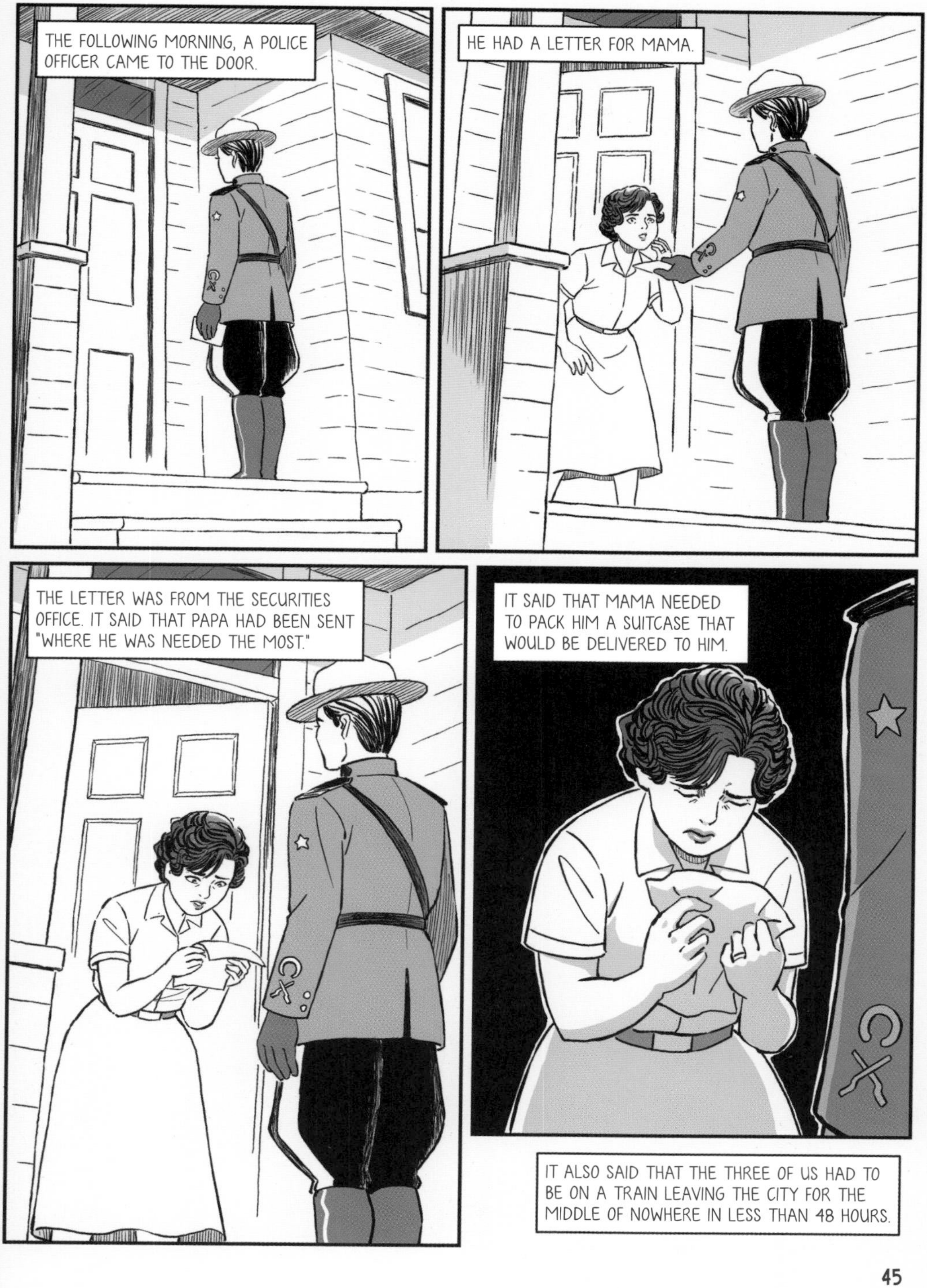
THE FOLLOWING MORNING, A POLICE OFFICER CAME TO THE DOOR.
HE HAD A LETTER FOR MAMA.
THE LETTER WAS FROM THE SECURITIES OFFICE. IT SAID THAT PAPA HAD BEEN SENT "WHERE HE WAS NEEDED THE MOST."
IT SAID THAT MAMA NEEDED TO PACK HIM A SUITCASE THAT WOULD BE DELIVERED TO HIM.
IT ALSO SAID THAT THE THREE OF US HAD TO BE ON A TRAIN LEAVING THE CITY FOR THE MIDDLE OF NOWHERE IN LESS THAN 48 HOURS.

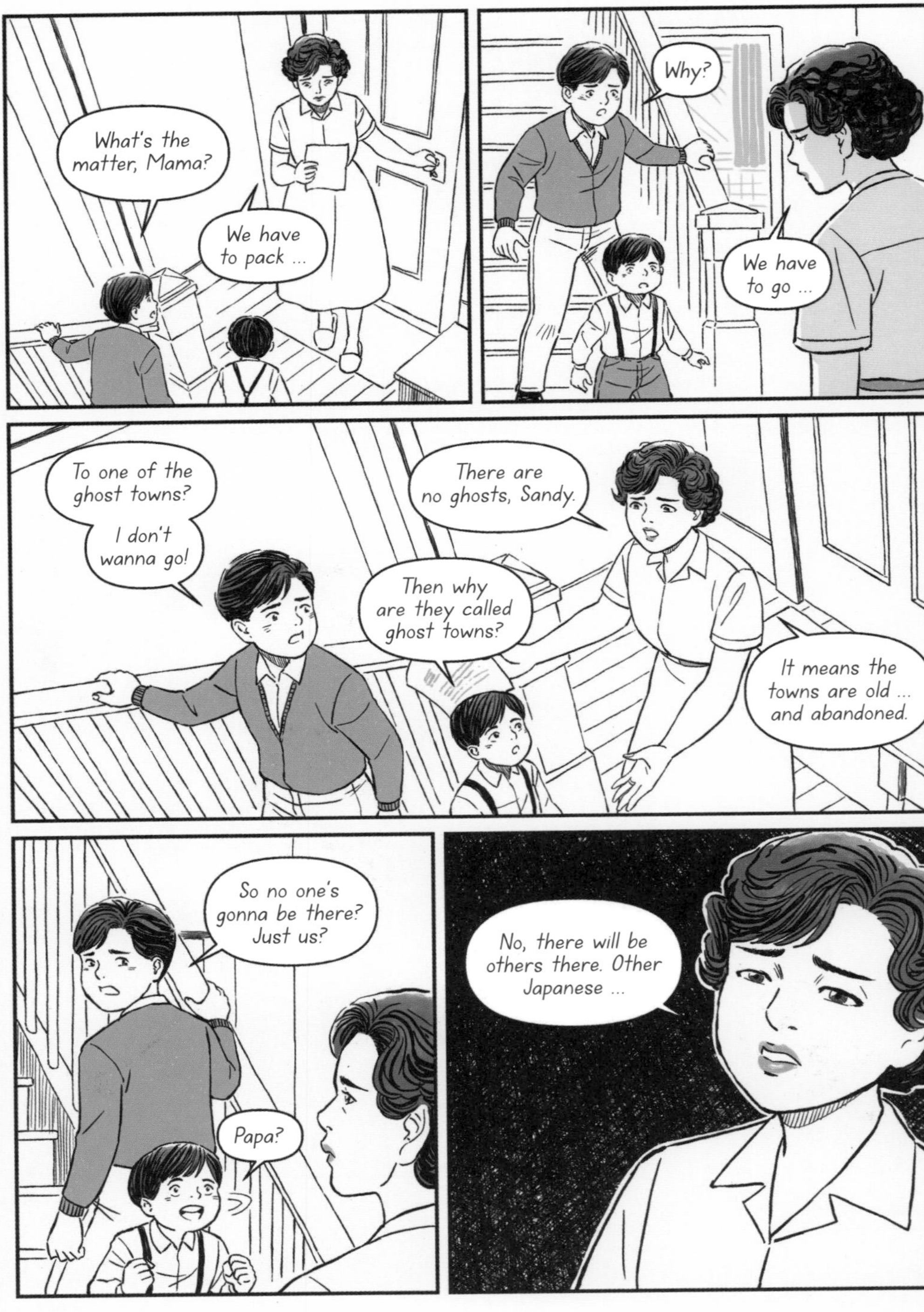
What's the matter, Mama?
We have to pack ...
Why?
We have to go ...
To one of the ghost towns?
I don't wanna go!
There are no ghosts, Sandy.
Then why are they called ghost towns?
It means the towns are old ... and abandoned.
So no one's gonna be there? Just us?
Papa?
No, there will be others there. Other Japanese ...

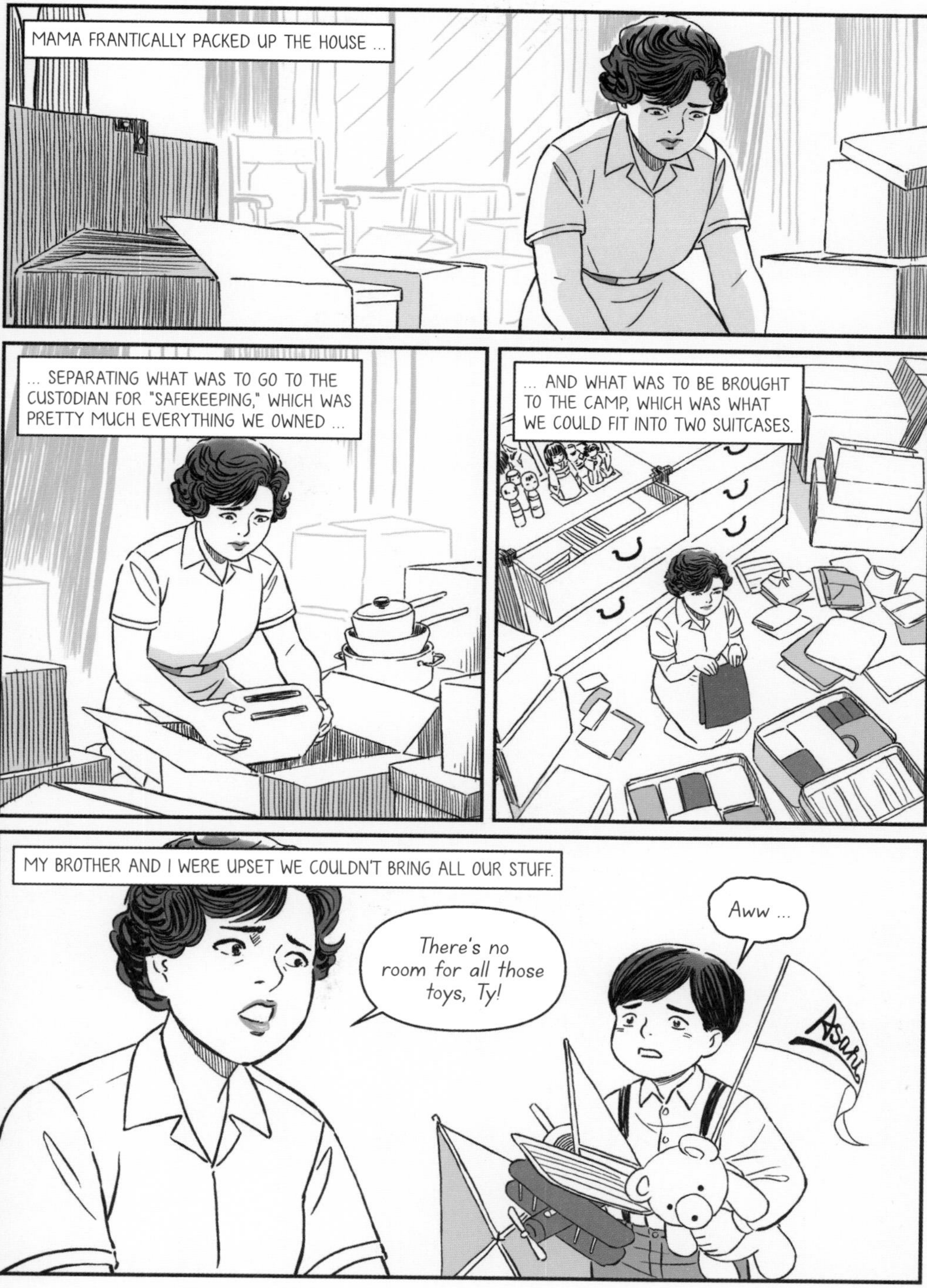
MAMA FRANTICALLY PACKED UP THE HOUSE ...
... SEPARATING WHAT WAS TO GO TO THE CUSTODIAN FOR "SAFEKEEPING," WHICH WAS PRETTY MUCH EVERYTHING WE OWNED ...
... AND WHAT WAS TO BE BROUGHT TO THE CAMP, WHICH WAS WHAT WE COULD FIT INTO TWO SUITCASES.
MY BROTHER AND I WERE UPSET WE COULDN'T BRING ALL OUR STUFF.
There's no room for all those toys, Ty!
Aww ...
Asahi

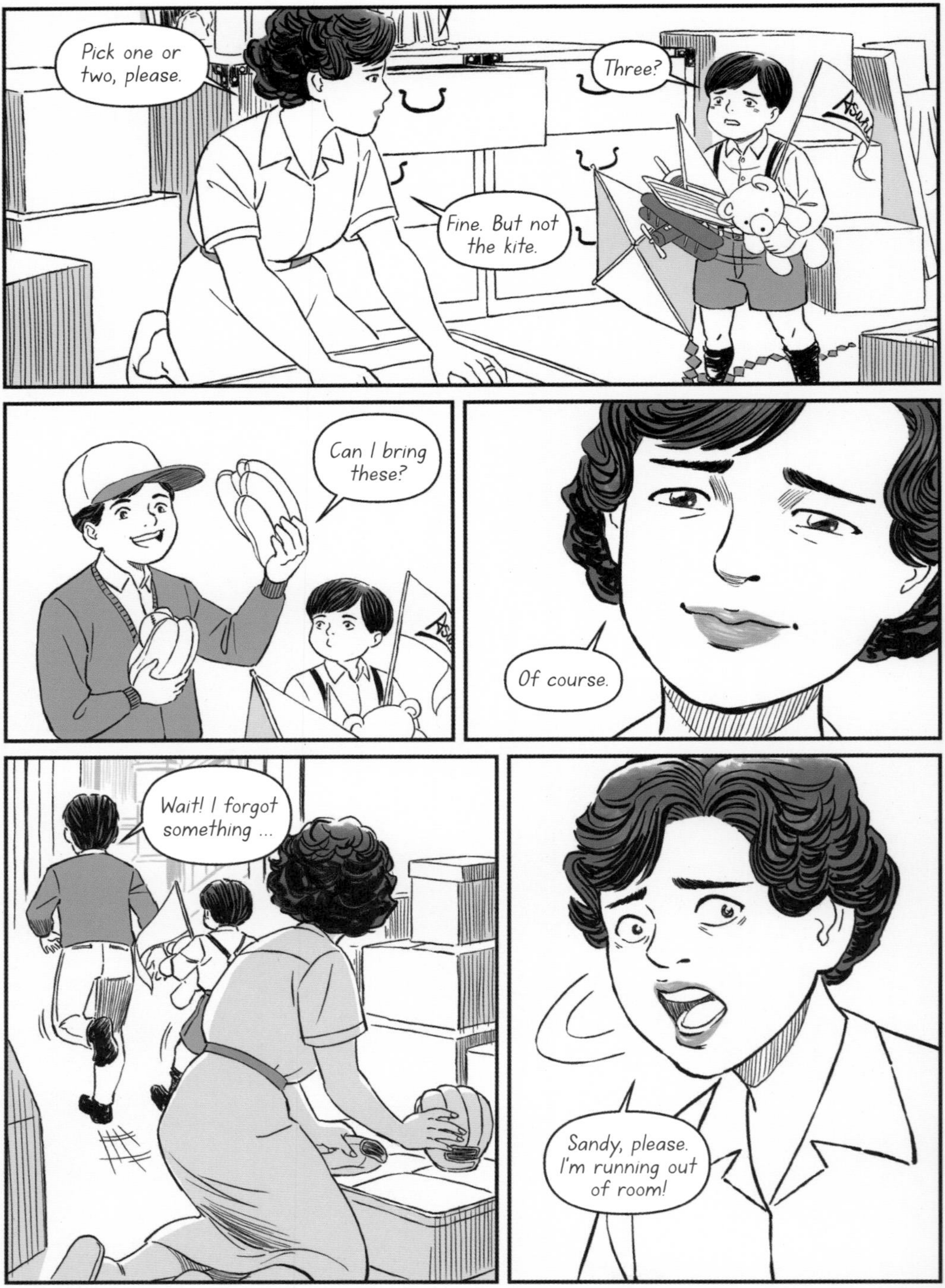
Pick one or two, please.
Three?
Fine. But not the kite.
Can I bring these?
Of course.
Wait! I forgot something ...
Sandy, please. I'm running out of room!

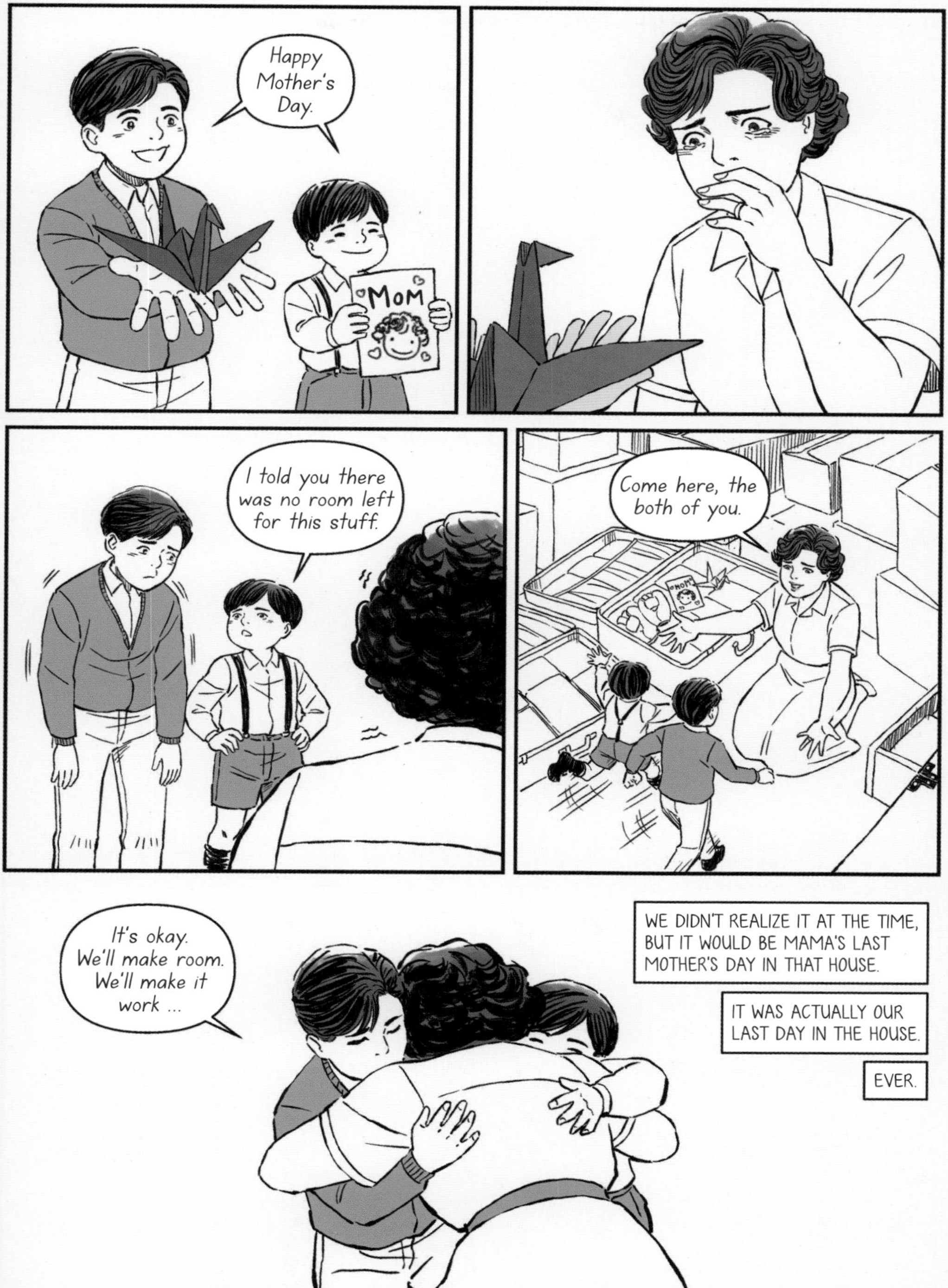
Happy Mother's Day.
MOM
I told you there was no room left for this stuff.
Come here, the both of you.
MOM
It's okay. We'll make room. We'll make it work ...
WE DIDN'T REALIZE IT AT THE TIME, BUT IT WOULD BE MAMA'S LAST MOTHER'S DAY IN THAT HOUSE.
IT WAS ACTUALLY OUR LAST DAY IN THE HOUSE.
EVER.

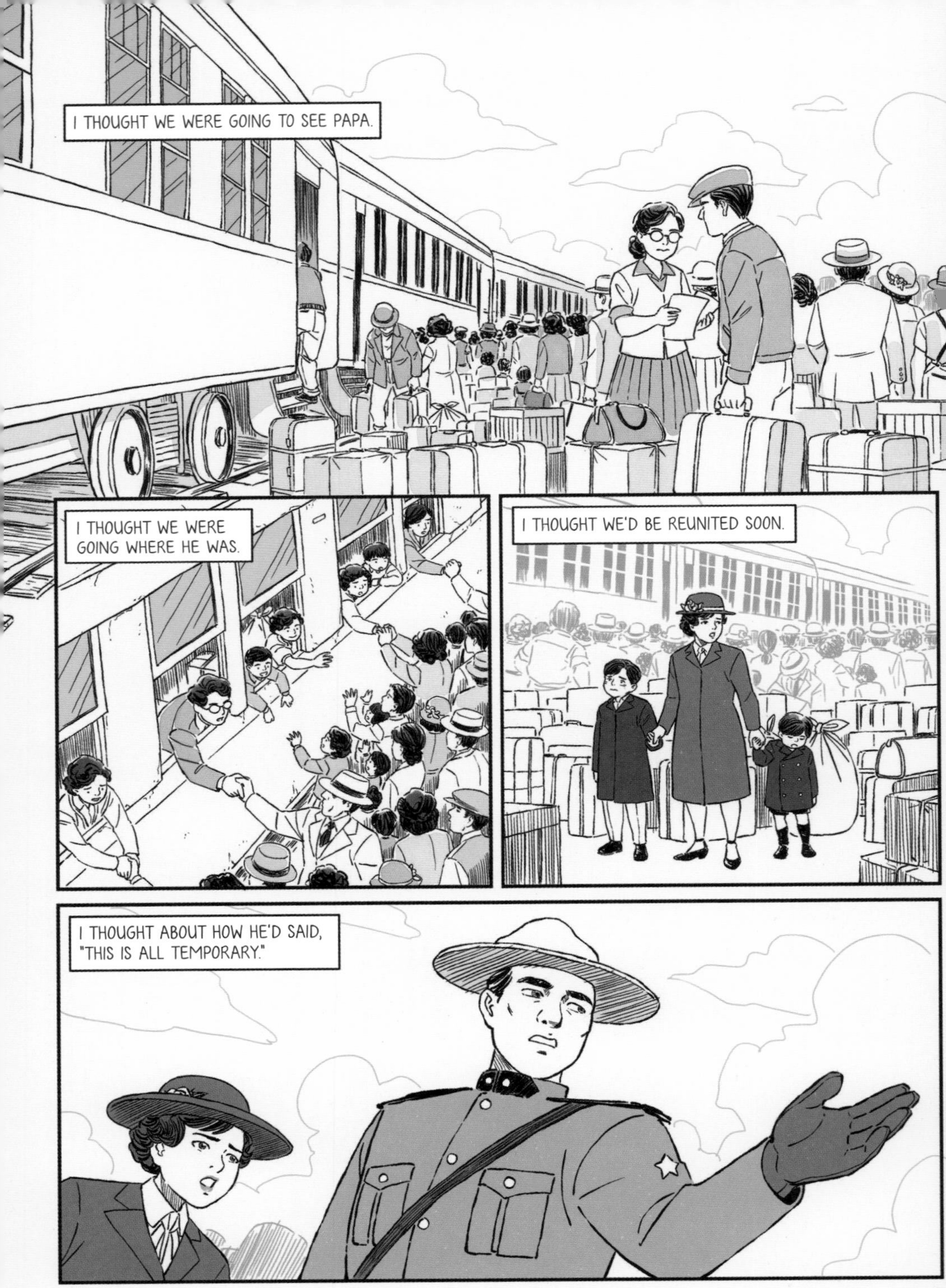
I THOUGHT WE WERE GOING TO SEE PAPA.
I THOUGHT WE WERE GOING WHERE HE WAS.
I THOUGHT WE'D BE REUNITED SOON.
I THOUGHT ABOUT HOW HE'D SAID, "THIS IS ALL TEMPORARY."

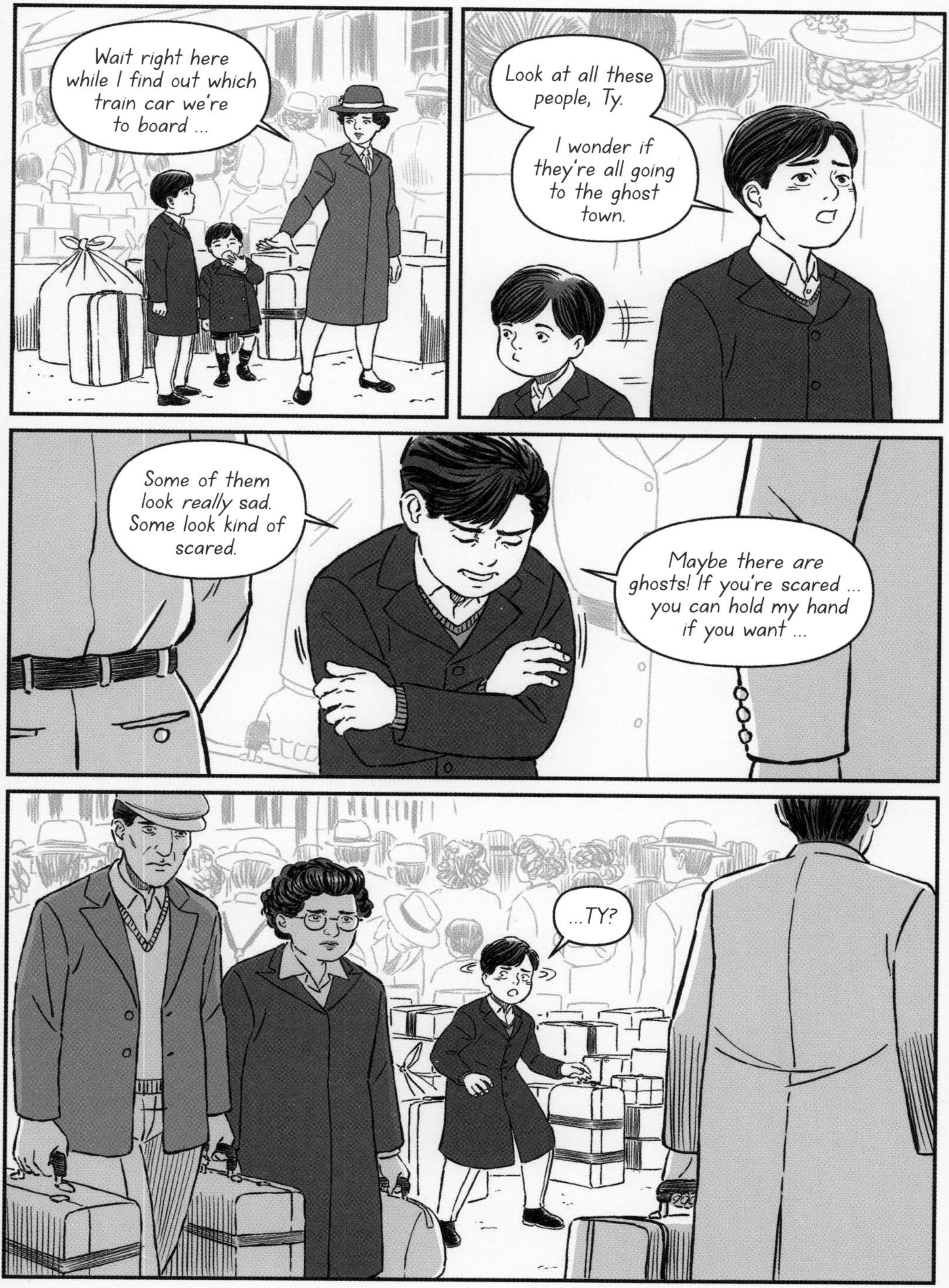
Wait right here while I find out which train car we're to board ...
Look at all these people, Ty.
I wonder if they're all going to the ghost town.
Some of them look *really* sad. Some look kind of scared.
Maybe there are ghosts! If you're scared ... you can hold my hand if you want ...
...TY?

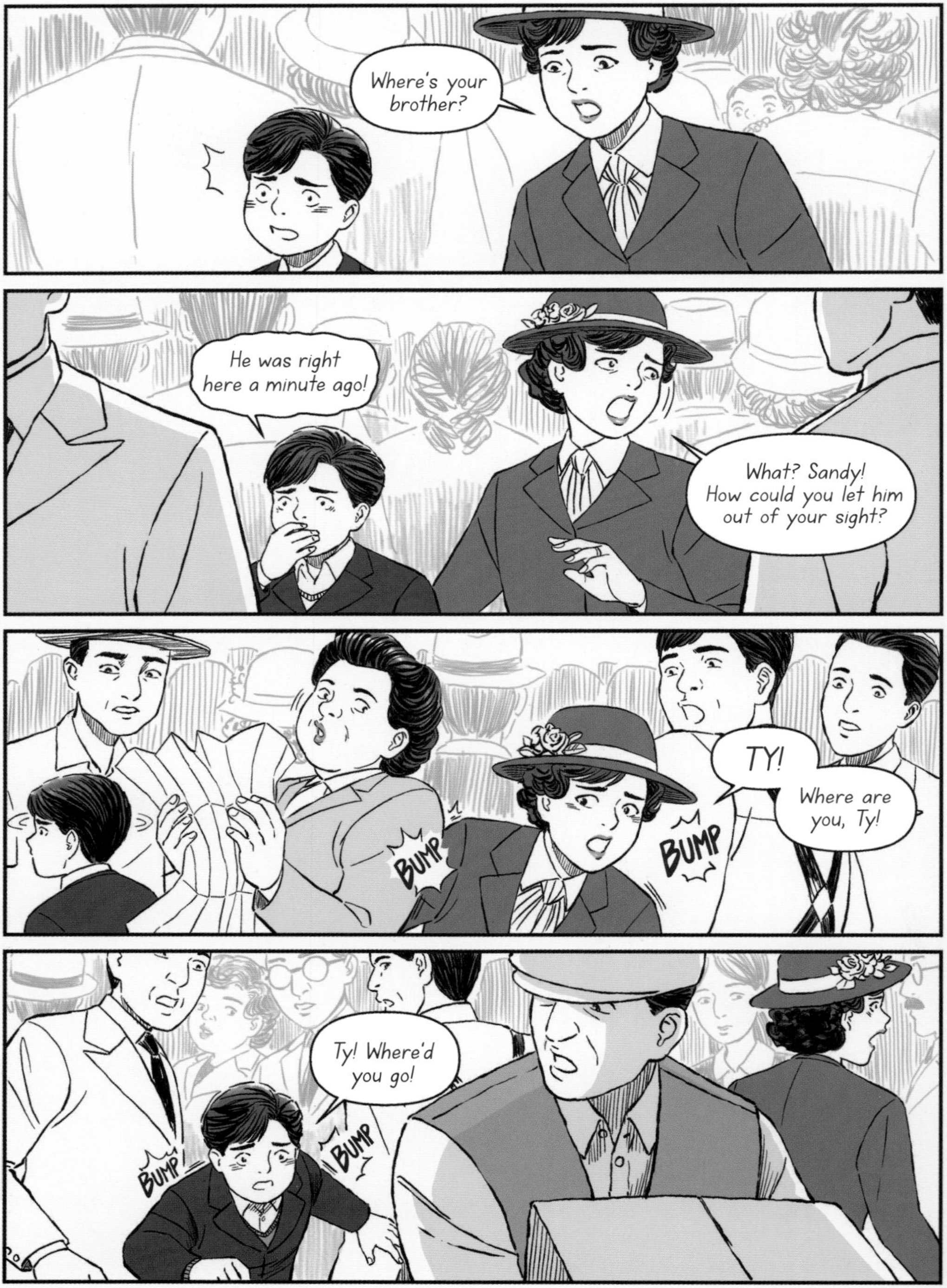

Where's your brother?
He was right here a minute ago!
What? Sandy! How could you let him out of your sight?
BUMP
BUMP
TY!
Where are you, Ty!
BUMP
Ty! Where'd you go!
BUMP

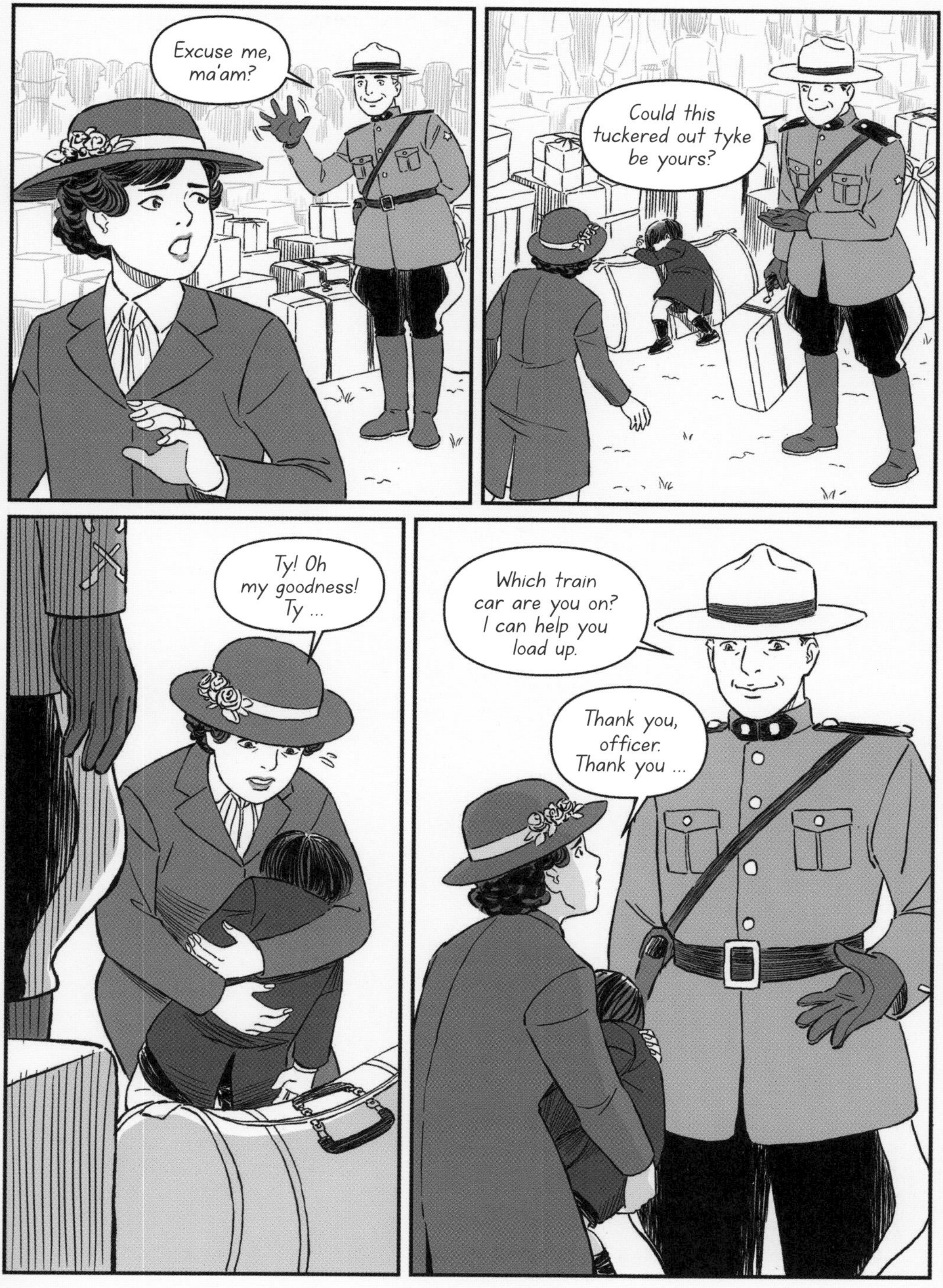
Excuse me, ma'am?
Could this tuckered out tyke be yours?
Ty! Oh my goodness! Ty ...
Which train car are you on? I can help you load up.
Thank you, officer. Thank you ...

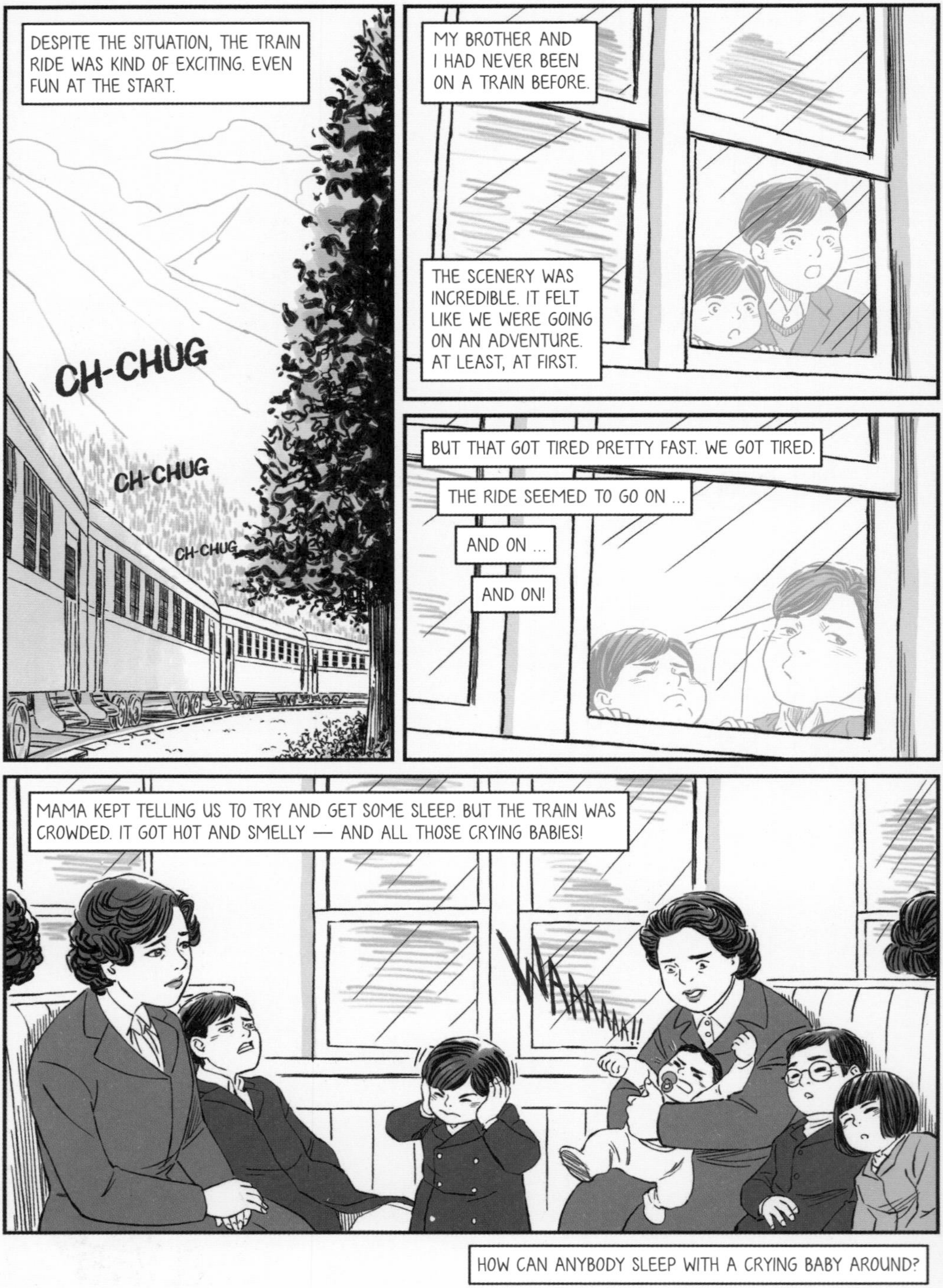
DESPITE THE SITUATION, THE TRAIN RIDE WAS KIND OF EXCITING. EVEN FUN AT THE START.
CH-CHUG
CH-CHUG
CH-CHUG
MY BROTHER AND I HAD NEVER BEEN ON A TRAIN BEFORE.
THE SCENERY WAS INCREDIBLE. IT FELT LIKE WE WERE GOING ON AN ADVENTURE. AT LEAST, AT FIRST.
BUT THAT GOT TIRED PRETTY FAST. WE GOT TIRED.
THE RIDE SEEMED TO GO ON ...
AND ON ...
AND ON!
MAMA KEPT TELLING US TO TRY AND GET SOME SLEEP. BUT THE TRAIN WAS CROWDED. IT GOT HOT AND SMELLY — AND ALL THOSE CRYING BABIES!
WAAAAAA!!
HOW CAN ANYBODY SLEEP WITH A CRYING BABY AROUND?

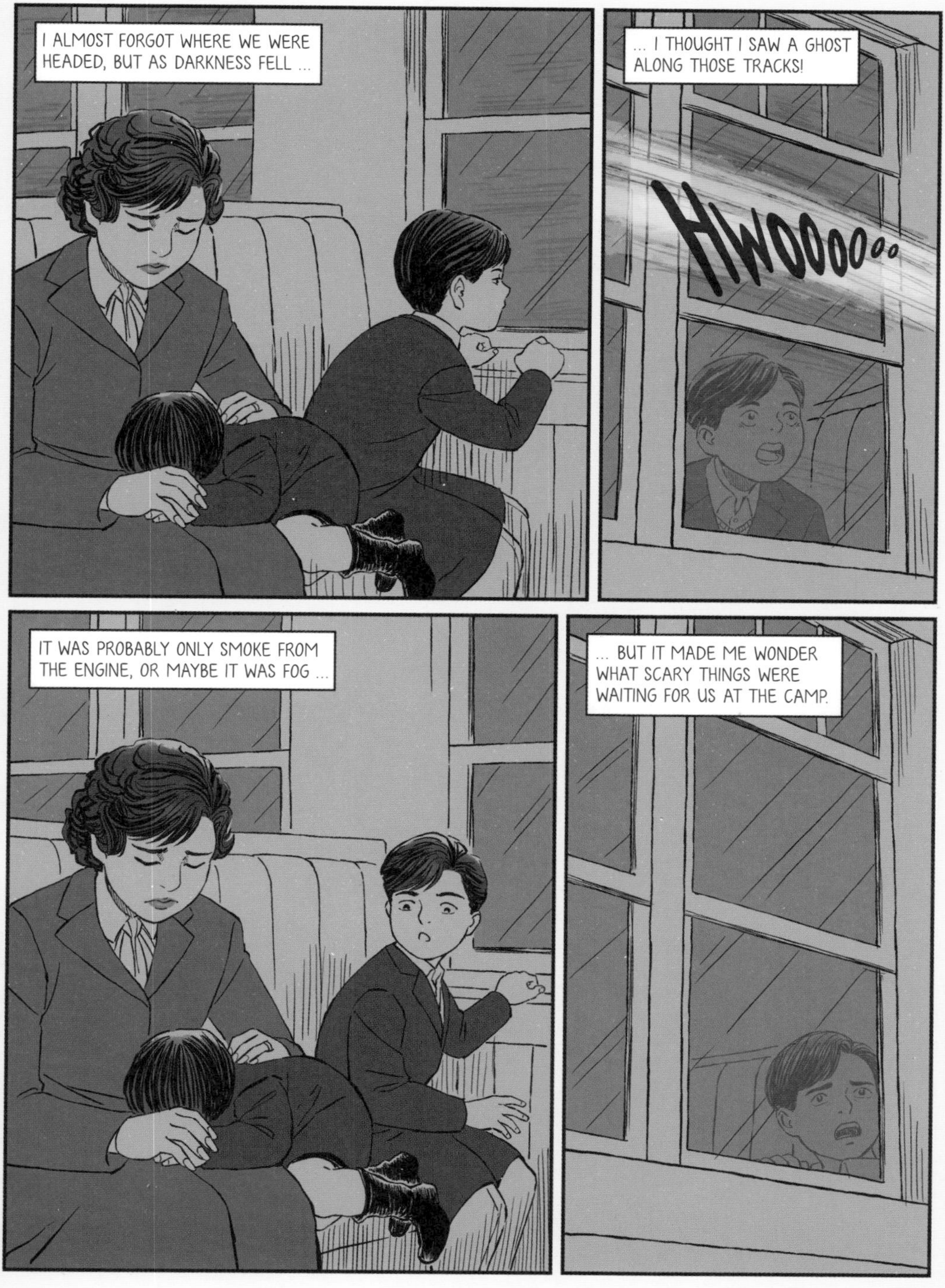
I ALMOST FORGOT WHERE WE WERE HEADED, BUT AS DARKNESS FELL ...
... I THOUGHT I SAW A GHOST ALONG THOSE TRACKS!
HWOOOOOo
IT WAS PROBABLY ONLY SMOKE FROM THE ENGINE, OR MAYBE IT WAS FOG ...
... BUT IT MADE ME WONDER WHAT SCARY THINGS WERE WAITING FOR US AT THE CAMP.

I DON'T REMEMBER GETTING OFF THE TRAIN.

I DON'T REMEMBER HOW I GOT ON THAT TRUCK.

MAYBE SOMEONE CARRIED ME THE WAY THAT OFFICER CARRIED TY ONTO THE TRAIN.

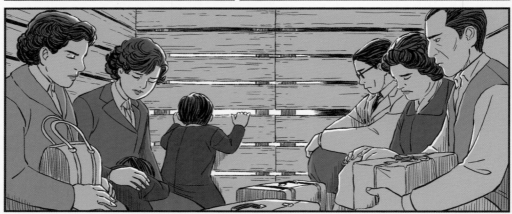

I REMEMBER IT BEING SO DARK. PITCH BLACK.

AND SO SO SO COLD.

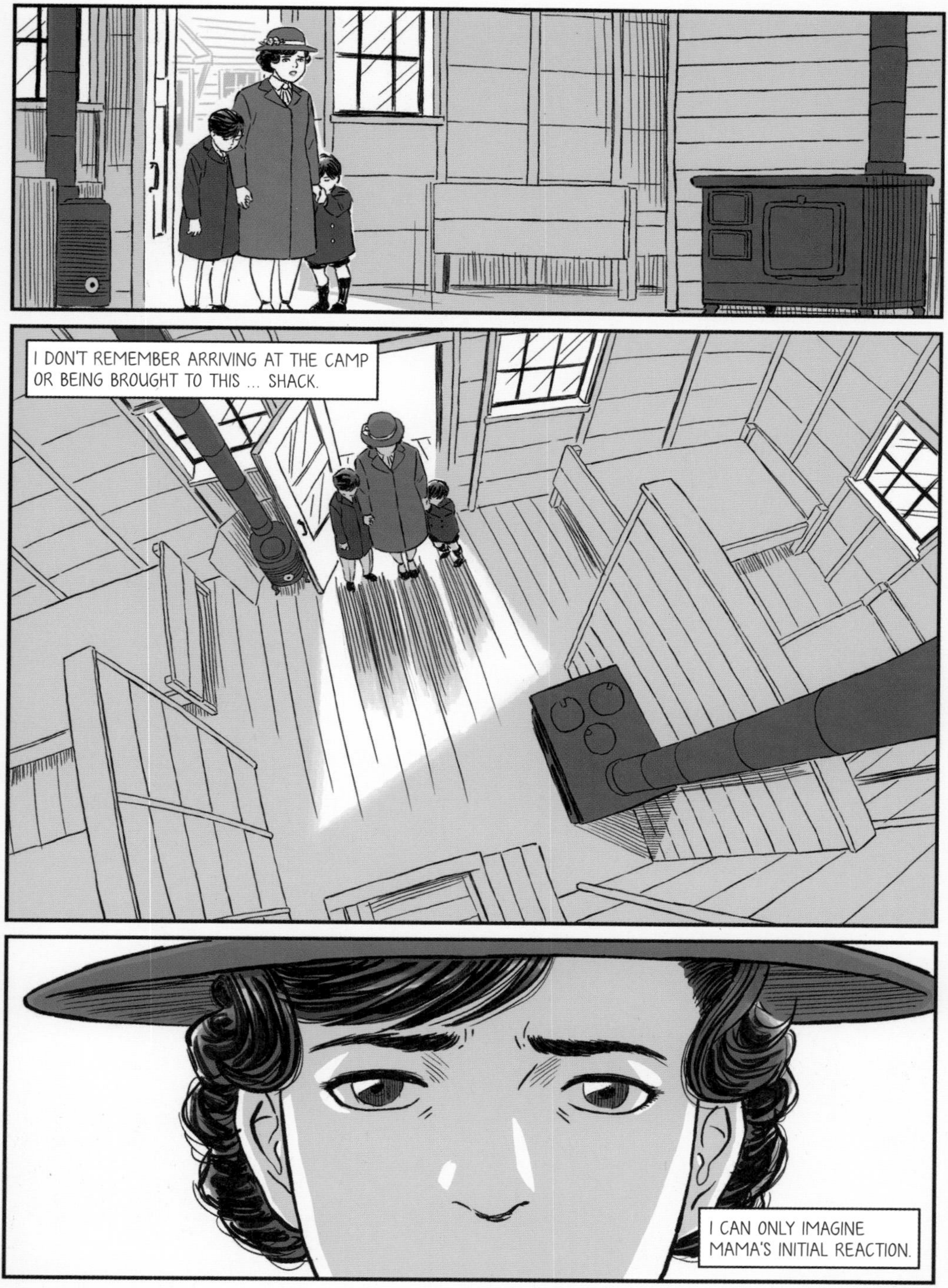
I DON'T REMEMBER ARRIVING AT THE CAMP OR BEING BROUGHT TO THIS ... SHACK.
I CAN ONLY IMAGINE MAMA'S INITIAL REACTION.

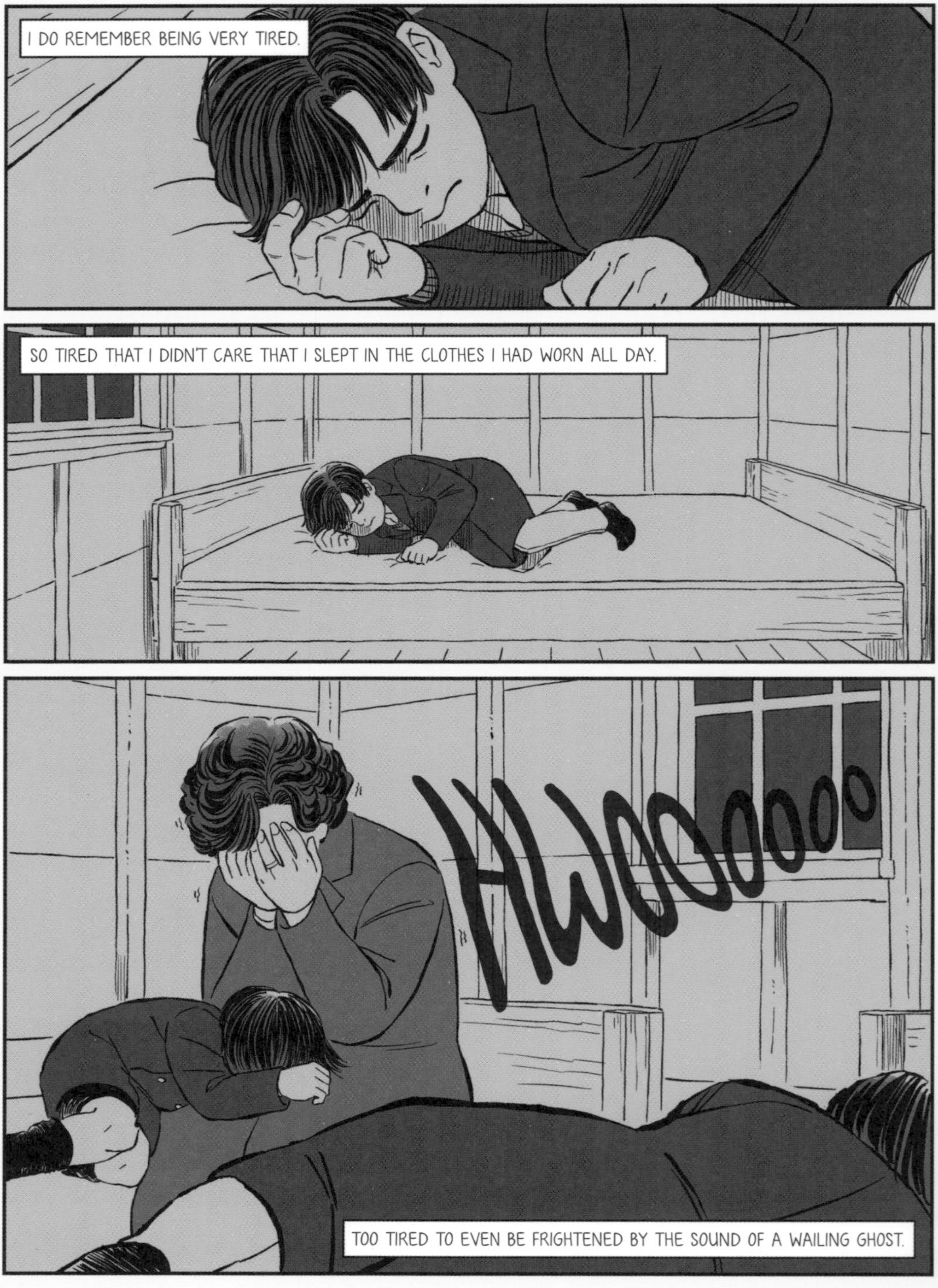
I DO REMEMBER BEING VERY TIRED.
SO TIRED THAT I DIDN'T CARE THAT I SLEPT IN THE CLOTHES I HAD WORN ALL DAY.
HWOOOOOOO
TOO TIRED TO EVEN BE FRIGHTENED BY THE SOUND OF A WAILING GHOST.

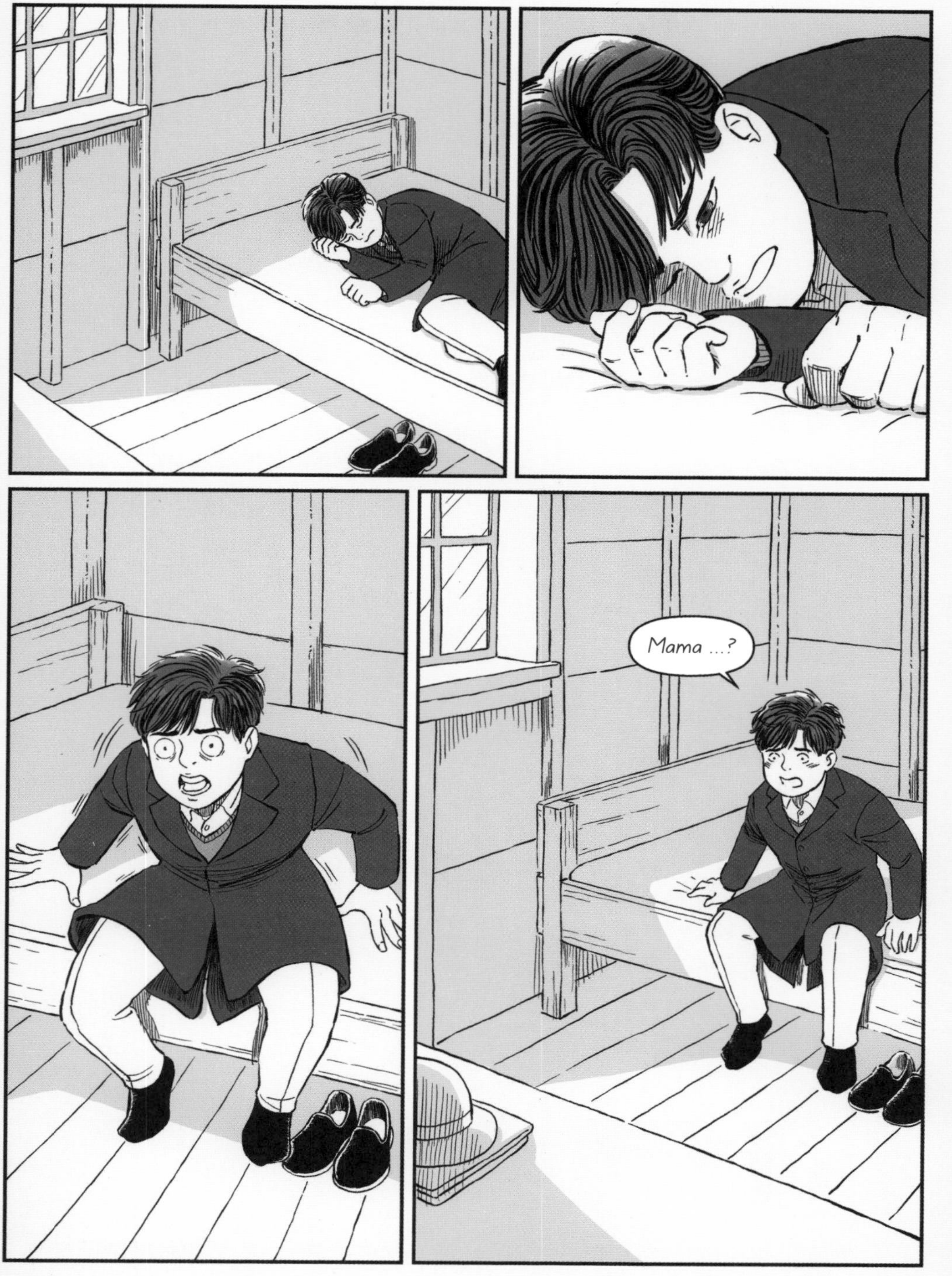
Mama ...?

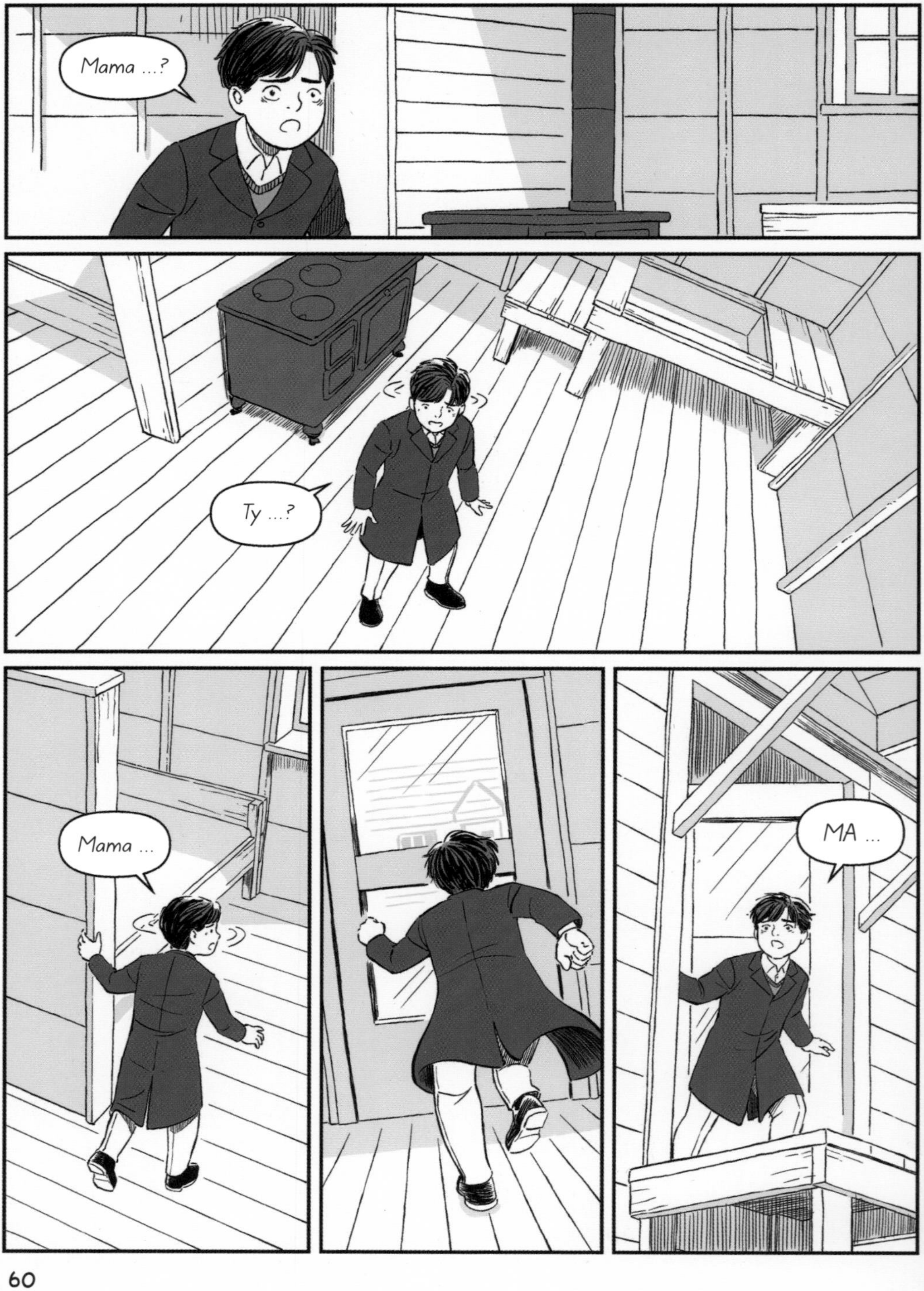
Mama ...?
Ty ...?
Mama ...
MA ...

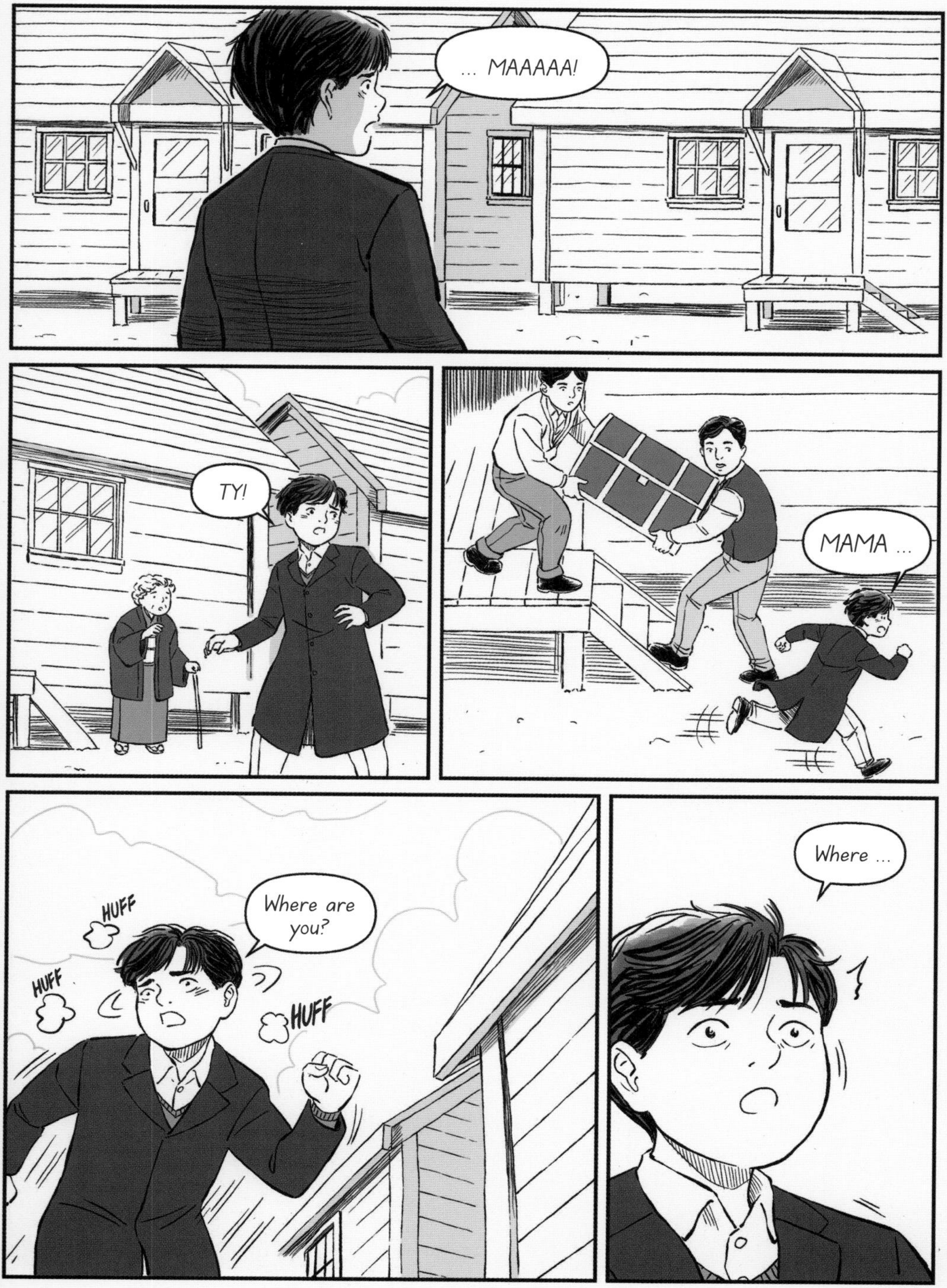
... MAAAAA!
TY!
MAMA ...
HUFF
HUFF
HUFF
Where are you?
Where ...

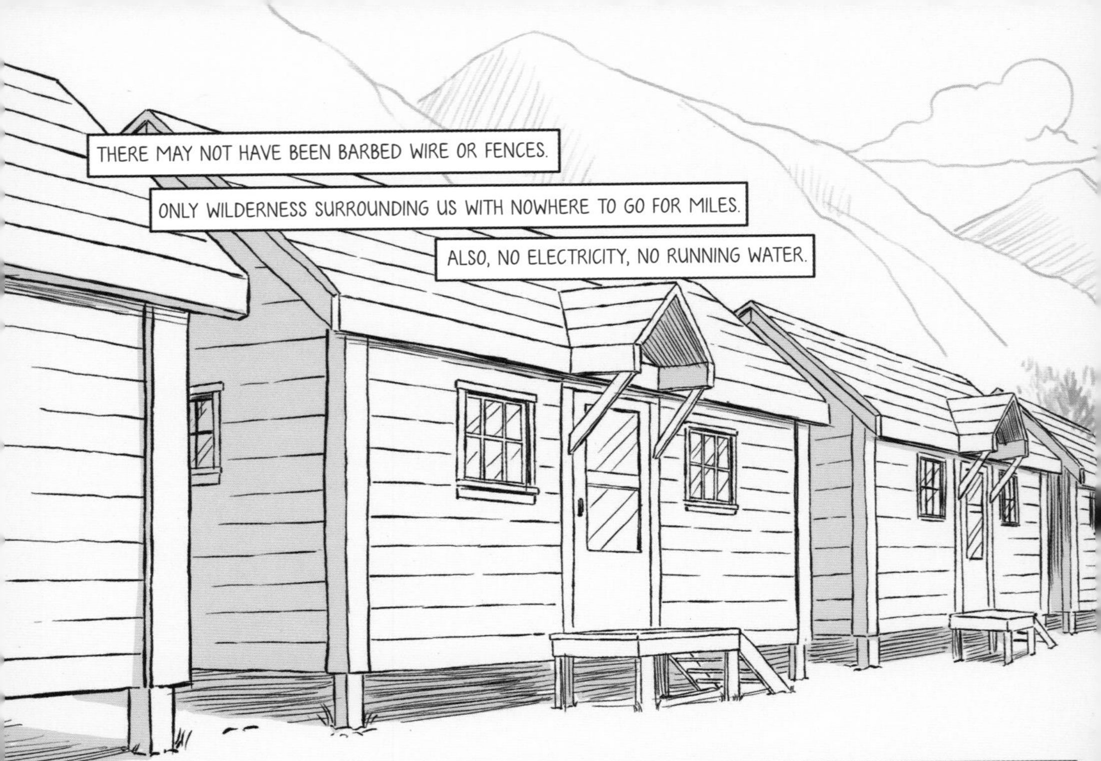
THERE MAY NOT HAVE BEEN BARBED WIRE OR FENCES.
ONLY WILDERNESS SURROUNDING US WITH NOWHERE TO GO FOR MILES.
ALSO, NO ELECTRICITY, NO RUNNING WATER.

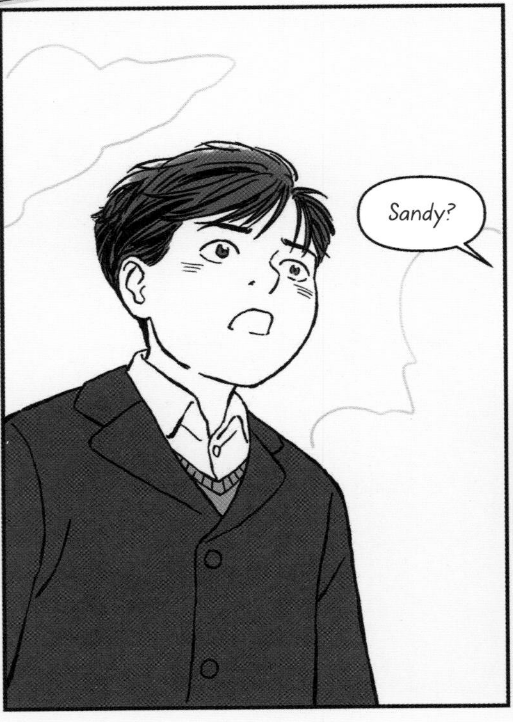
Sandy?

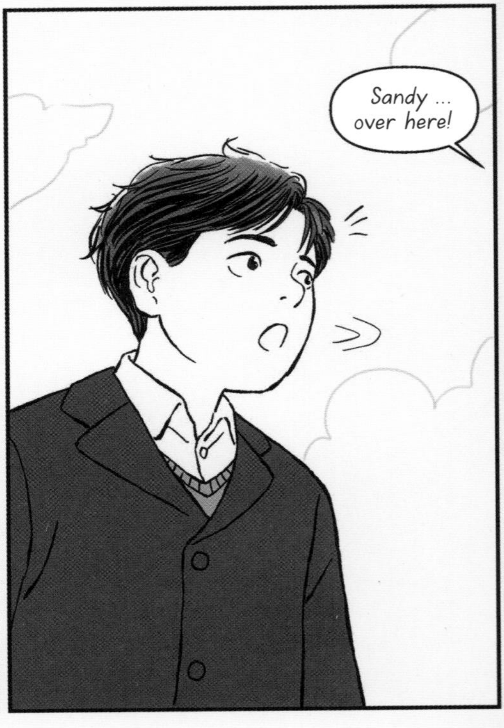
Sandy ... over here!

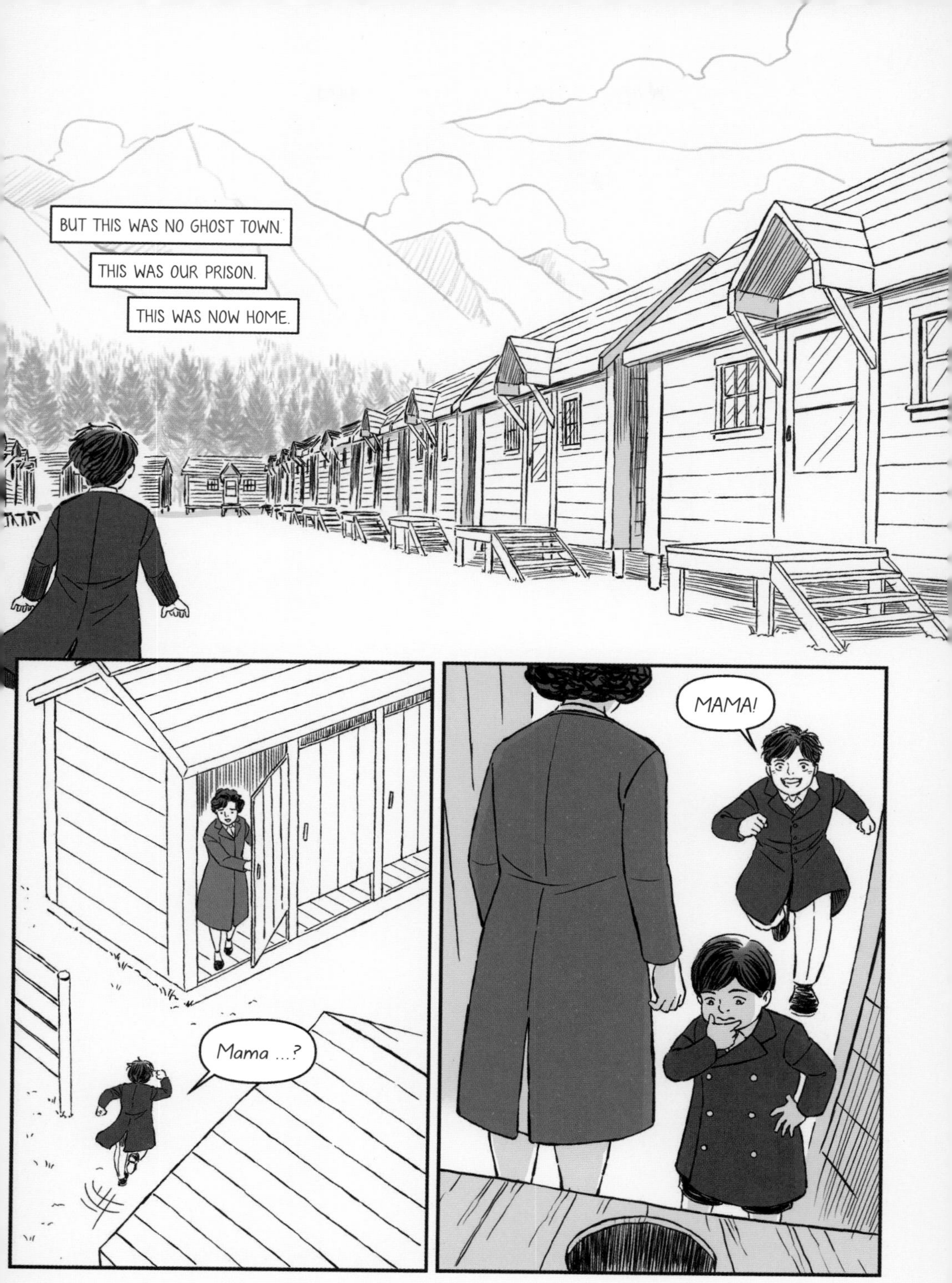
BUT THIS WAS NO GHOST TOWN.
THIS WAS OUR PRISON.
THIS WAS NOW HOME.
Mama ...?
MAMA!

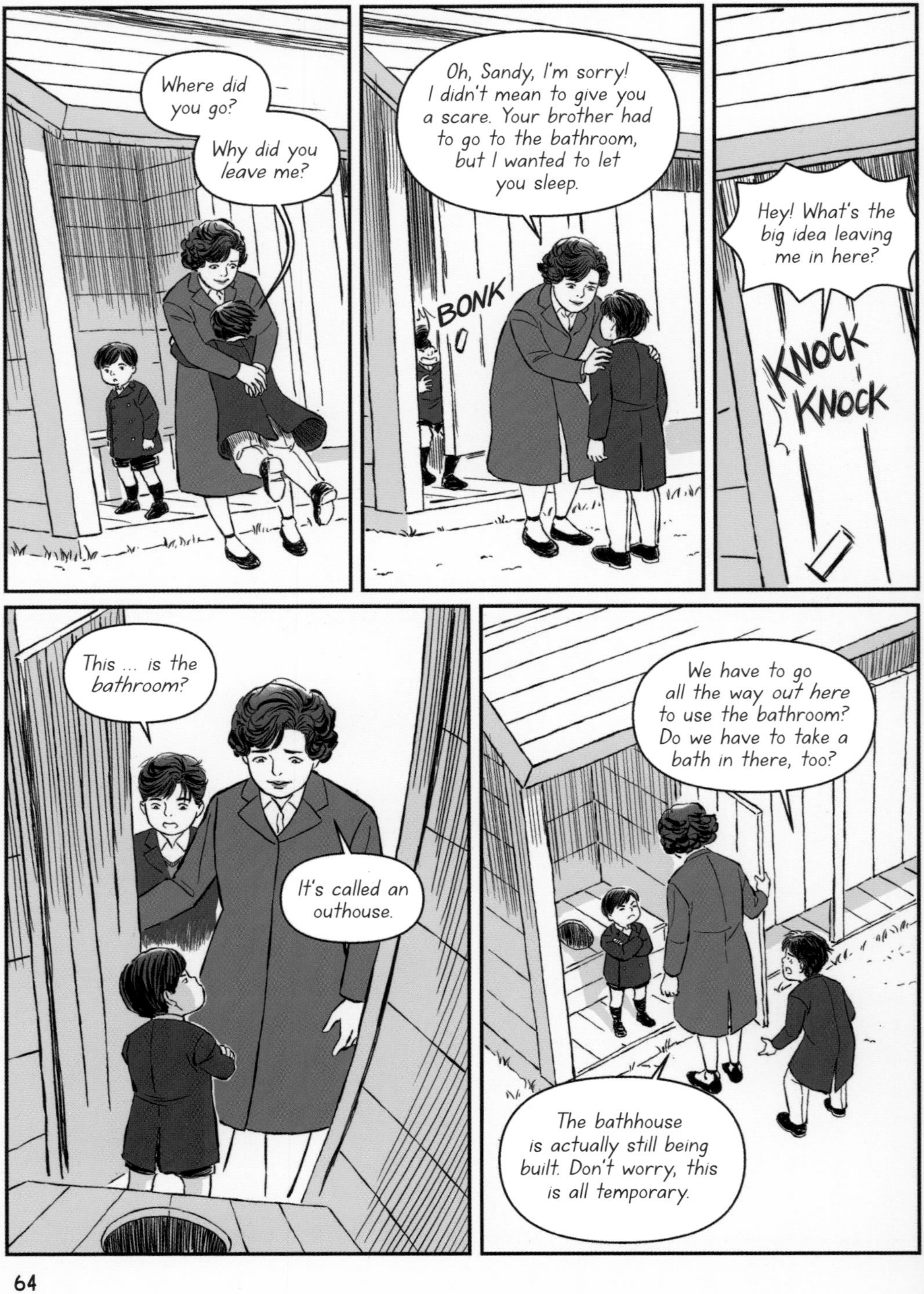
Where did you go?
Why did you leave me?
Oh, Sandy, I'm sorry! I didn't mean to give you a scare. Your brother had to go to the bathroom, but I wanted to let you sleep.
BONK
Hey! What's the big idea leaving me in here?
KNOCK KNOCK
This ... is the bathroom?
It's called an outhouse.
We have to go all the way out here to use the bathroom? Do we have to take a bath in there, too?
The bathhouse is actually still being built. Don't worry, this is all temporary.

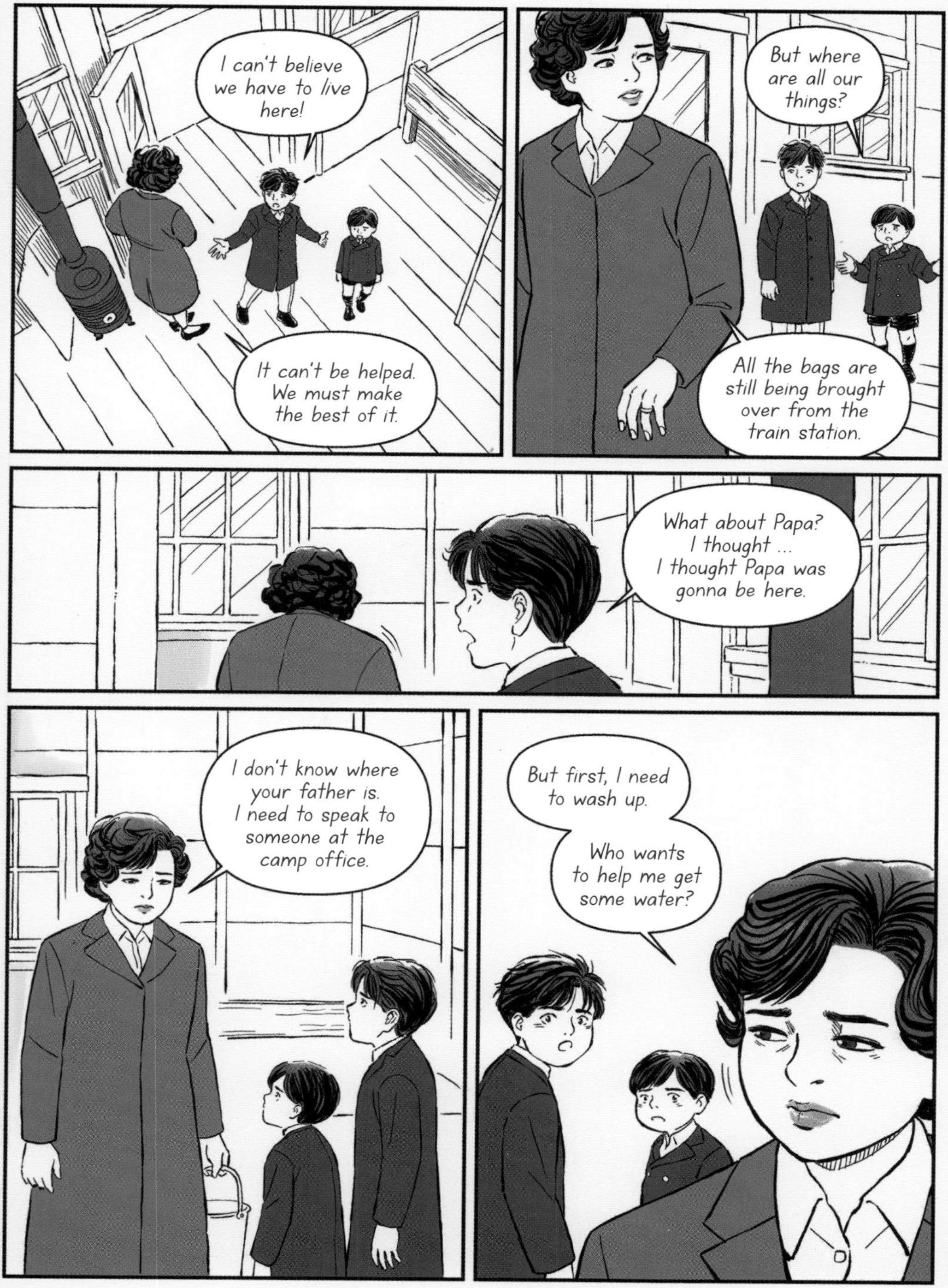
I can't believe we have to live here!
It can't be helped. We must make the best of it.
But where are all our things?
All the bags are still being brought over from the train station.
What about Papa? I thought ... I thought Papa was gonna be here.
I don't know where your father is. I need to speak to someone at the camp office.
But first, I need to wash up.
Who wants to help me get some water?

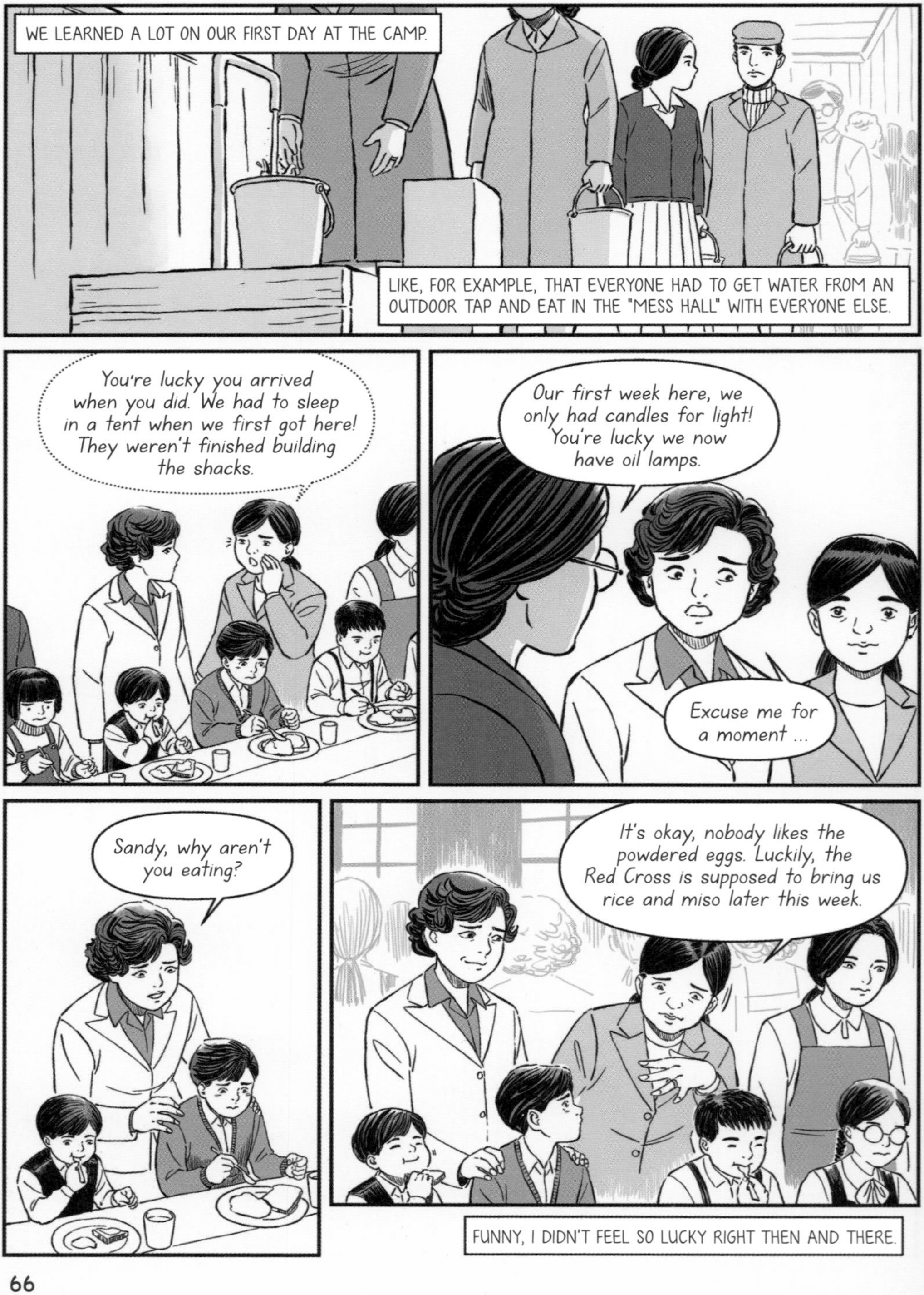
WE LEARNED A LOT ON OUR FIRST DAY AT THE CAMP.
LIKE, FOR EXAMPLE, THAT EVERYONE HAD TO GET WATER FROM AN OUTDOOR TAP AND EAT IN THE "MESS HALL" WITH EVERYONE ELSE.
You're lucky you arrived when you did. We had to sleep in a tent when we first got here! They weren't finished building the shacks.
Our first week here, we only had candles for light! You're lucky we now have oil lamps.
Excuse me for a moment ...
Sandy, why aren't you eating?
It's okay, nobody likes the powdered eggs. Luckily, the Red Cross is supposed to bring us rice and miso later this week.
FUNNY, I DIDN'T FEEL SO LUCKY RIGHT THEN AND THERE.

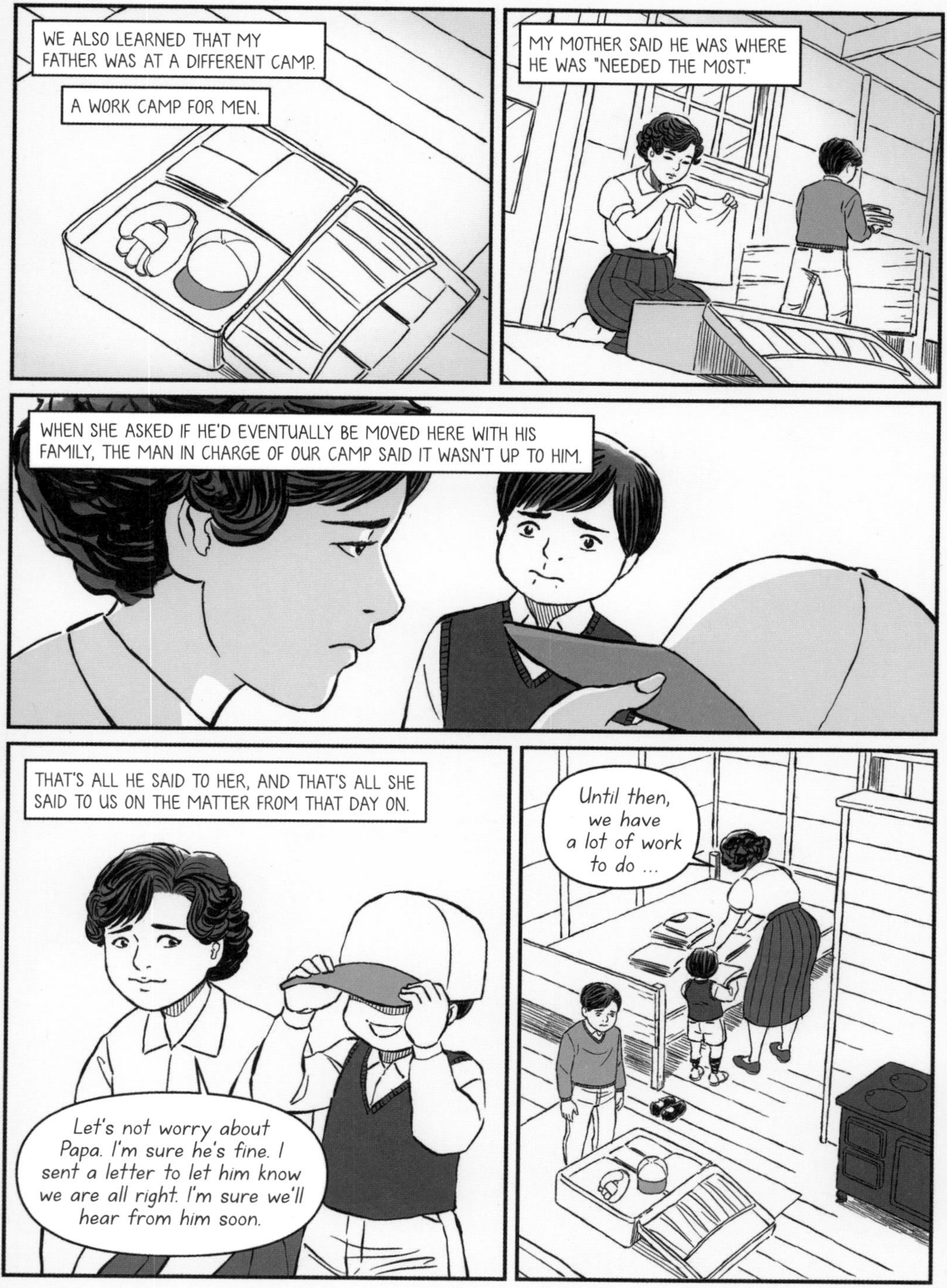
WE ALSO LEARNED THAT MY FATHER WAS AT A DIFFERENT CAMP.
A WORK CAMP FOR MEN.
MY MOTHER SAID HE WAS WHERE HE WAS "NEEDED THE MOST."
WHEN SHE ASKED IF HE'D EVENTUALLY BE MOVED HERE WITH HIS FAMILY, THE MAN IN CHARGE OF OUR CAMP SAID IT WASN'T UP TO HIM.
THAT'S ALL HE SAID TO HER, AND THAT'S ALL SHE SAID TO US ON THE MATTER FROM THAT DAY ON.
Let's not worry about Papa. I'm sure he's fine. I sent a letter to let him know we are all right. I'm sure we'll hear from him soon.
Until then, we have a lot of work to do ...

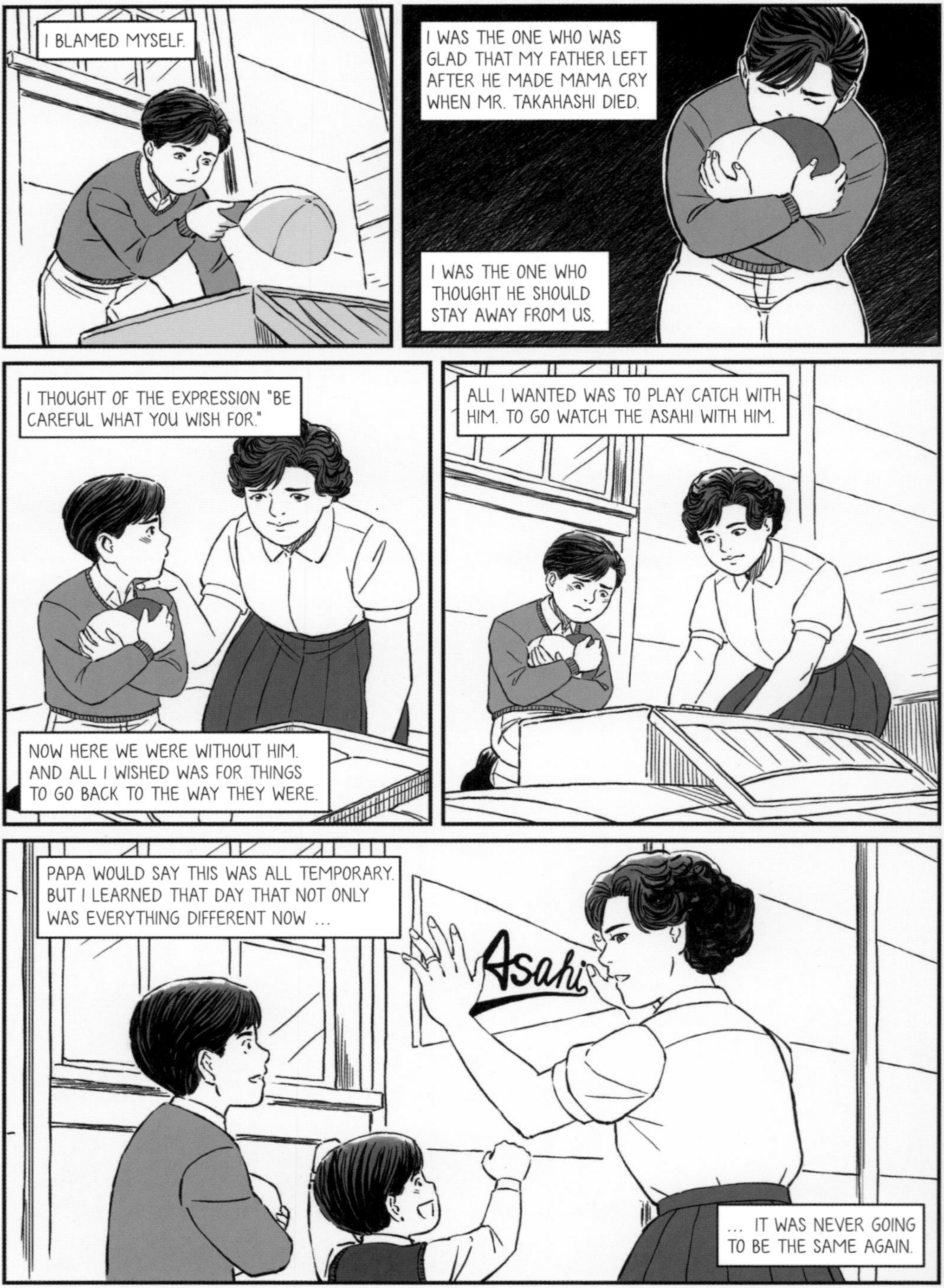
I BLAMED MYSELF.
I WAS THE ONE WHO WAS GLAD THAT MY FATHER LEFT AFTER HE MADE MAMA CRY WHEN MR. TAKAHASHI DIED.
I WAS THE ONE WHO THOUGHT HE SHOULD STAY AWAY FROM US.
I THOUGHT OF THE EXPRESSION "BE CAREFUL WHAT YOU WISH FOR."
NOW HERE WE WERE WITHOUT HIM. AND ALL I WISHED WAS FOR THINGS TO GO BACK TO THE WAY THEY WERE.
ALL I WANTED WAS TO PLAY CATCH WITH HIM. TO GO WATCH THE ASAHI WITH HIM.
PAPA WOULD SAY THIS WAS ALL TEMPORARY. BUT I LEARNED THAT DAY THAT NOT ONLY WAS EVERYTHING DIFFERENT NOW ...
Asahi
... IT WAS NEVER GOING TO BE THE SAME AGAIN.

IT WASN'T LONG BEFORE WE SETTLED INTO A ROUTINE AT THE CAMP.

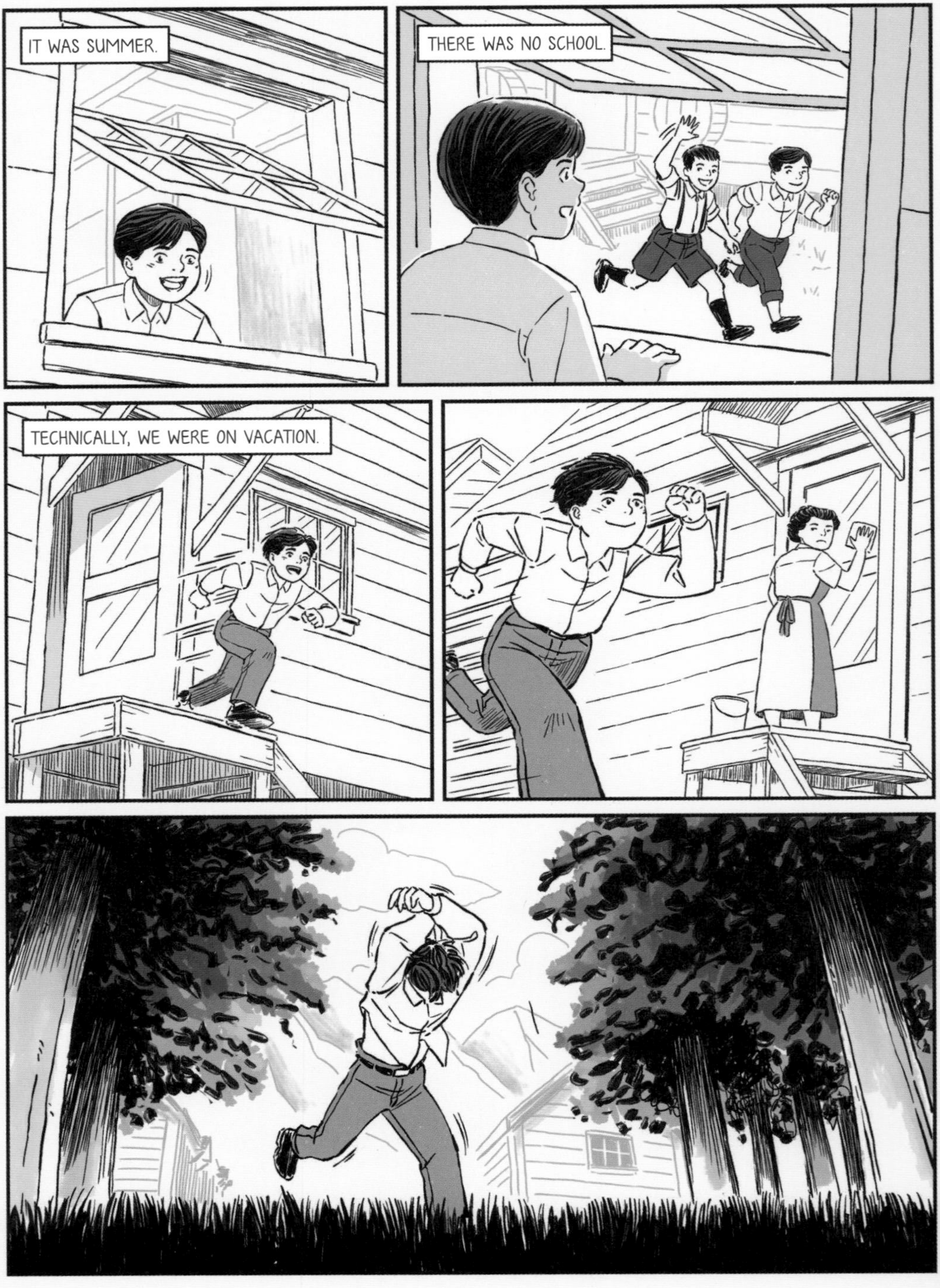
IT WAS SUMMER.
THERE WAS NO SCHOOL.
TECHNICALLY, WE WERE ON VACATION.

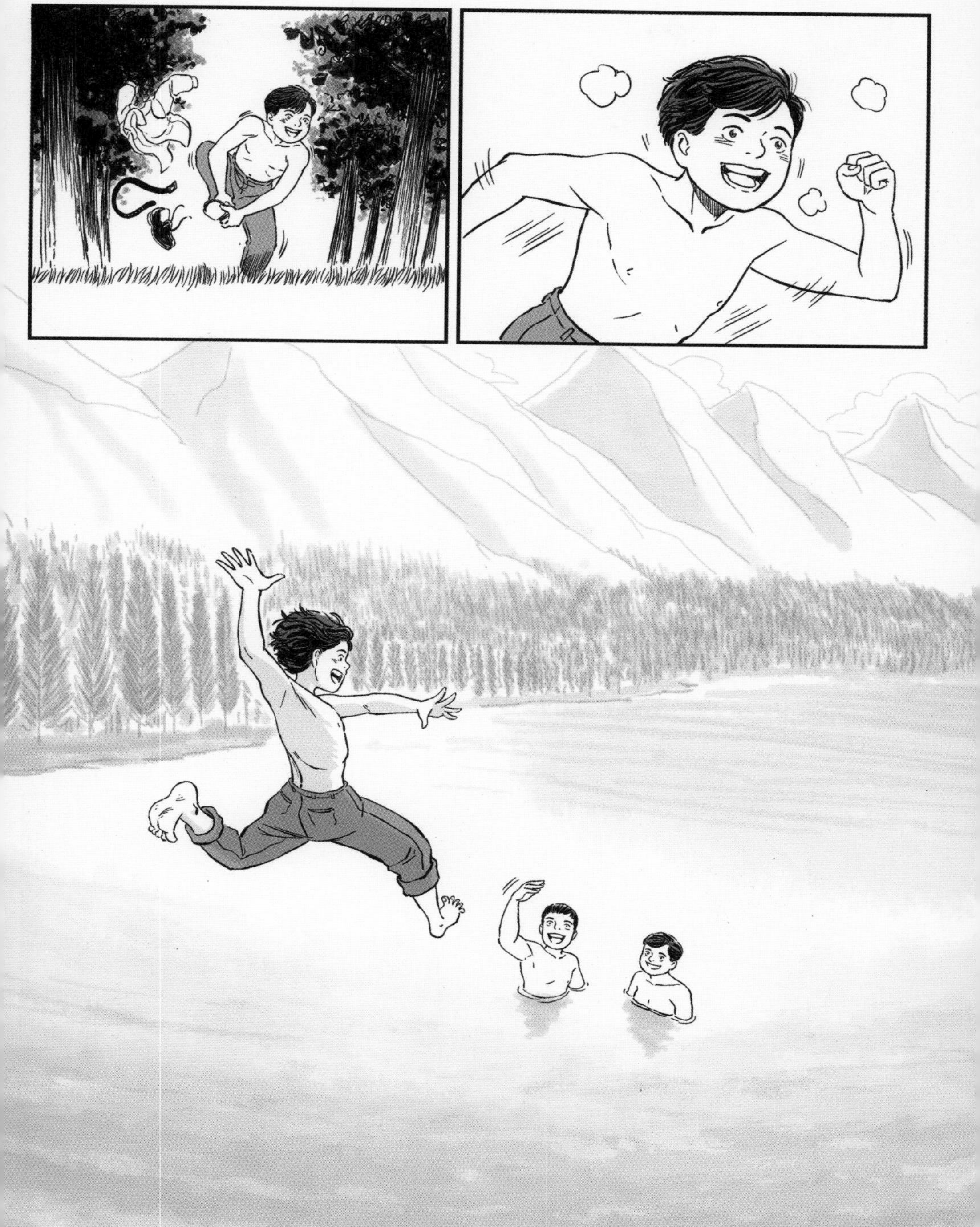

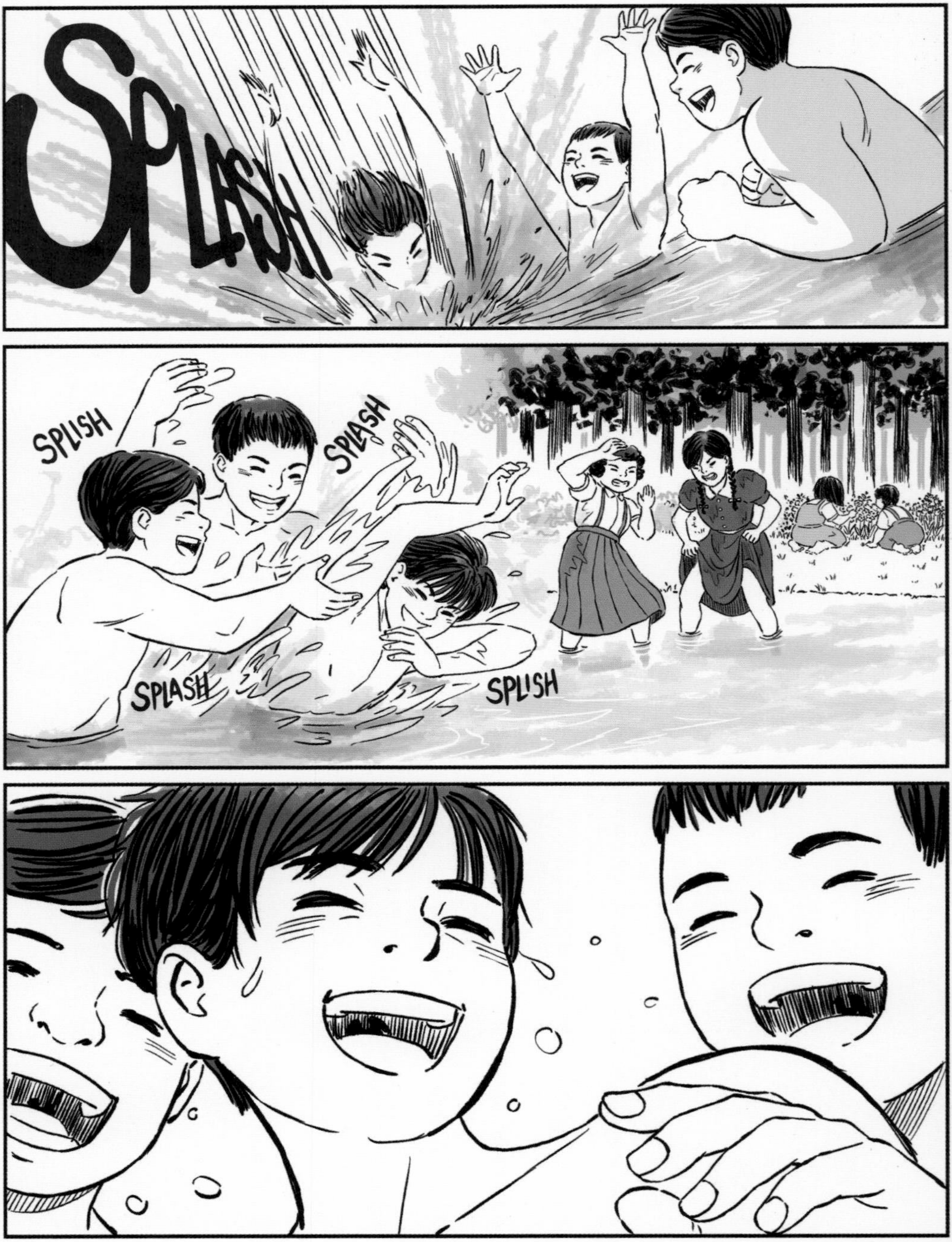
SPLASH
SPLISH
SPLASH
SPLASH
SPLISH

STRANGELY, IT FELT LIKE WE WERE AT SOME KIND OF SUMMER CAMP.

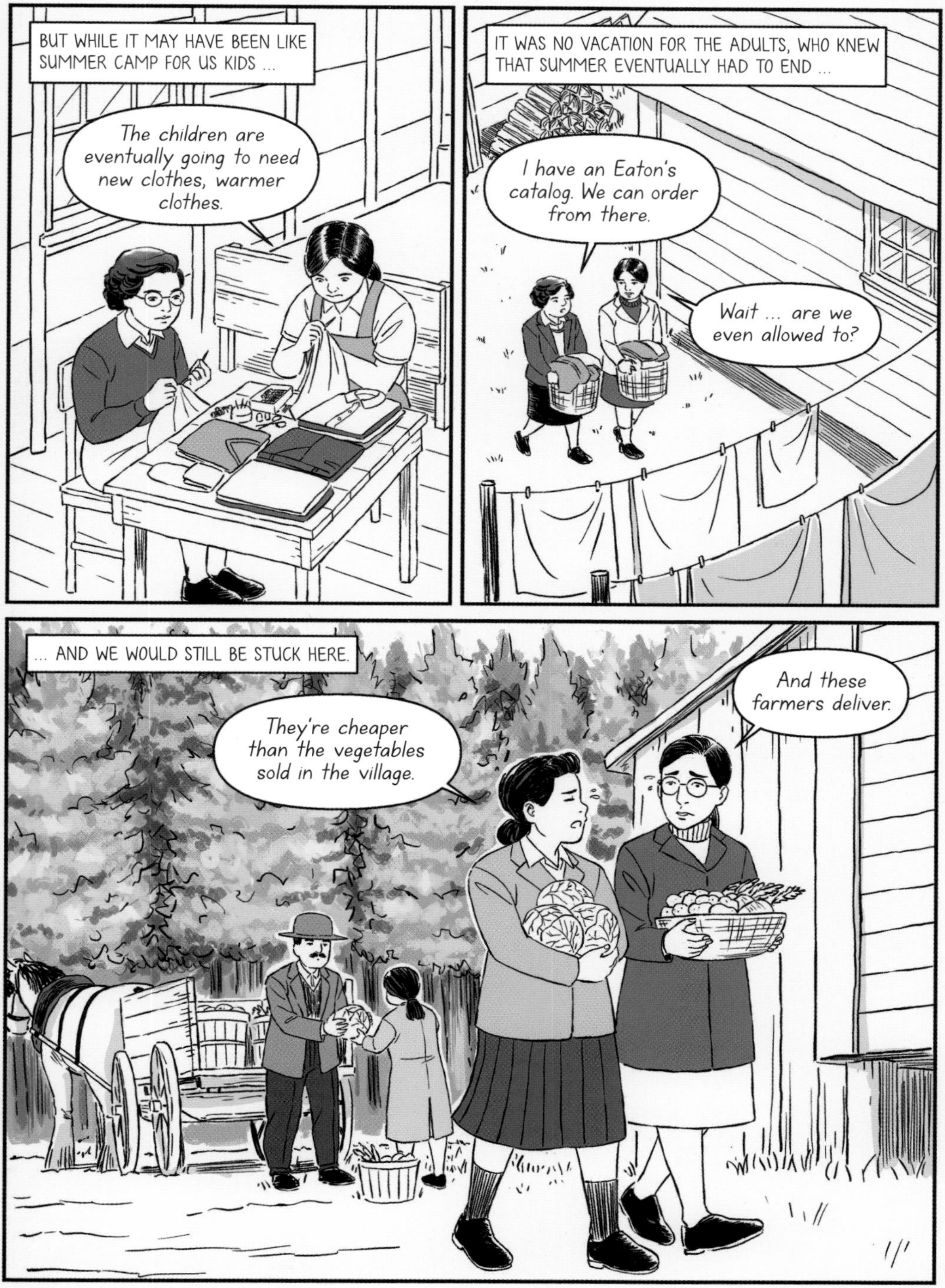
BUT WHILE IT MAY HAVE BEEN LIKE SUMMER CAMP FOR US KIDS ...
The children are eventually going to need new clothes, warmer clothes.
IT WAS NO VACATION FOR THE ADULTS, WHO KNEW THAT SUMMER EVENTUALLY HAD TO END ...
I have an Eaton's catalog. We can order from there.
Wait ... are we even allowed to?
... AND WE WOULD STILL BE STUCK HERE.
They're cheaper than the vegetables sold in the village.
And these farmers deliver.

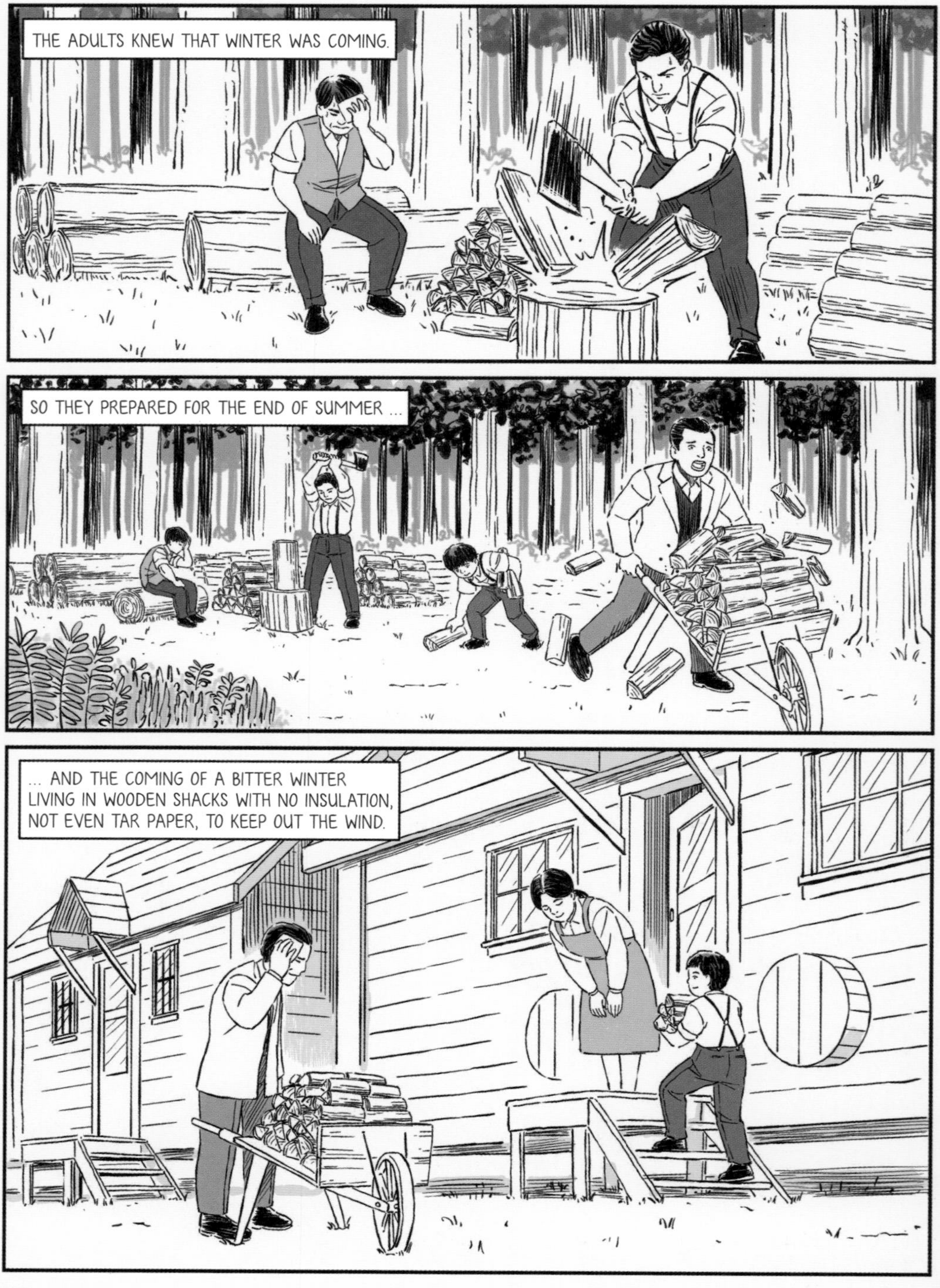
THE ADULTS KNEW THAT WINTER WAS COMING.
SO THEY PREPARED FOR THE END OF SUMMER ...
... AND THE COMING OF A BITTER WINTER LIVING IN WOODEN SHACKS WITH NO INSULATION, NOT EVEN TAR PAPER, TO KEEP OUT THE WIND.

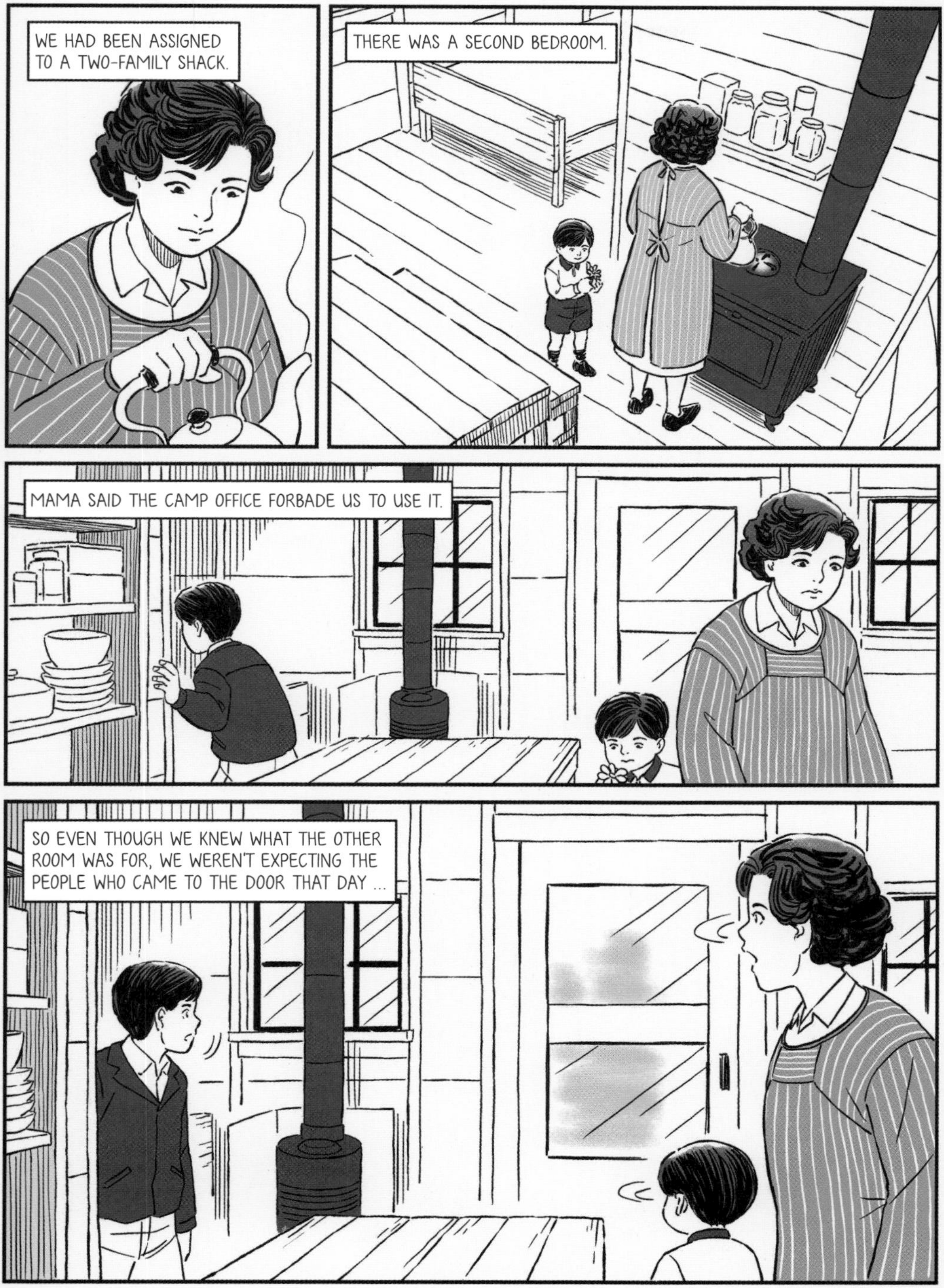
WE HAD BEEN ASSIGNED TO A TWO-FAMILY SHACK.
THERE WAS A SECOND BEDROOM.
MAMA SAID THE CAMP OFFICE FORBADE US TO USE IT.
SO EVEN THOUGH WE KNEW WHAT THE OTHER ROOM WAS FOR, WE WEREN'T EXPECTING THE PEOPLE WHO CAME TO THE DOOR THAT DAY ...

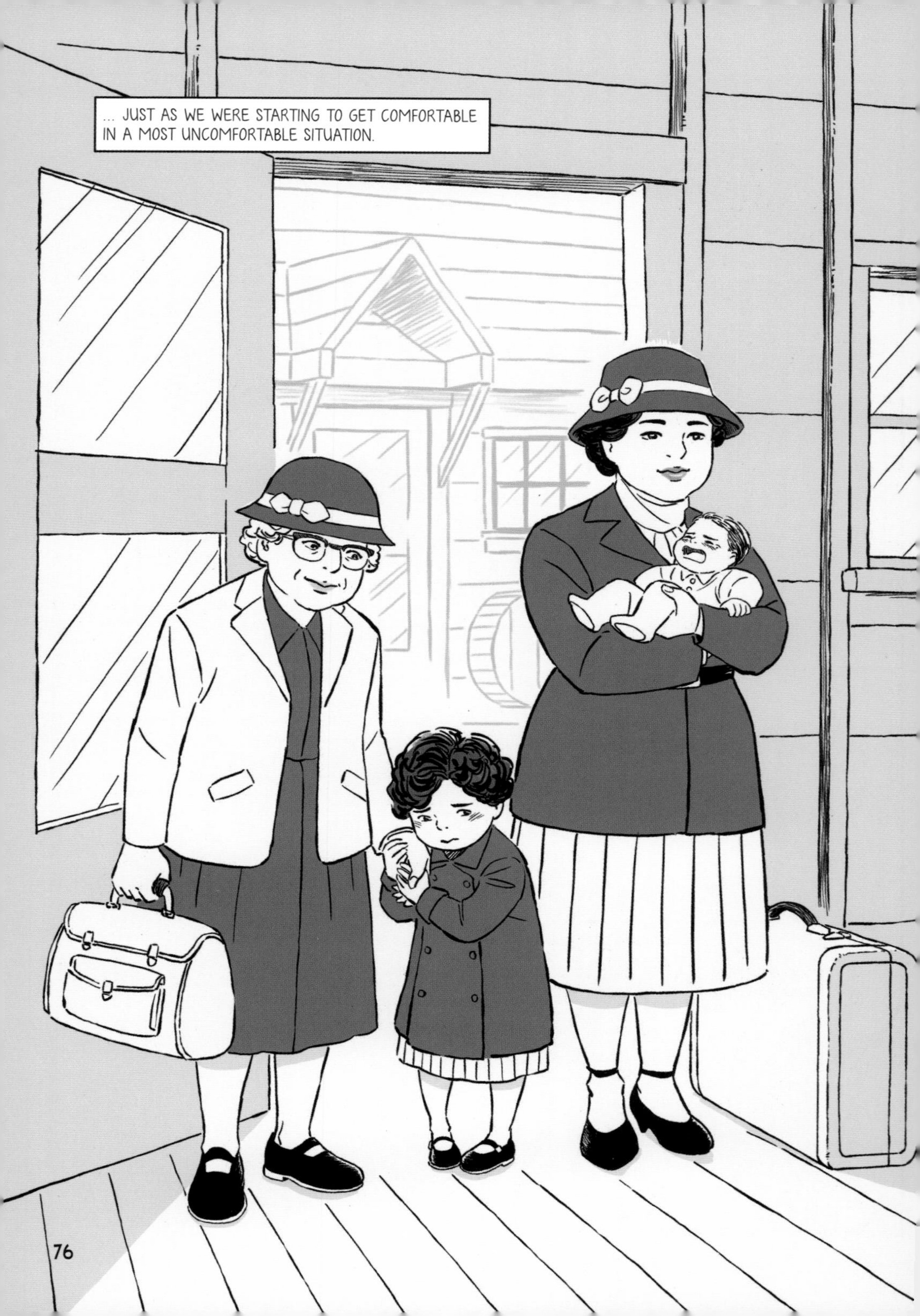
... JUST AS WE WERE STARTING TO GET COMFORTABLE IN A MOST UNCOMFORTABLE SITUATION.

MAMA WAS VERY ACCOMMODATING TO THE ITO FAMILY.

VERY HELPFUL. VERY PATIENT.

WAAAAAAAA

SHE MADE IT WORK.

BUT TO ME, THE SHACK FELT SMALL ENOUGH WITH JUST THE THREE OF US. AND NOW IT WAS LIKE THAT TRAIN CAR ALL OVER AGAIN!

BUMP

CROWDED, HOT, SMELLY.

WAAAAAAAA

AND THAT CRYING BABY!

WAAAAA
WAAA WAAAAA
WAAAAAAAA
WAAAAAAAA

WAAA
WAAAAA
WAAAA
WAM

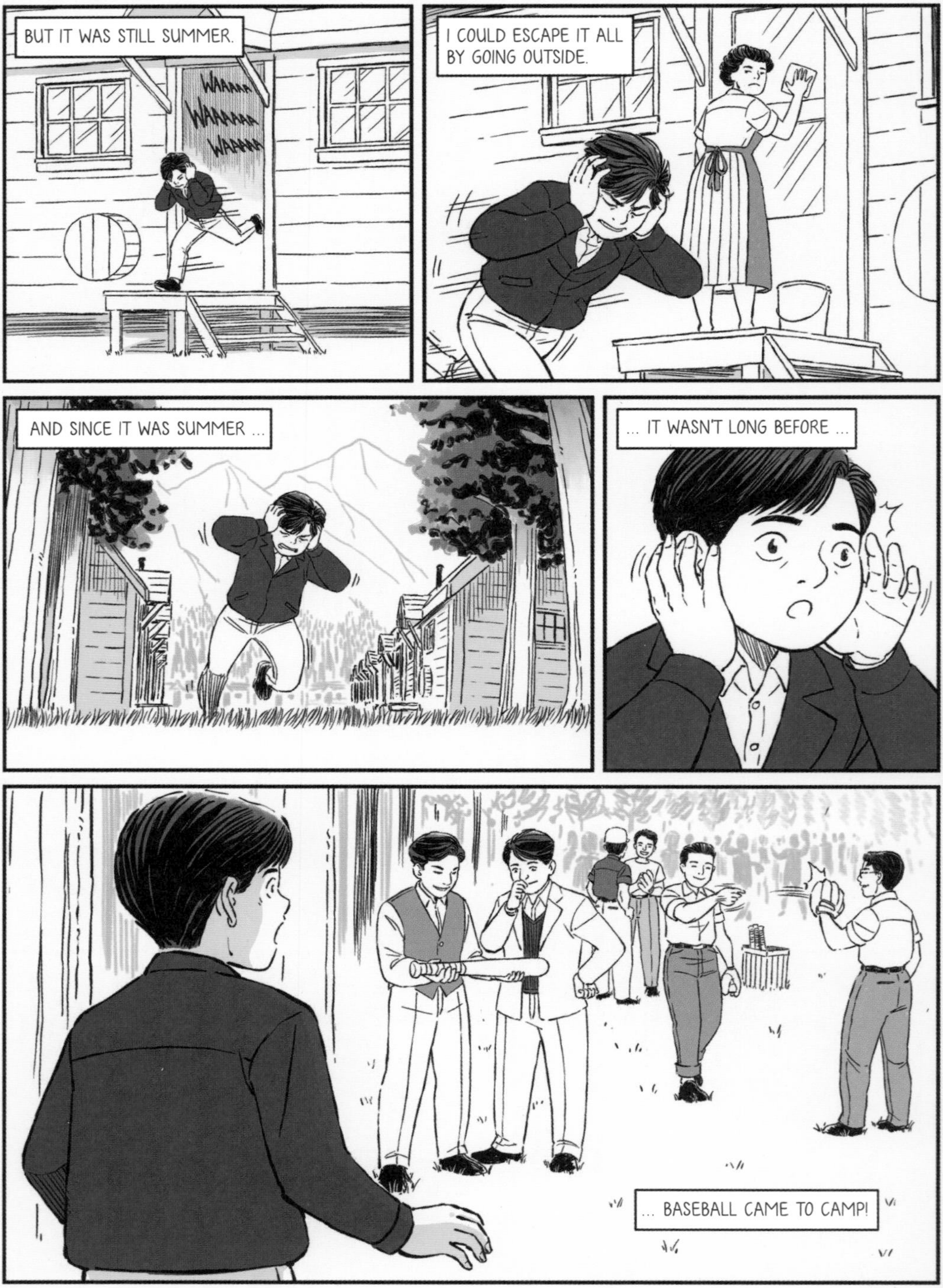
BUT IT WAS STILL SUMMER.
WAAAAA
WAAAAAA
WAAAAA
I COULD ESCAPE IT ALL BY GOING OUTSIDE.
AND SINCE IT WAS SUMMER ...
... IT WASN'T LONG BEFORE ...
... BASEBALL CAME TO CAMP!

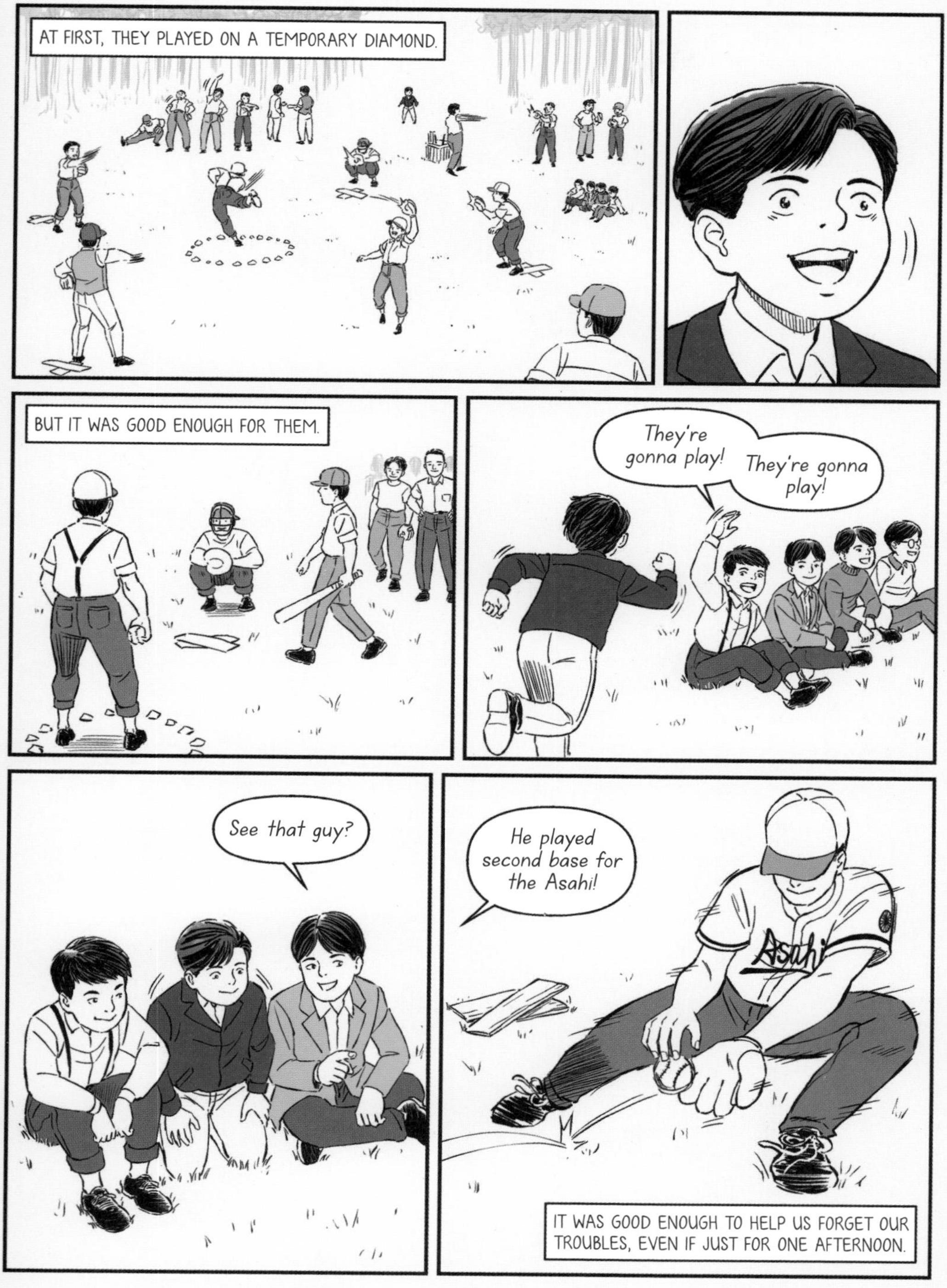
AT FIRST, THEY PLAYED ON A TEMPORARY DIAMOND.
BUT IT WAS GOOD ENOUGH FOR THEM.
They're gonna play!
They're gonna play!
See that guy?
He played second base for the Asahi!
Asahi
IT WAS GOOD ENOUGH TO HELP US FORGET OUR TROUBLES, EVEN IF JUST FOR ONE AFTERNOON.

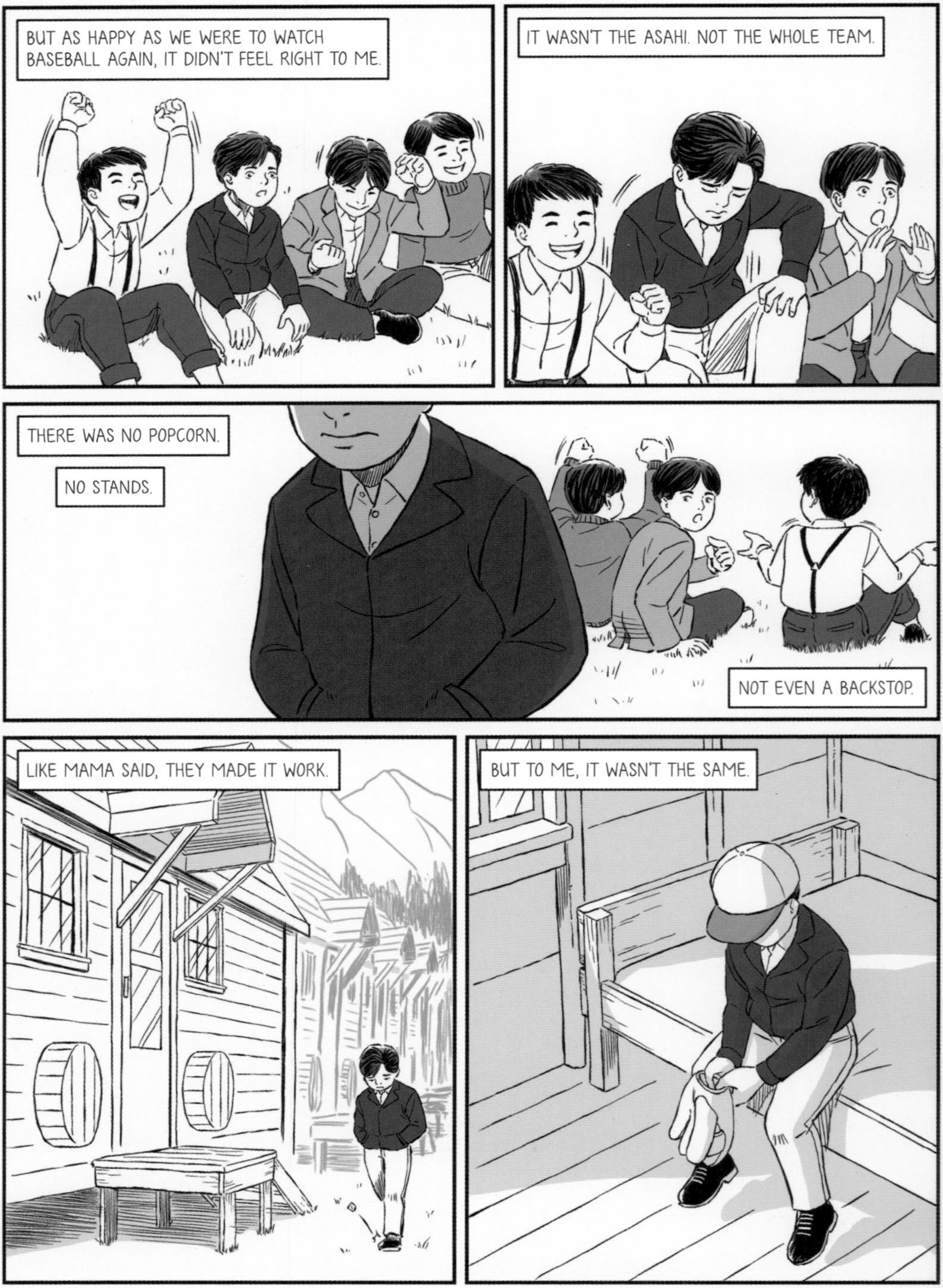
BUT AS HAPPY AS WE WERE TO WATCH BASEBALL AGAIN, IT DIDN'T FEEL RIGHT TO ME.
IT WASN'T THE ASAHI. NOT THE WHOLE TEAM.
THERE WAS NO POPCORN.
NO STANDS.
NOT EVEN A BACKSTOP.
LIKE MAMA SAID, THEY MADE IT WORK.
BUT TO ME, IT WASN'T THE SAME.

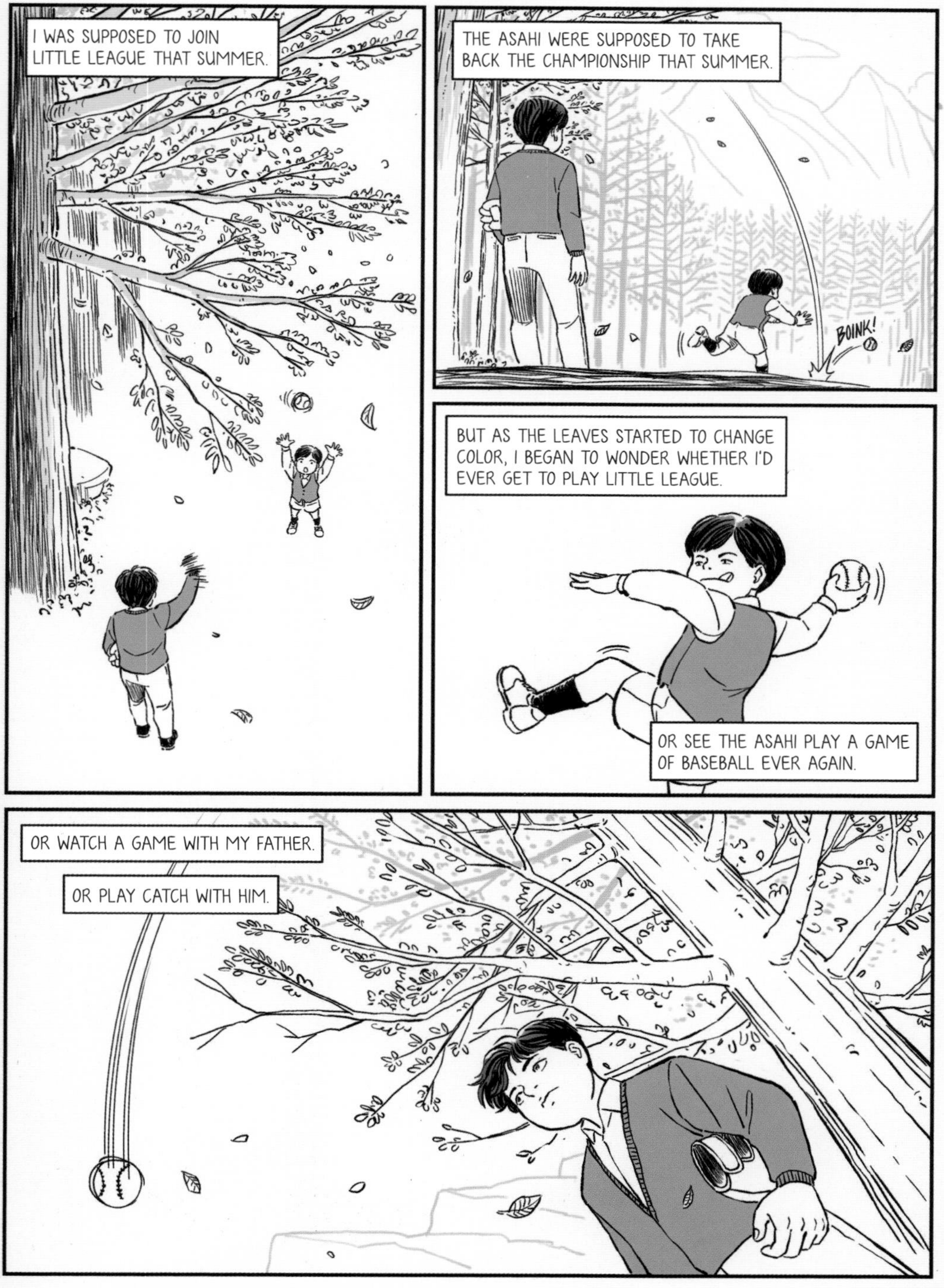
I WAS SUPPOSED TO JOIN LITTLE LEAGUE THAT SUMMER.
THE ASAHI WERE SUPPOSED TO TAKE BACK THE CHAMPIONSHIP THAT SUMMER.
BOINK!
BUT AS THE LEAVES STARTED TO CHANGE COLOR, I BEGAN TO WONDER WHETHER I'D EVER GET TO PLAY LITTLE LEAGUE.
OR SEE THE ASAHI PLAY A GAME OF BASEBALL EVER AGAIN.
OR WATCH A GAME WITH MY FATHER.
OR PLAY CATCH WITH HIM.

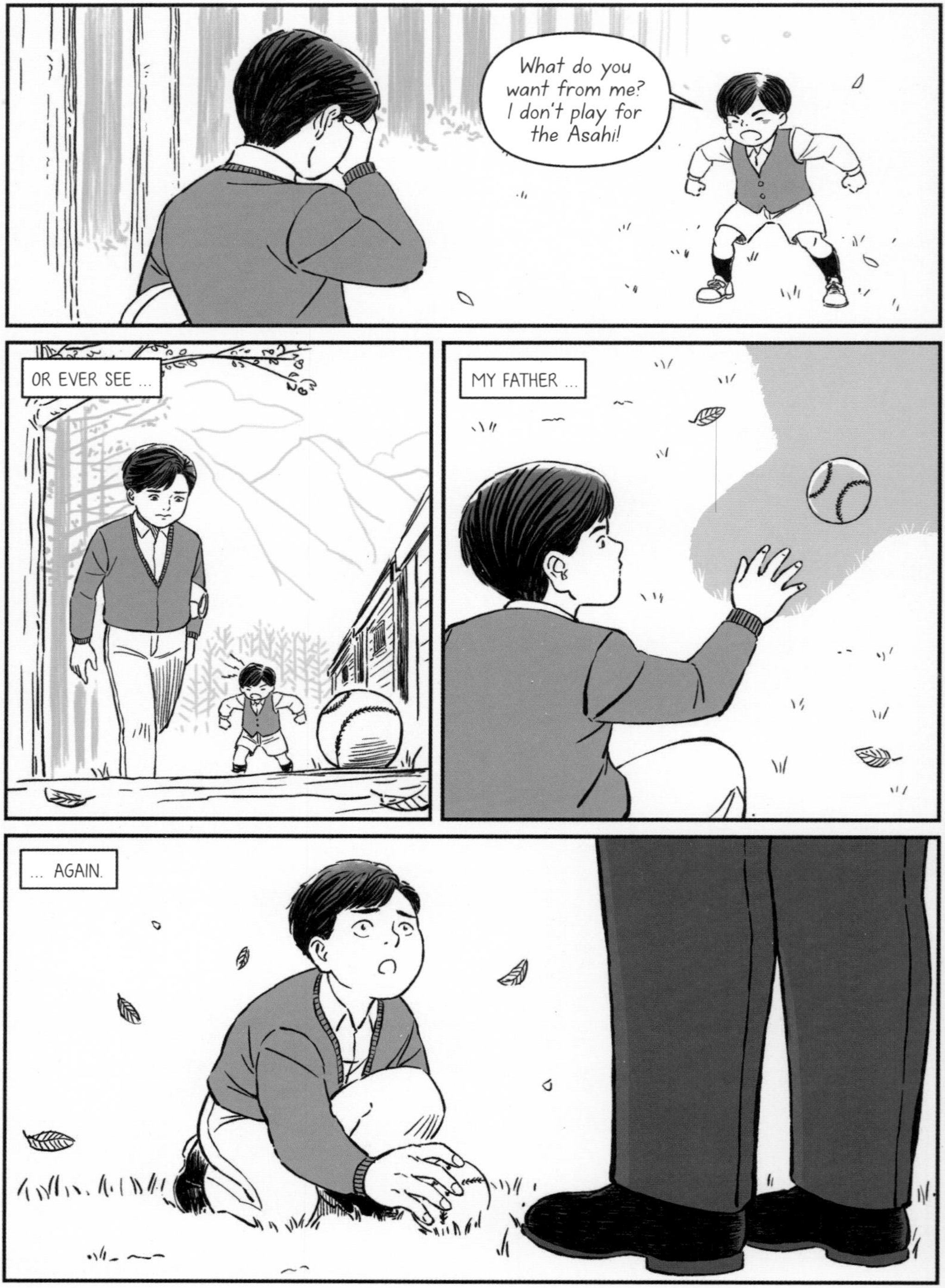
What do you want from me? I don't play for the Asahi!
OR EVER SEE ...
MY FATHER ...
... AGAIN.

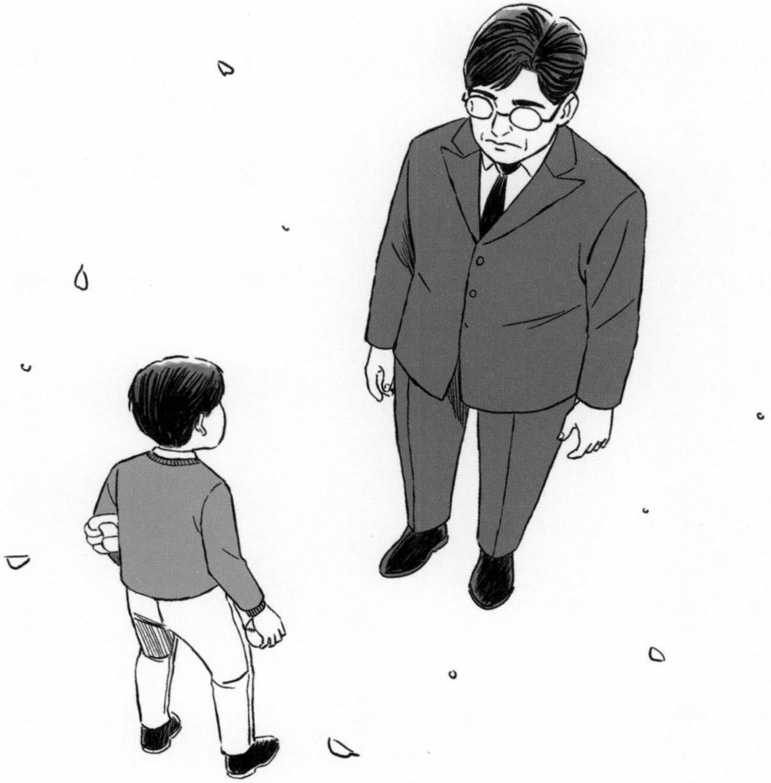

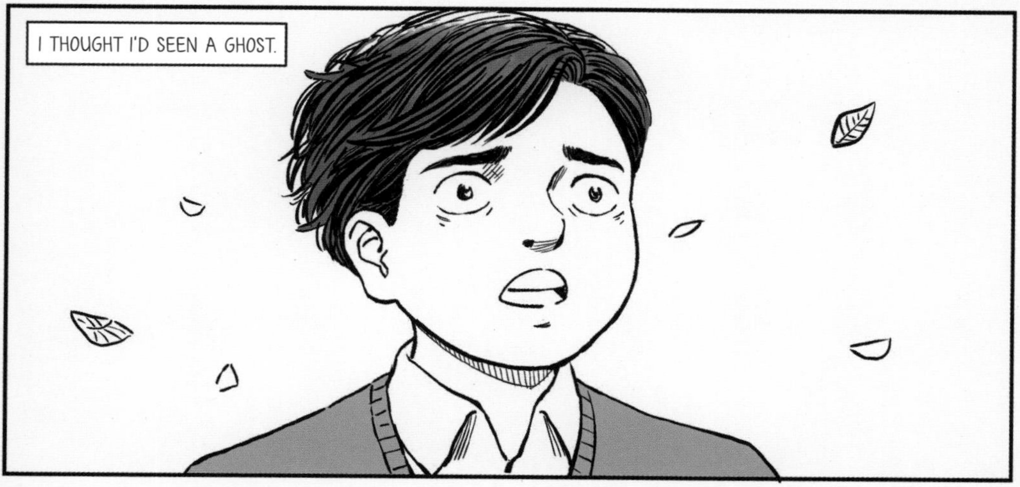
I THOUGHT I'D SEEN A GHOST.

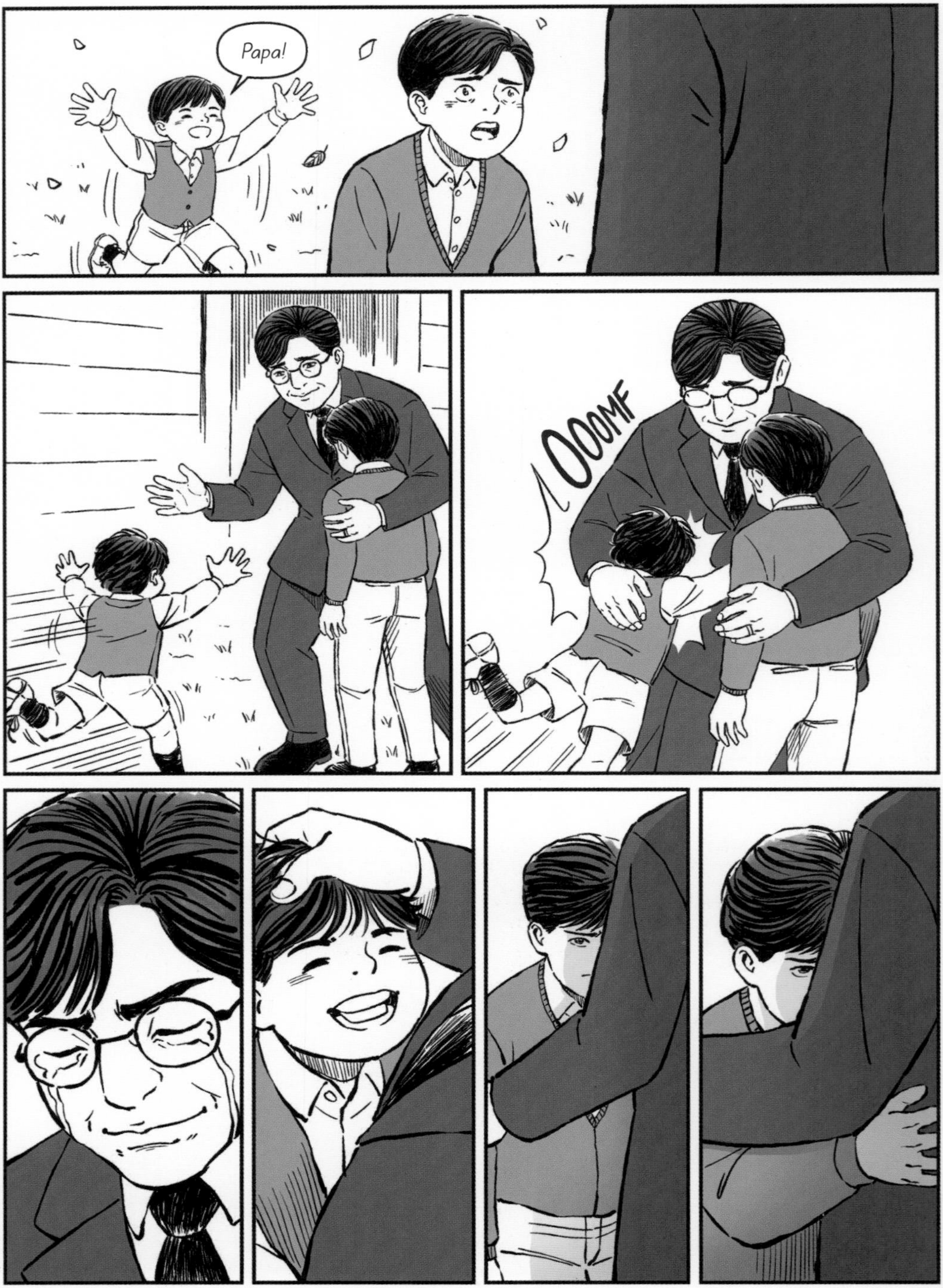
Papa!
OOOMF

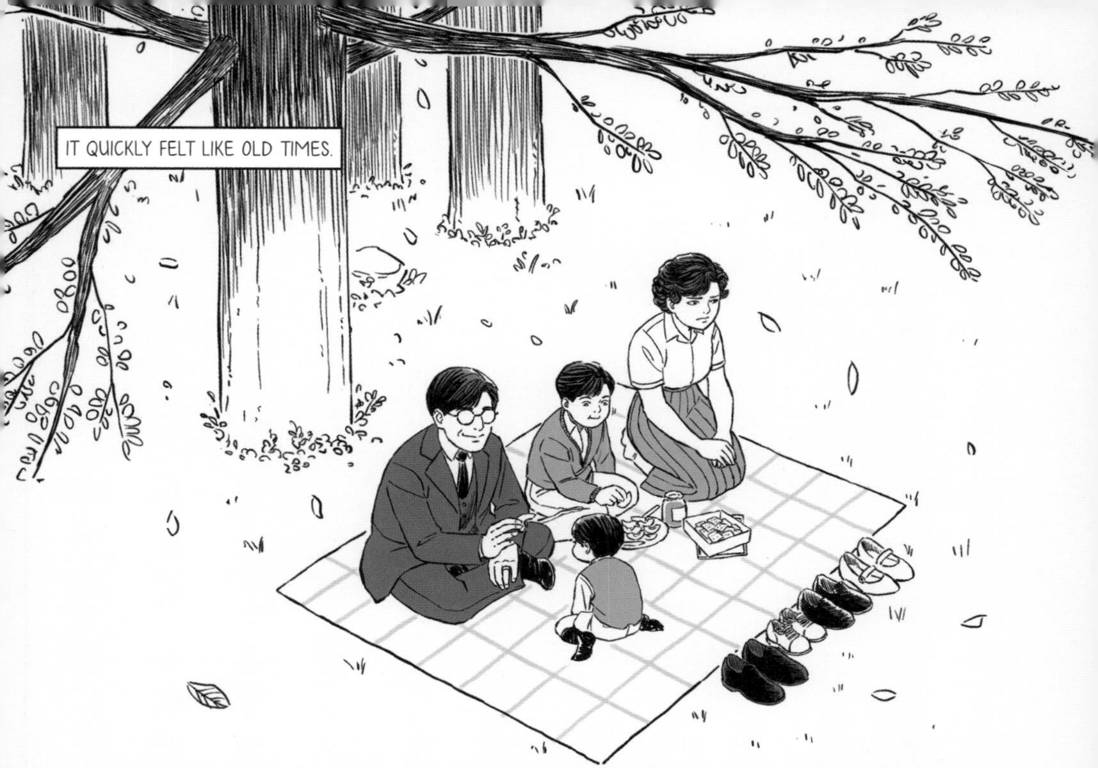
IT QUICKLY FELT LIKE OLD TIMES.

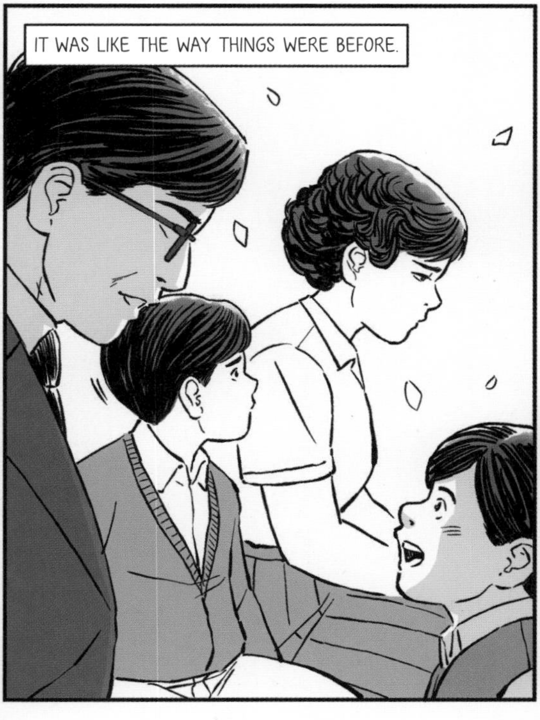
IT WAS LIKE THE WAY THINGS WERE BEFORE.

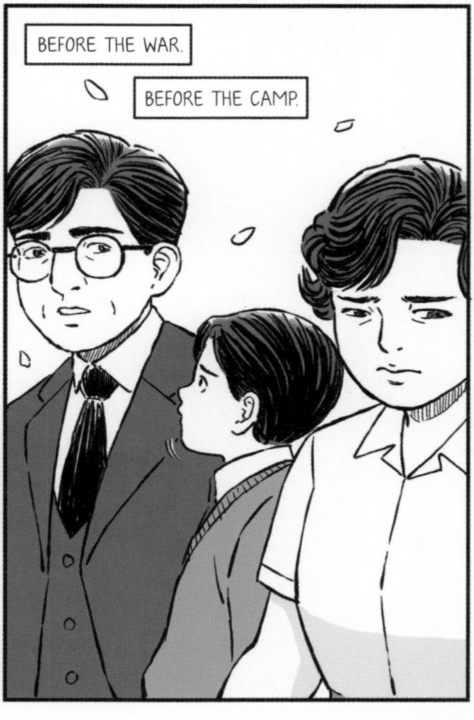
BEFORE THE WAR.
BEFORE THE CAMP.

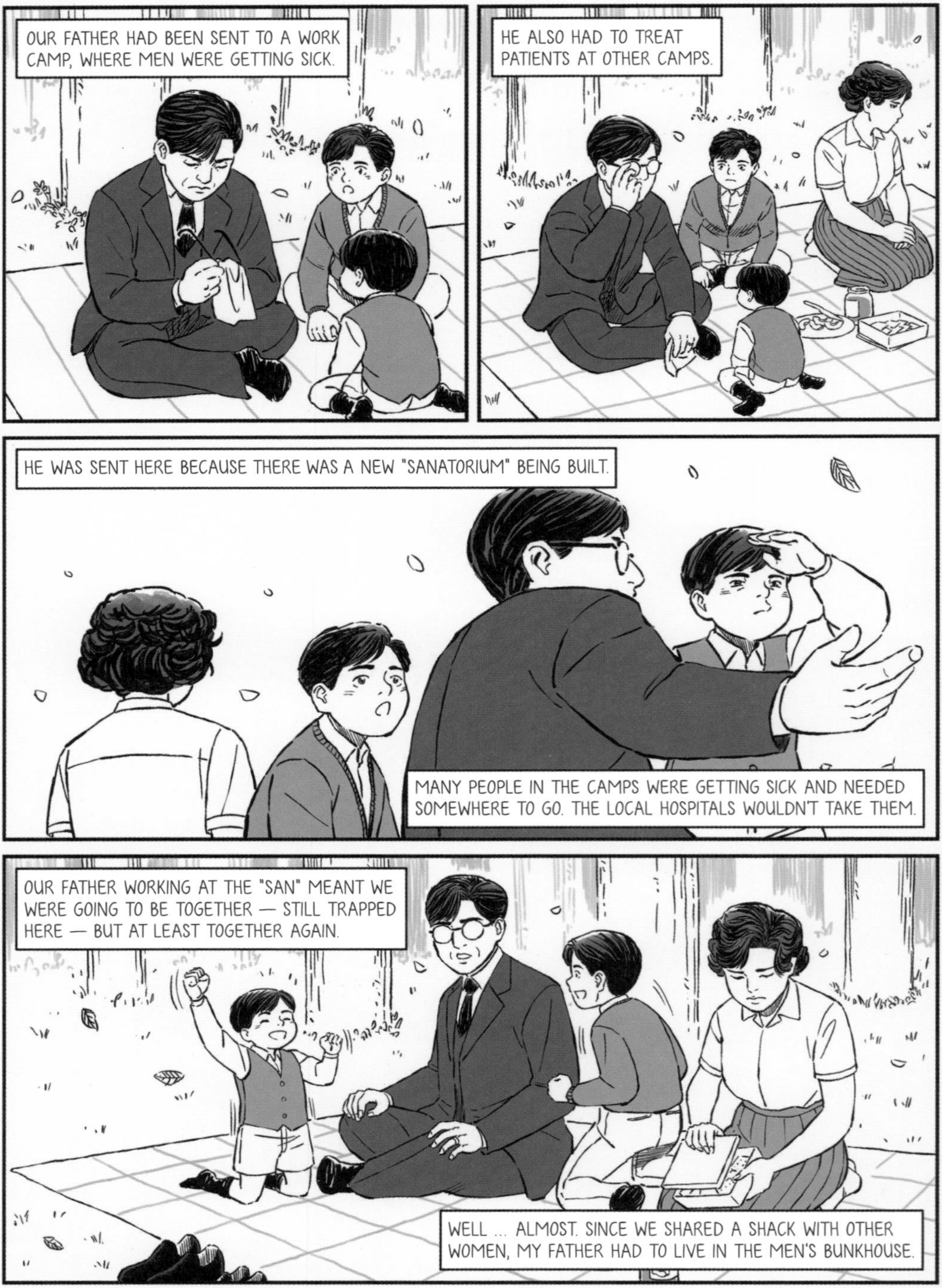
OUR FATHER HAD BEEN SENT TO A WORK CAMP, WHERE MEN WERE GETTING SICK.
HE ALSO HAD TO TREAT PATIENTS AT OTHER CAMPS.
HE WAS SENT HERE BECAUSE THERE WAS A NEW "SANATORIUM" BEING BUILT.
MANY PEOPLE IN THE CAMPS WERE GETTING SICK AND NEEDED SOMEWHERE TO GO. THE LOCAL HOSPITALS WOULDN'T TAKE THEM.
OUR FATHER WORKING AT THE "SAN" MEANT WE WERE GOING TO BE TOGETHER — STILL TRAPPED HERE — BUT AT LEAST TOGETHER AGAIN.
WELL ... ALMOST. SINCE WE SHARED A SHACK WITH OTHER WOMEN, MY FATHER HAD TO LIVE IN THE MEN'S BUNKHOUSE.

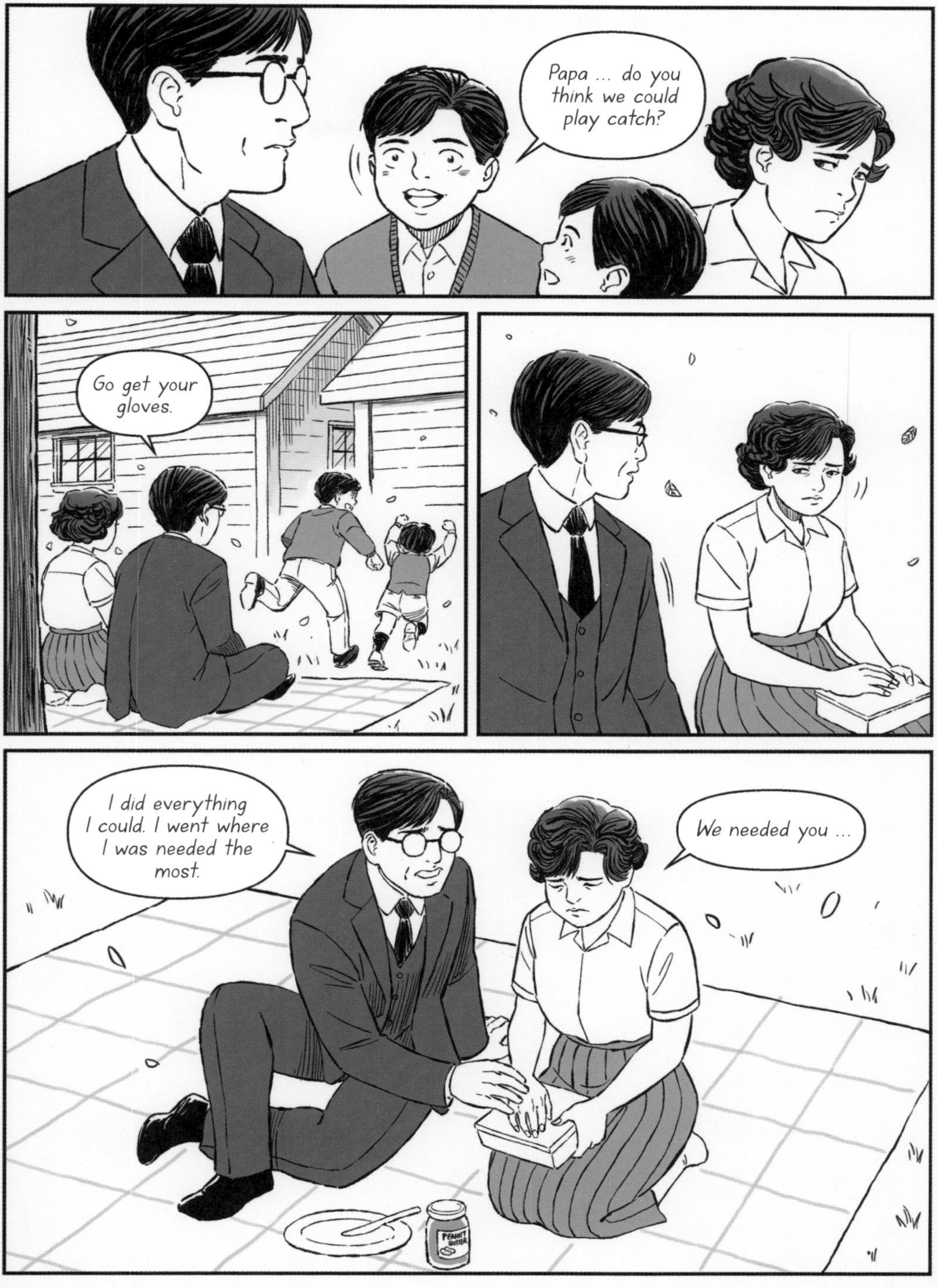
Papa ... do you think we could play catch?
Go get your gloves.
I did everything I could. I went where I was needed the most.
We needed you ...
PEANUT BUTTER

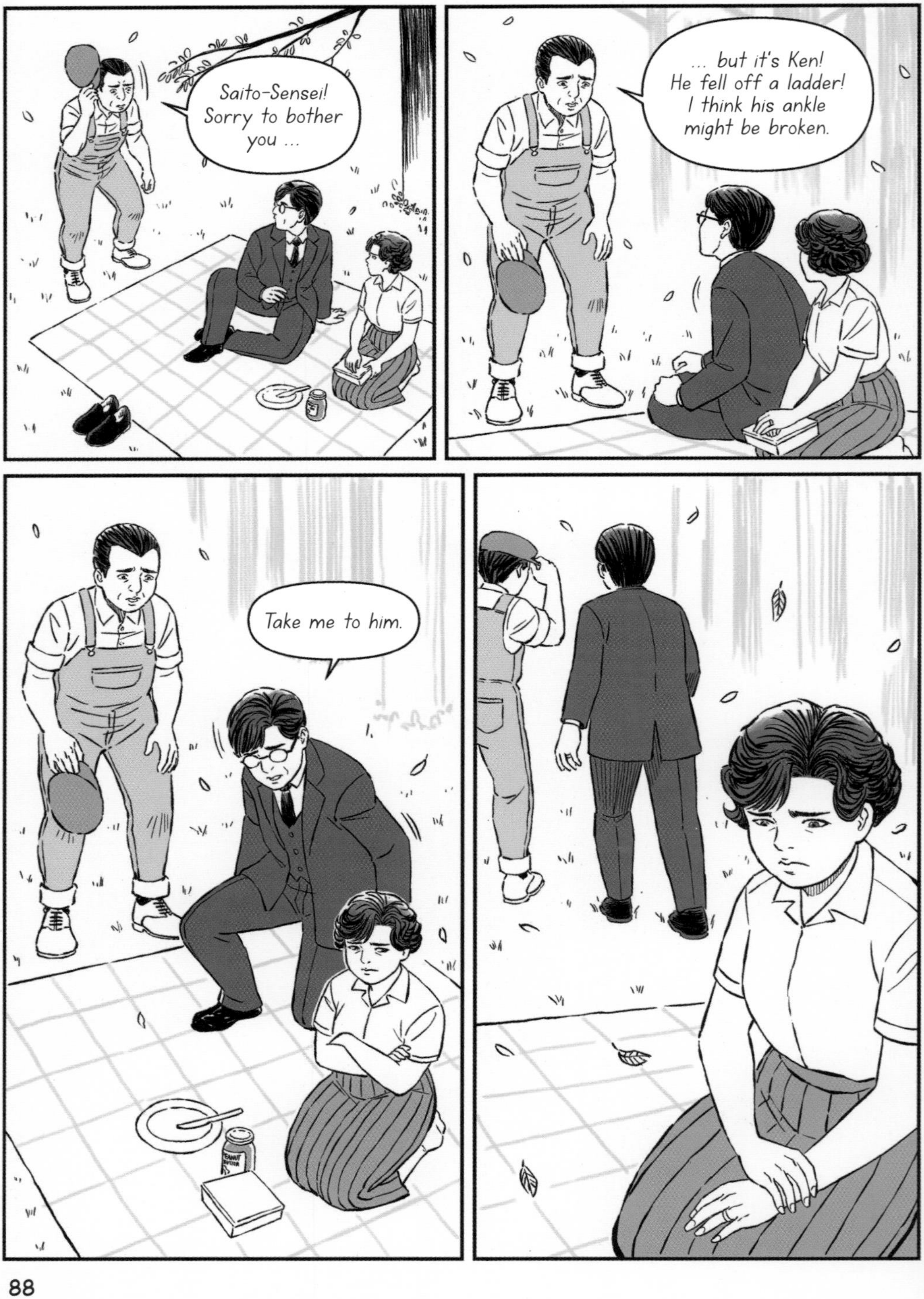
Saito-Sensei! Sorry to bother you ...
... but it's Ken! He fell off a ladder! I think his ankle might be broken.
Take me to him.

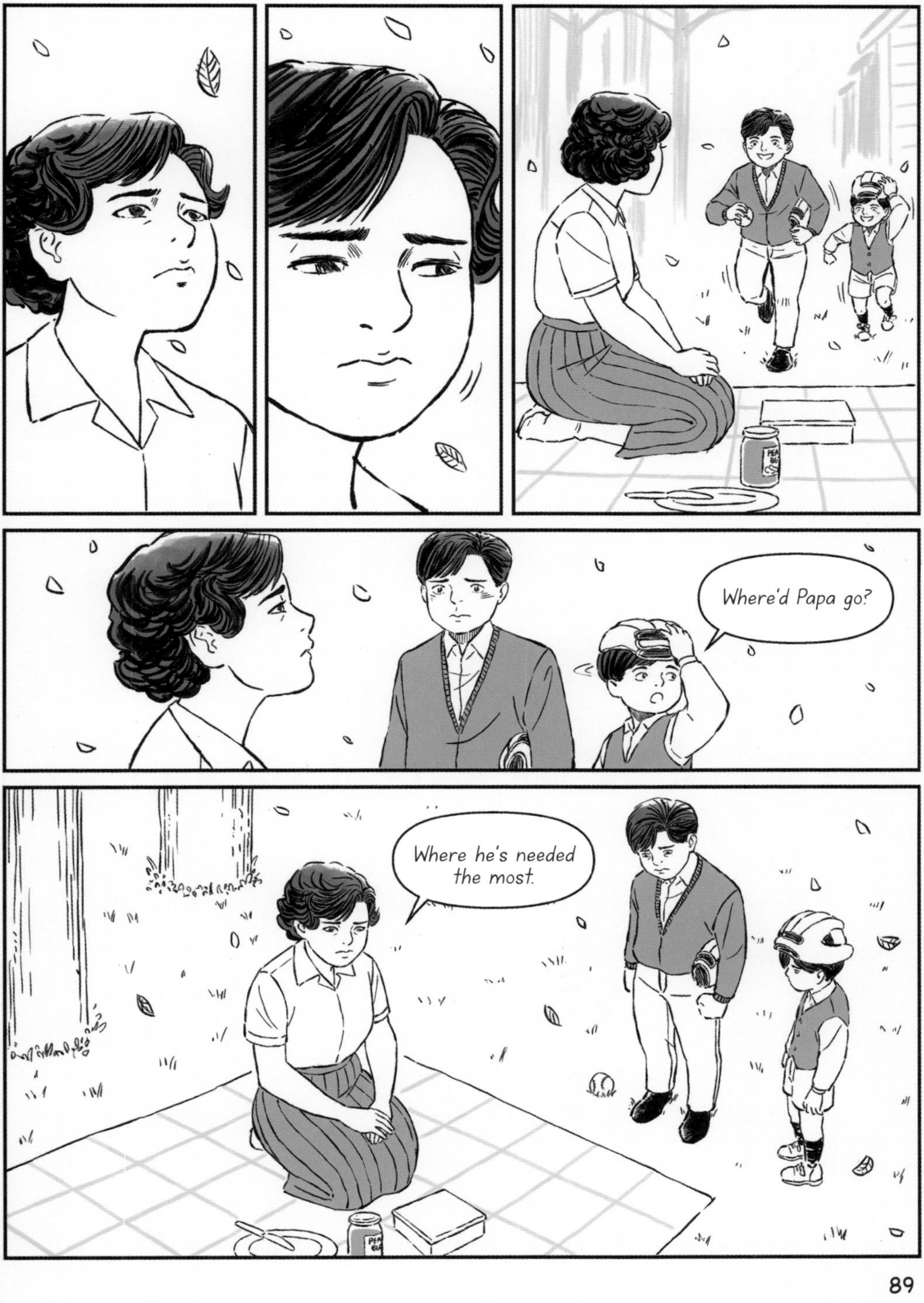
Where'd Papa go?
Where he's needed the most.

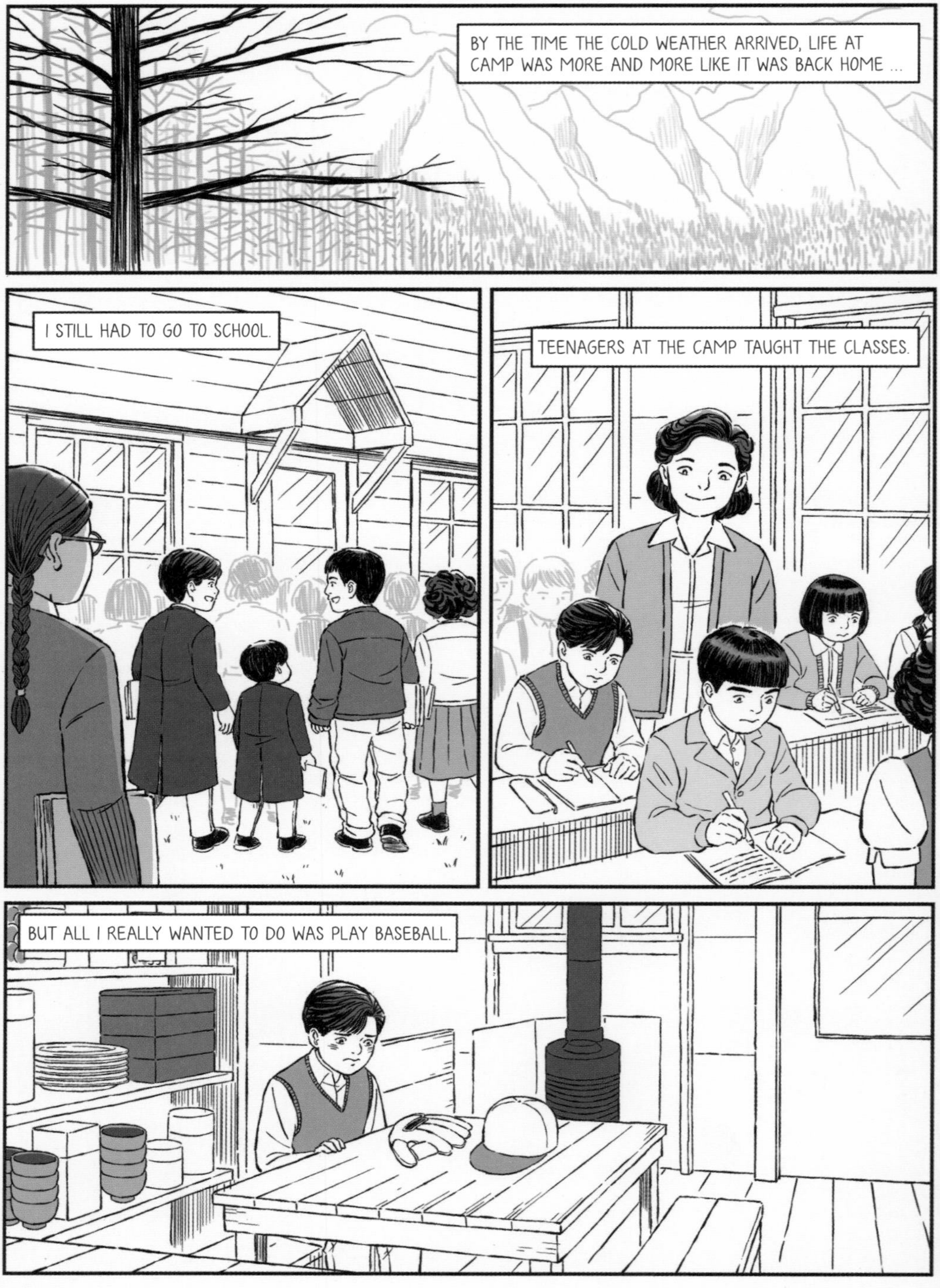
BY THE TIME THE COLD WEATHER ARRIVED, LIFE AT CAMP WAS MORE AND MORE LIKE IT WAS BACK HOME ...
I STILL HAD TO GO TO SCHOOL.
TEENAGERS AT THE CAMP TAUGHT THE CLASSES.
BUT ALL I REALLY WANTED TO DO WAS PLAY BASEBALL.

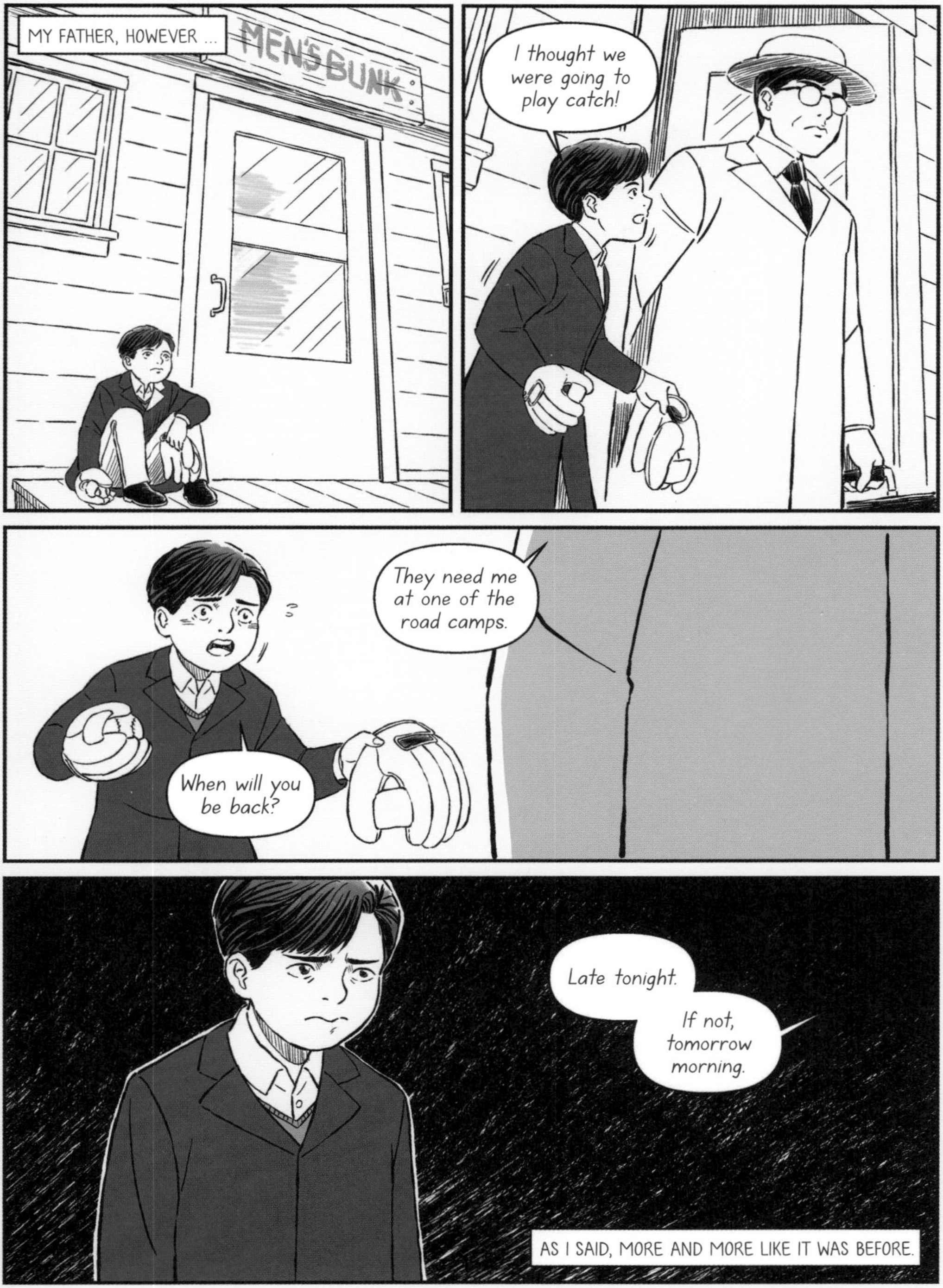
MY FATHER, HOWEVER ...
MEN'S BUNK
I thought we were going to play catch!
They need me at one of the road camps.
When will you be back?
Late tonight.
If not, tomorrow morning.
AS I SAID, MORE AND MORE LIKE IT WAS BEFORE.

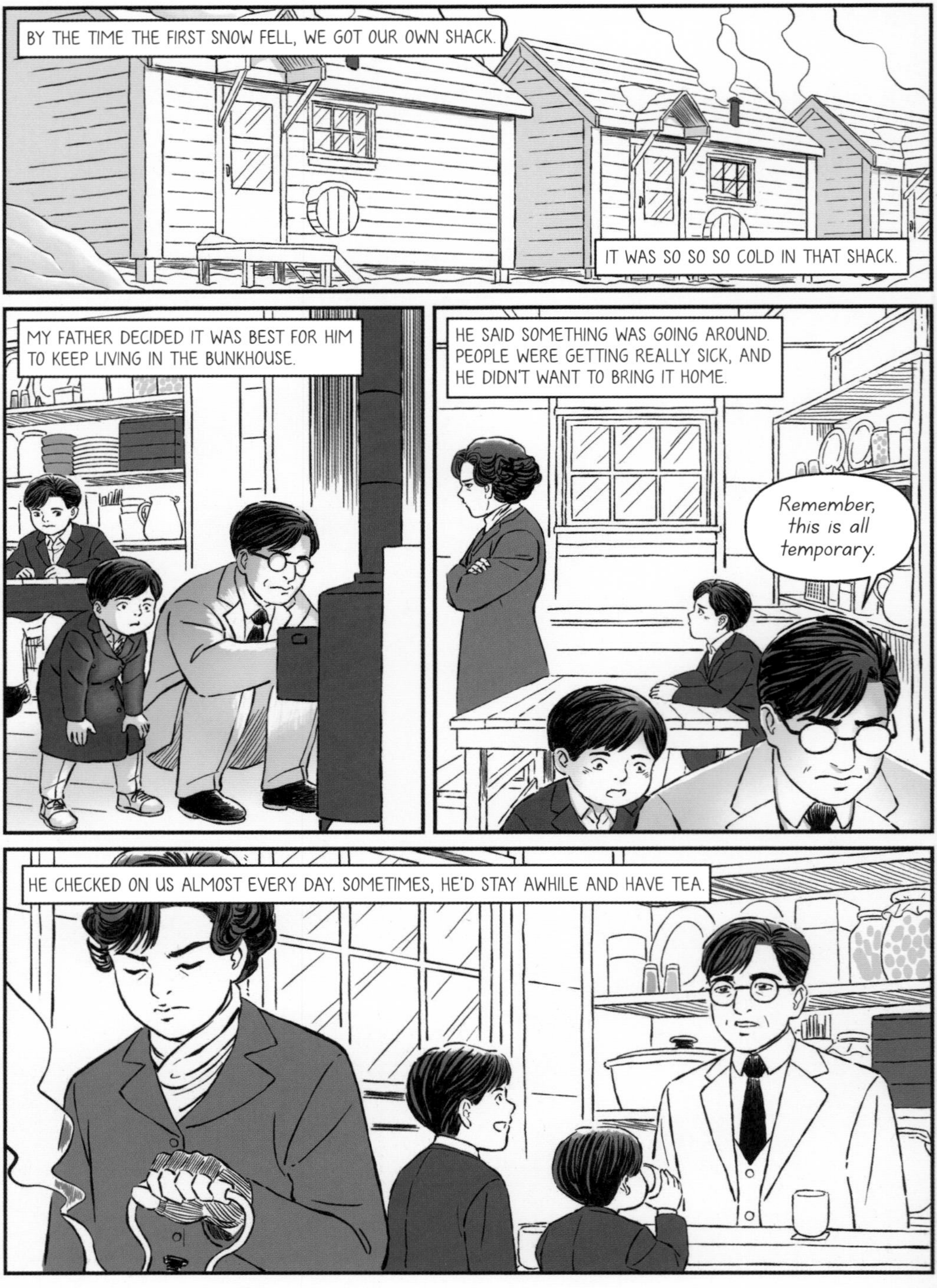
BY THE TIME THE FIRST SNOW FELL, WE GOT OUR OWN SHACK.
IT WAS SO SO SO COLD IN THAT SHACK.
MY FATHER DECIDED IT WAS BEST FOR HIM TO KEEP LIVING IN THE BUNKHOUSE.
HE SAID SOMETHING WAS GOING AROUND. PEOPLE WERE GETTING REALLY SICK, AND HE DIDN'T WANT TO BRING IT HOME.
Remember, this is all temporary.
HE CHECKED ON US ALMOST EVERY DAY. SOMETIMES, HE'D STAY AWHILE AND HAVE TEA.

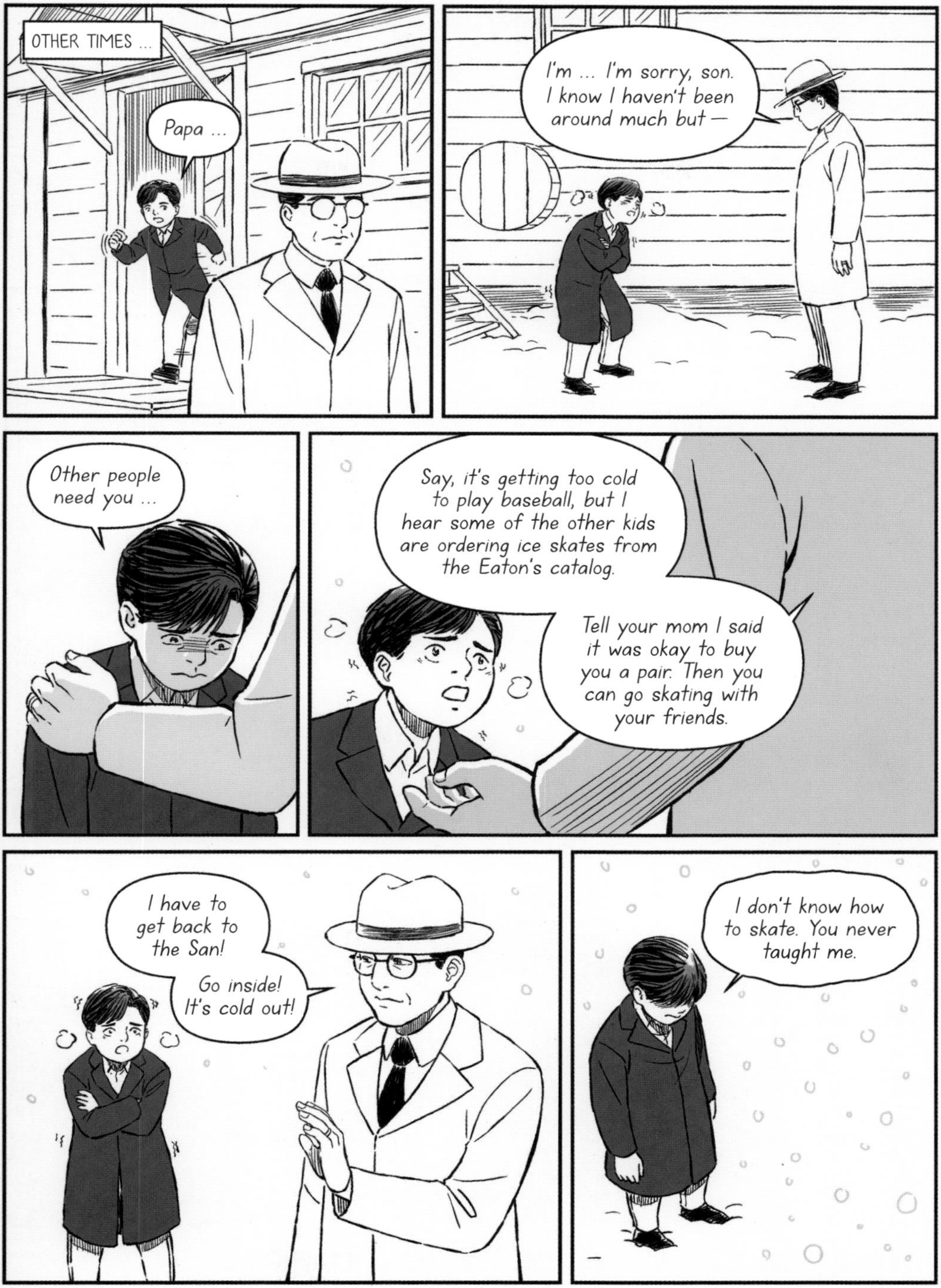
OTHER TIMES ...
Papa ...
I'm ... I'm sorry, son. I know I haven't been around much but —
Other people need you ...
Say, it's getting too cold to play baseball, but I hear some of the other kids are ordering ice skates from the Eaton's catalog.
Tell your mom I said it was okay to buy you a pair. Then you can go skating with your friends.
I have to get back to the San!
Go inside! It's cold out!
I don't know how to skate. You never taught me.

WHATEVER WAS GOING AROUND THE CAMP EVENTUALLY MADE MAMA SICK.

KOFF
KOFF
KOFF

SHE DIDN'T CALL ON MY FATHER BECAUSE SHE DIDN'T WANT TO BOTHER HIM. IT WAS WINTER, AND MORE PEOPLE GOT SICK IN WINTER.

THE SAN WAS COMPLETELY BUILT BY THEN — AND REALLY FULL — SO SOMETIMES WE WOULDN'T SEE MY FATHER FOR DAYS ON END.

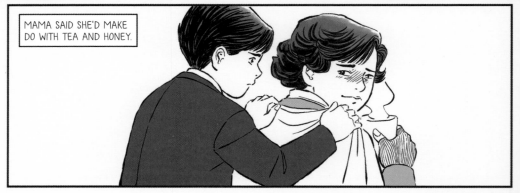

MAMA SAID SHE'D MAKE DO WITH TEA AND HONEY.

BUT I KNEW SHE NEEDED MORE THAN TEA AND HONEY.

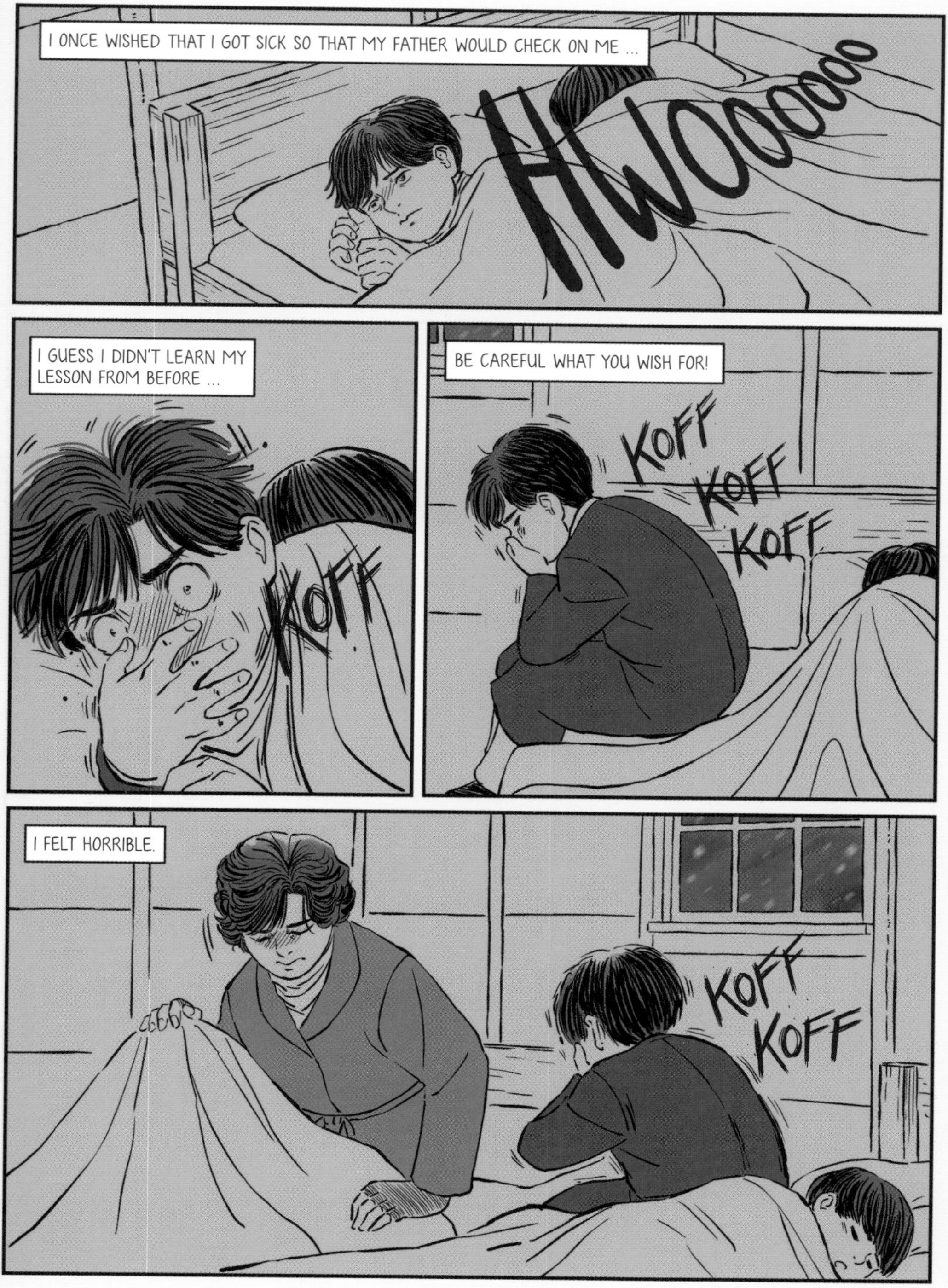
I ONCE WISHED THAT I GOT SICK SO THAT MY FATHER WOULD CHECK ON ME ...
HWOOOOOO
I GUESS I DIDN'T LEARN MY LESSON FROM BEFORE ...
KOFF
BE CAREFUL WHAT YOU WISH FOR!
KOFF
KOFF
KOFF
I FELT HORRIBLE.
KOFF
KOFF

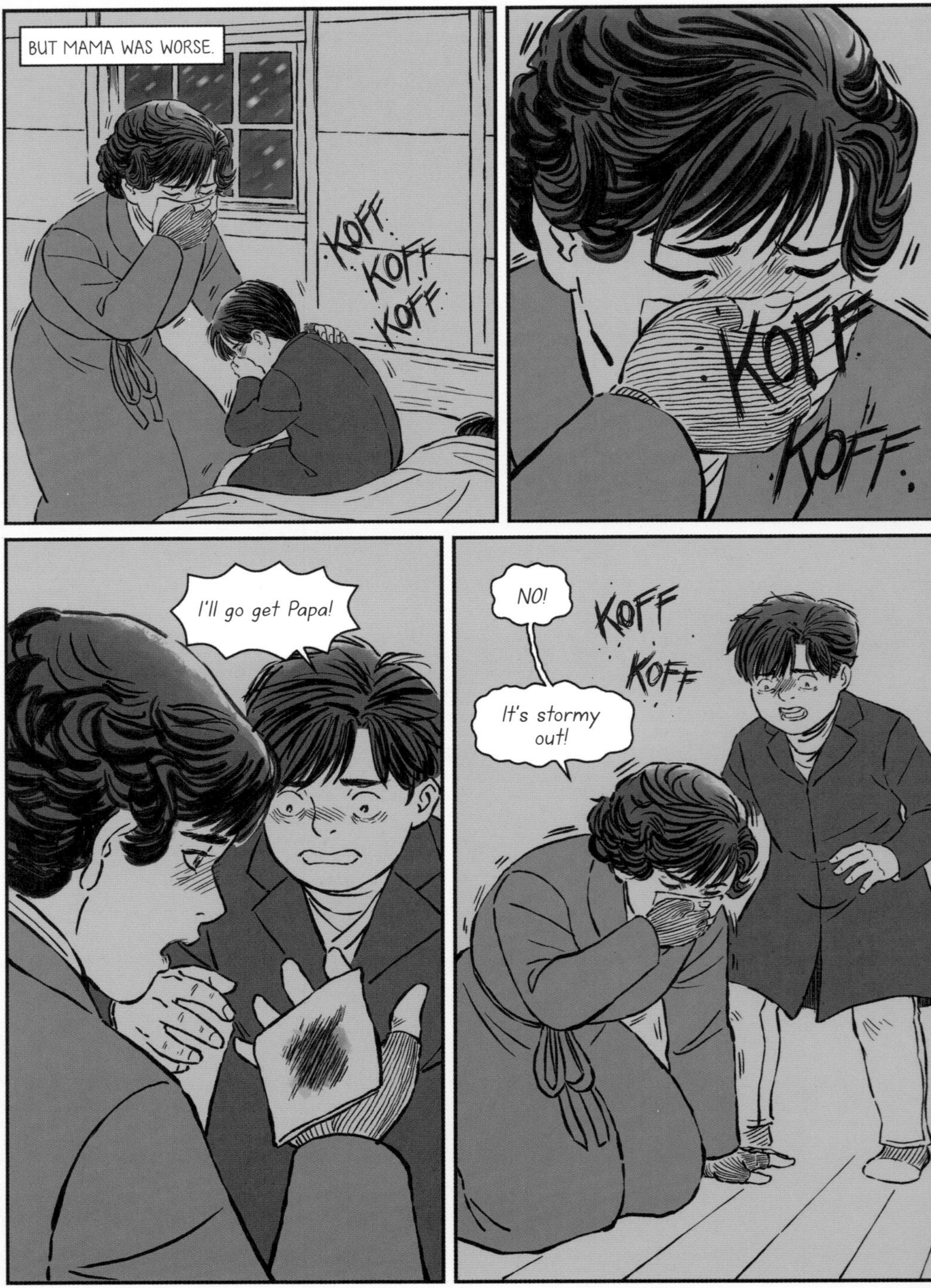
BUT MAMA WAS WORSE.
KOFF... KOFF KOFF
KOFF KOFF
I'll go get Papa!
NO!
KOFF KOFF
It's stormy out!

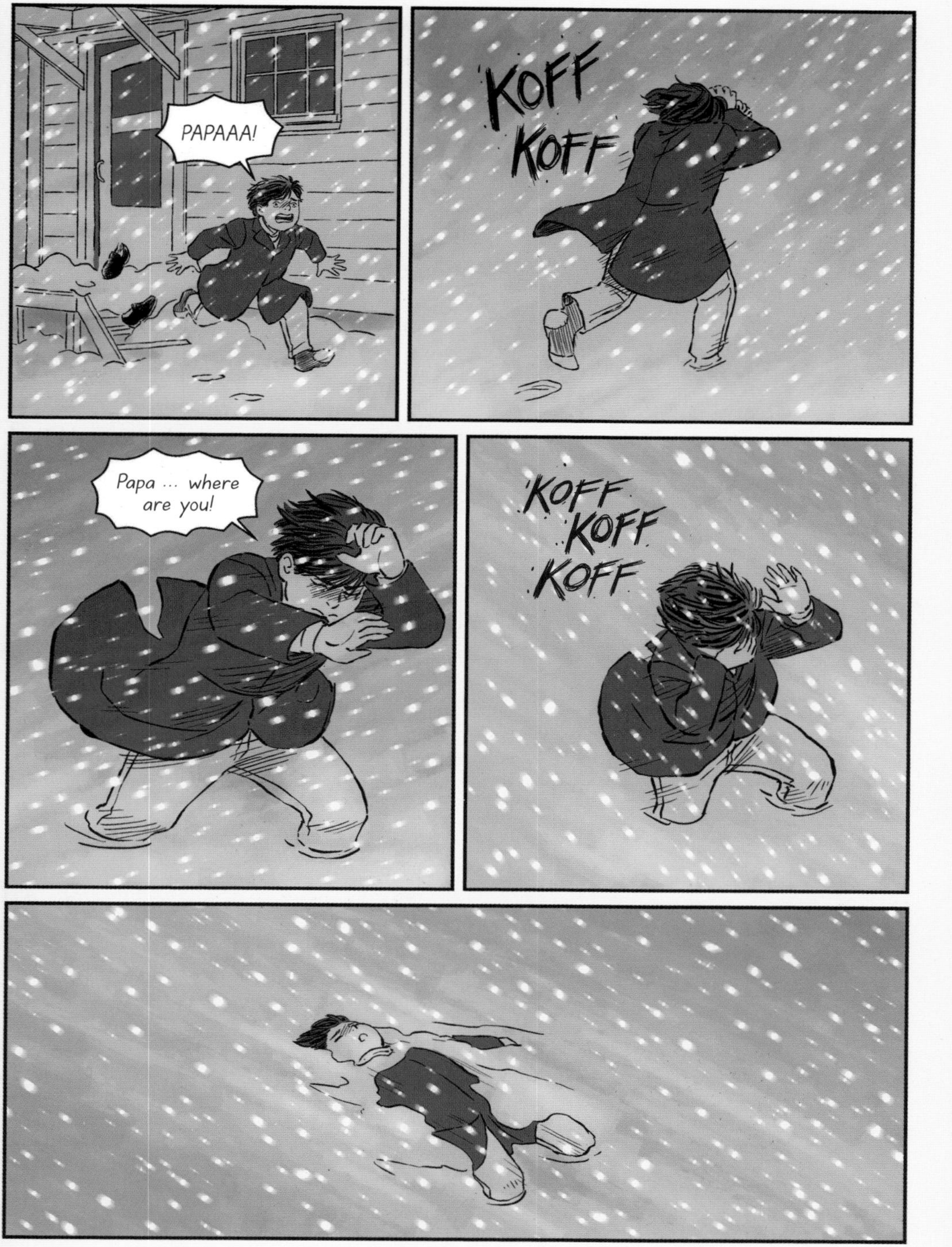
PAPAAA!
KOFF KOFF
Papa ... where are you!
KOFF KOFF KOFF

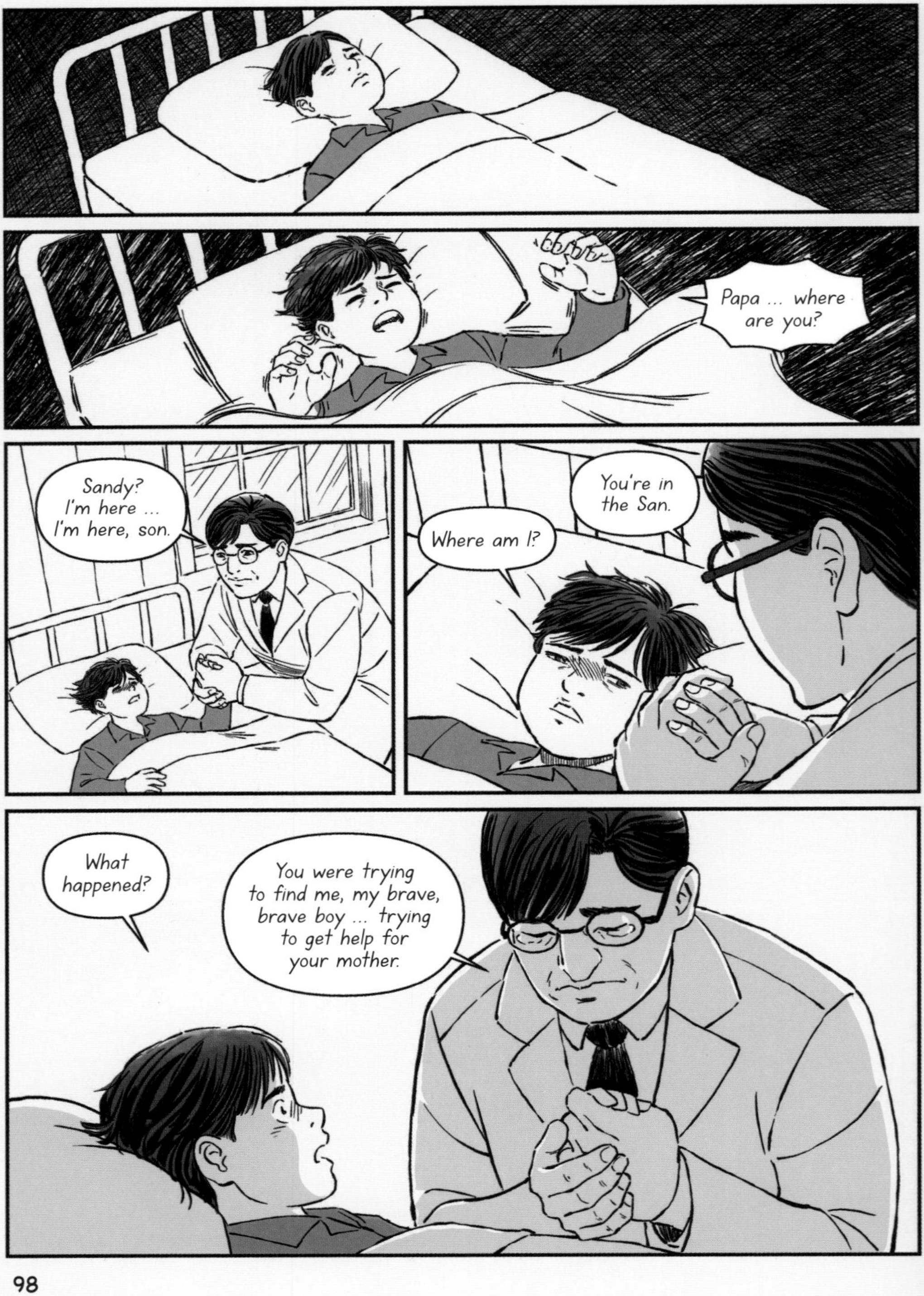
Papa ... where are you?
Sandy? I'm here ... I'm here, son.
Where am I?
You're in the San.
What happened?
You were trying to find me, my brave, brave boy ... trying to get help for your mother.

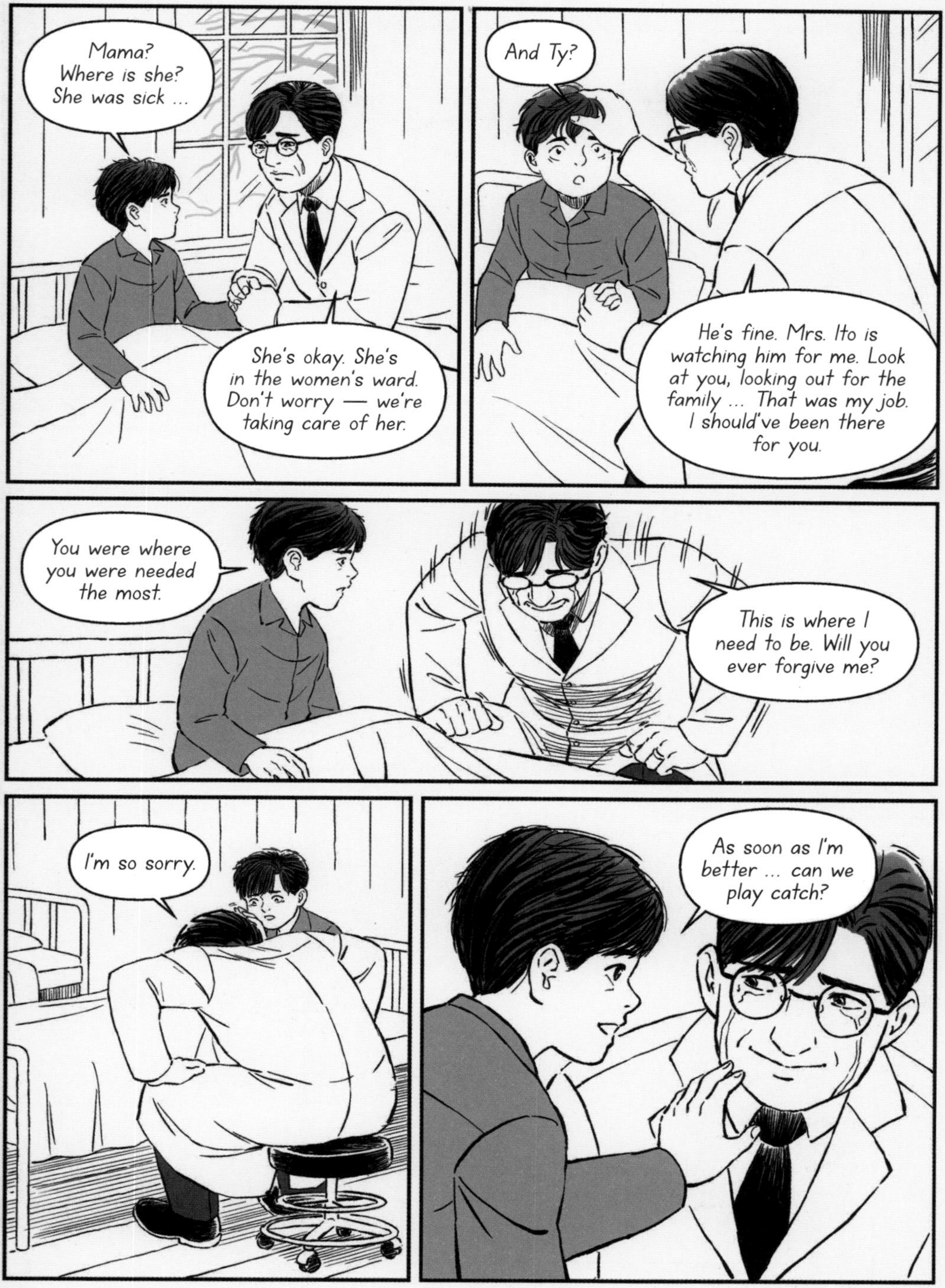

Mama? Where is she? She was sick ...
She's okay. She's in the women's ward. Don't worry — we're taking care of her.
And Ty?
He's fine. Mrs. Ito is watching him for me. Look at you, looking out for the family ... That was my job. I should've been there for you.
You were where you were needed the most.
This is where I need to be. Will you ever forgive me?
I'm so sorry.
As soon as I'm better ... can we play catch?

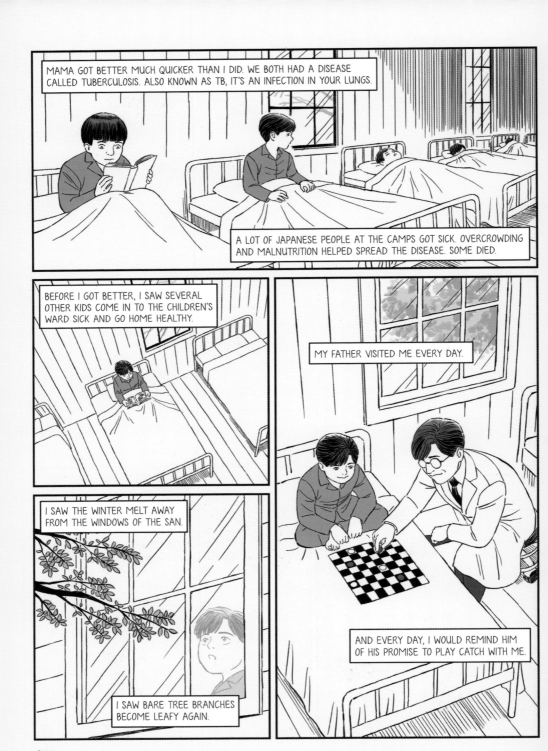

MAMA GOT BETTER MUCH QUICKER THAN I DID. WE BOTH HAD A DISEASE CALLED TUBERCULOSIS. ALSO KNOWN AS TB, IT'S AN INFECTION IN YOUR LUNGS.

A LOT OF JAPANESE PEOPLE AT THE CAMPS GOT SICK. OVERCROWDING AND MALNUTRITION HELPED SPREAD THE DISEASE. SOME DIED.

BEFORE I GOT BETTER, I SAW SEVERAL OTHER KIDS COME IN TO THE CHILDREN'S WARD SICK AND GO HOME HEALTHY.

MY FATHER VISITED ME EVERY DAY.

I SAW THE WINTER MELT AWAY FROM THE WINDOWS OF THE SAN.

I SAW BARE TREE BRANCHES BECOME LEAFY AGAIN.

AND EVERY DAY, I WOULD REMIND HIM OF HIS PROMISE TO PLAY CATCH WITH ME.

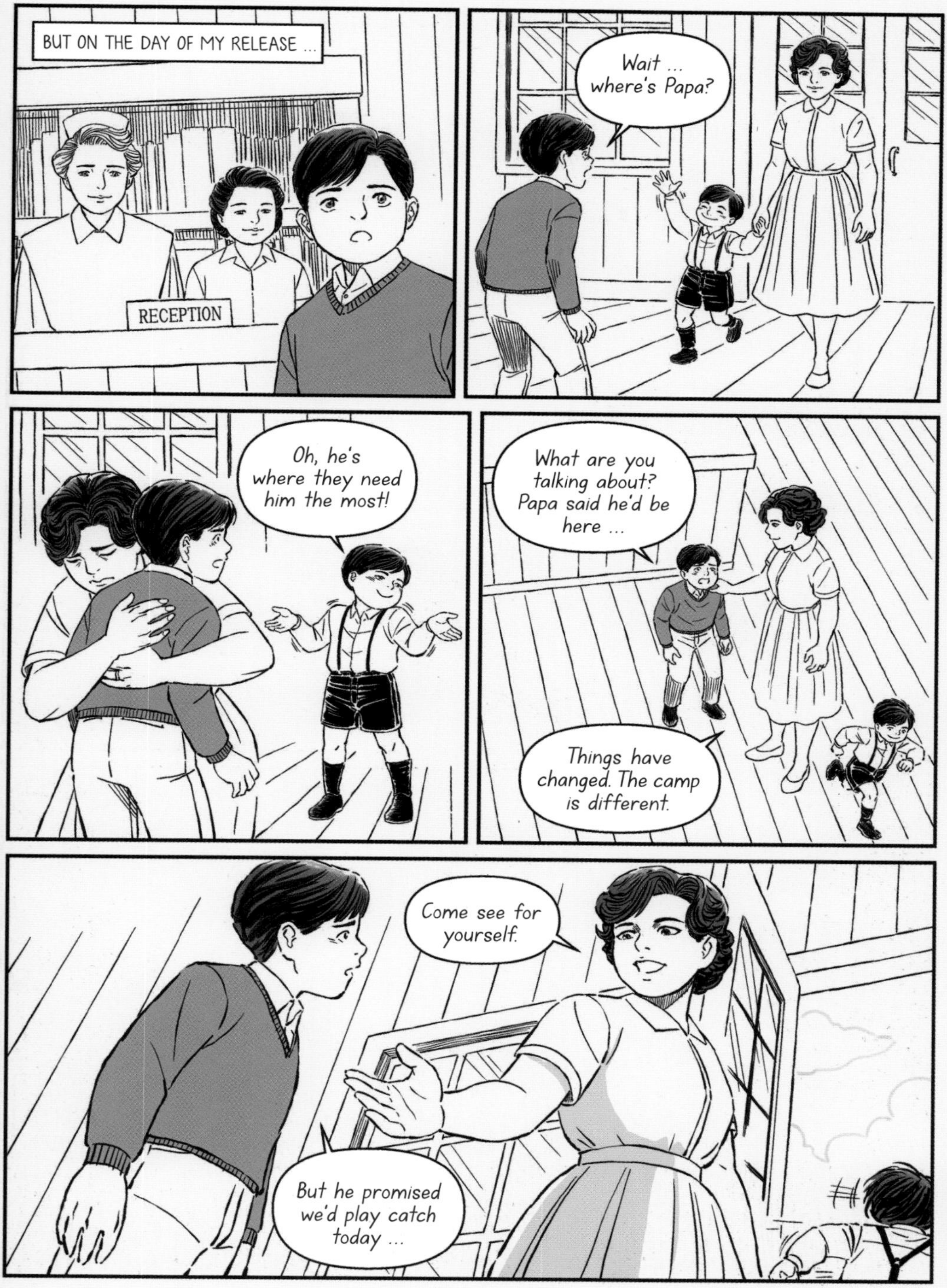
BUT ON THE DAY OF MY RELEASE ...
RECEPTION
Wait ... where's Papa?
Oh, he's where they need him the most!
What are you talking about? Papa said he'd be here ...
Things have changed. The camp is different.
Come see for yourself.
But he promised we'd play catch today ...

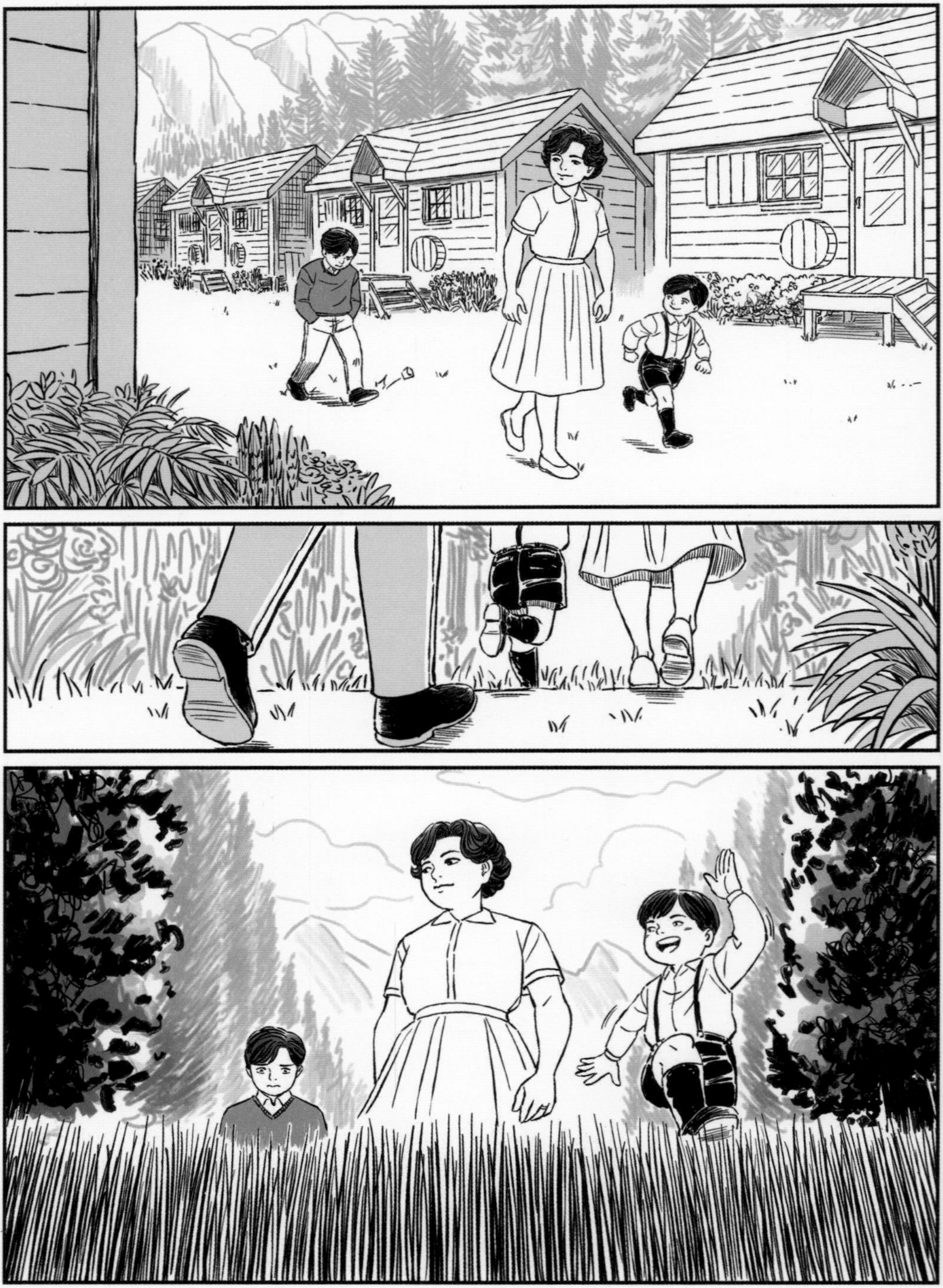

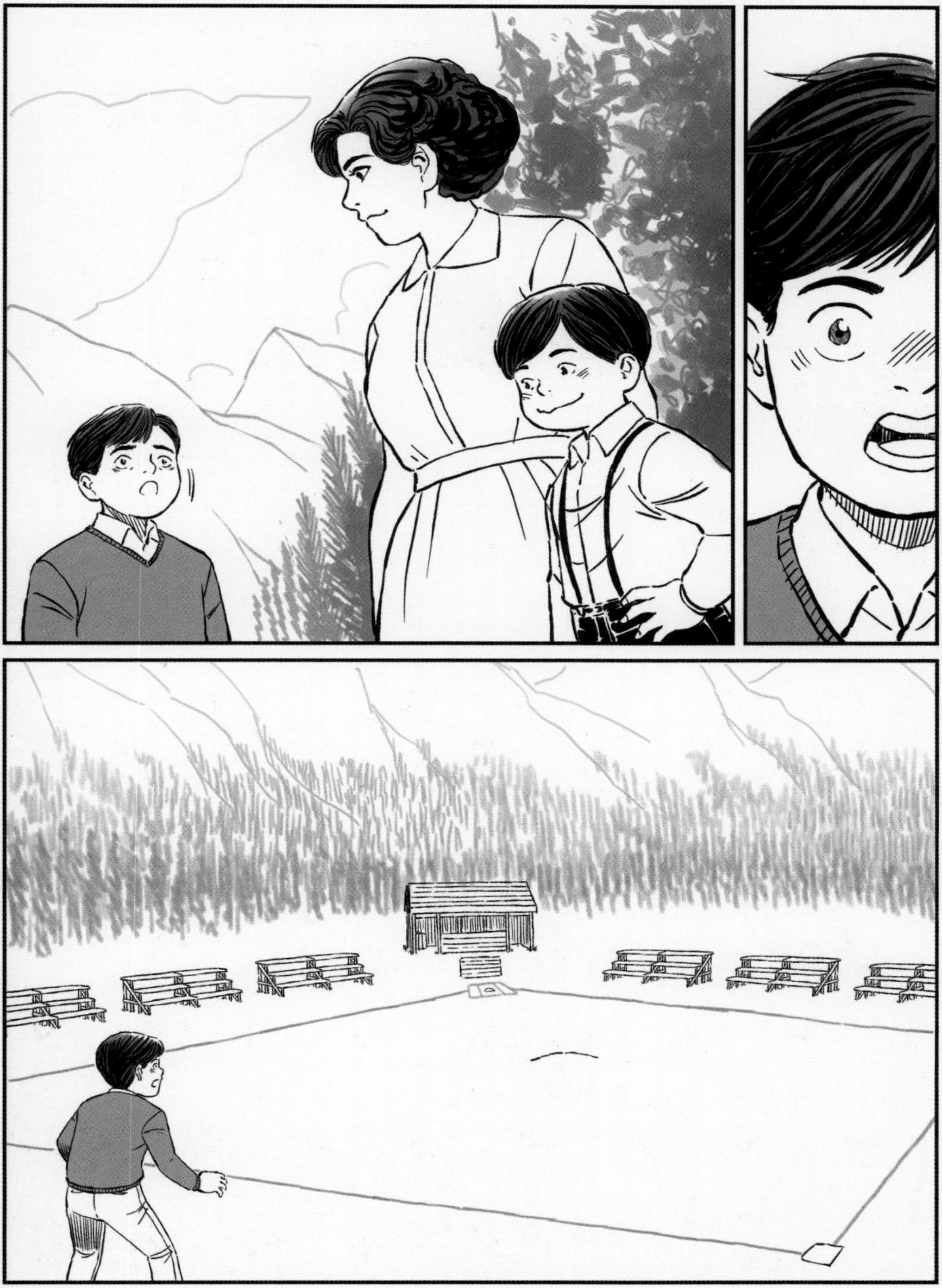

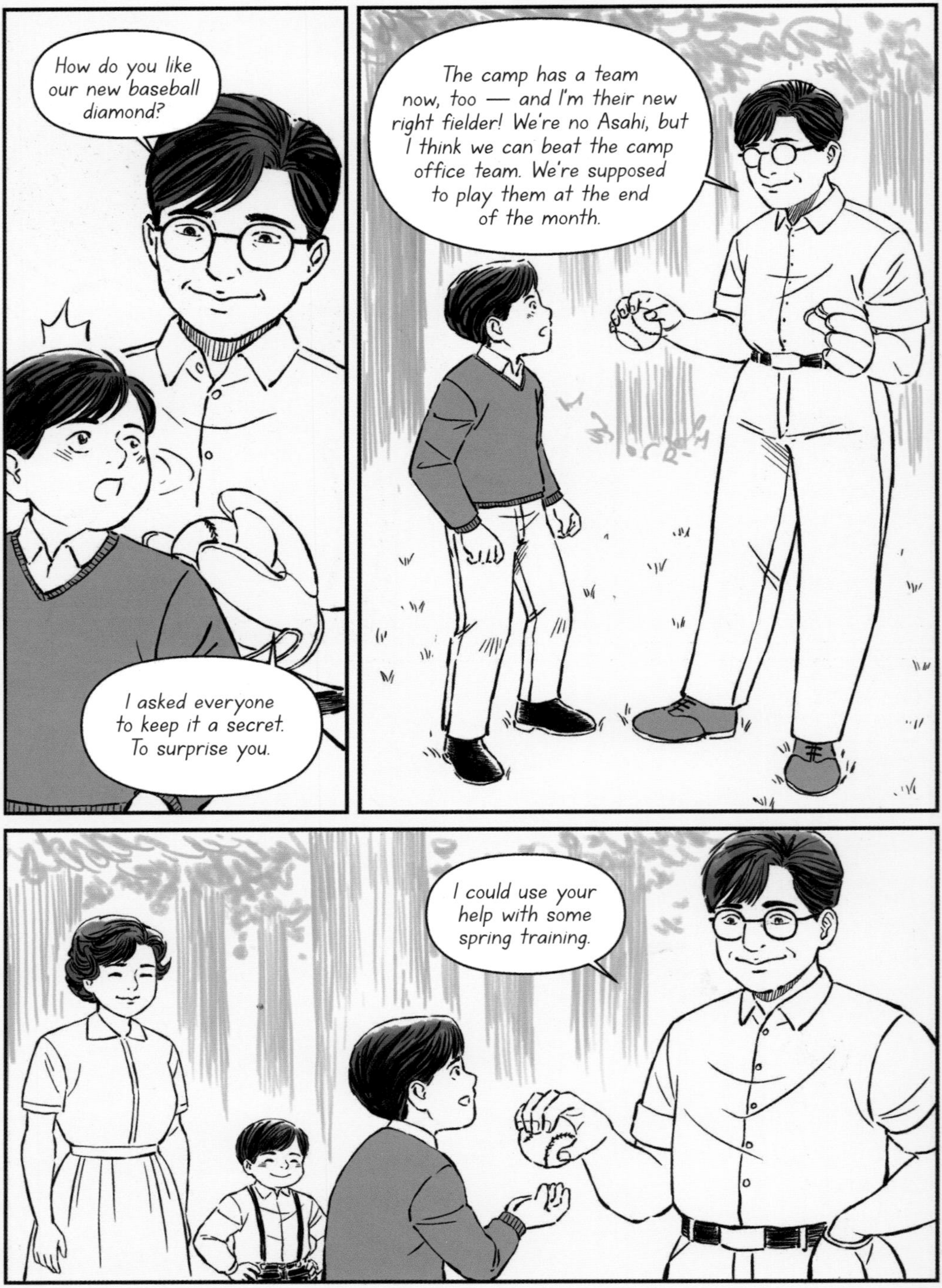
How do you like our new baseball diamond?
I asked everyone to keep it a secret. To surprise you.
The camp has a team now, too — and I'm their new right fielder! We're no Asahi, but I think we can beat the camp office team. We're supposed to play them at the end of the month.
I could use your help with some spring training.

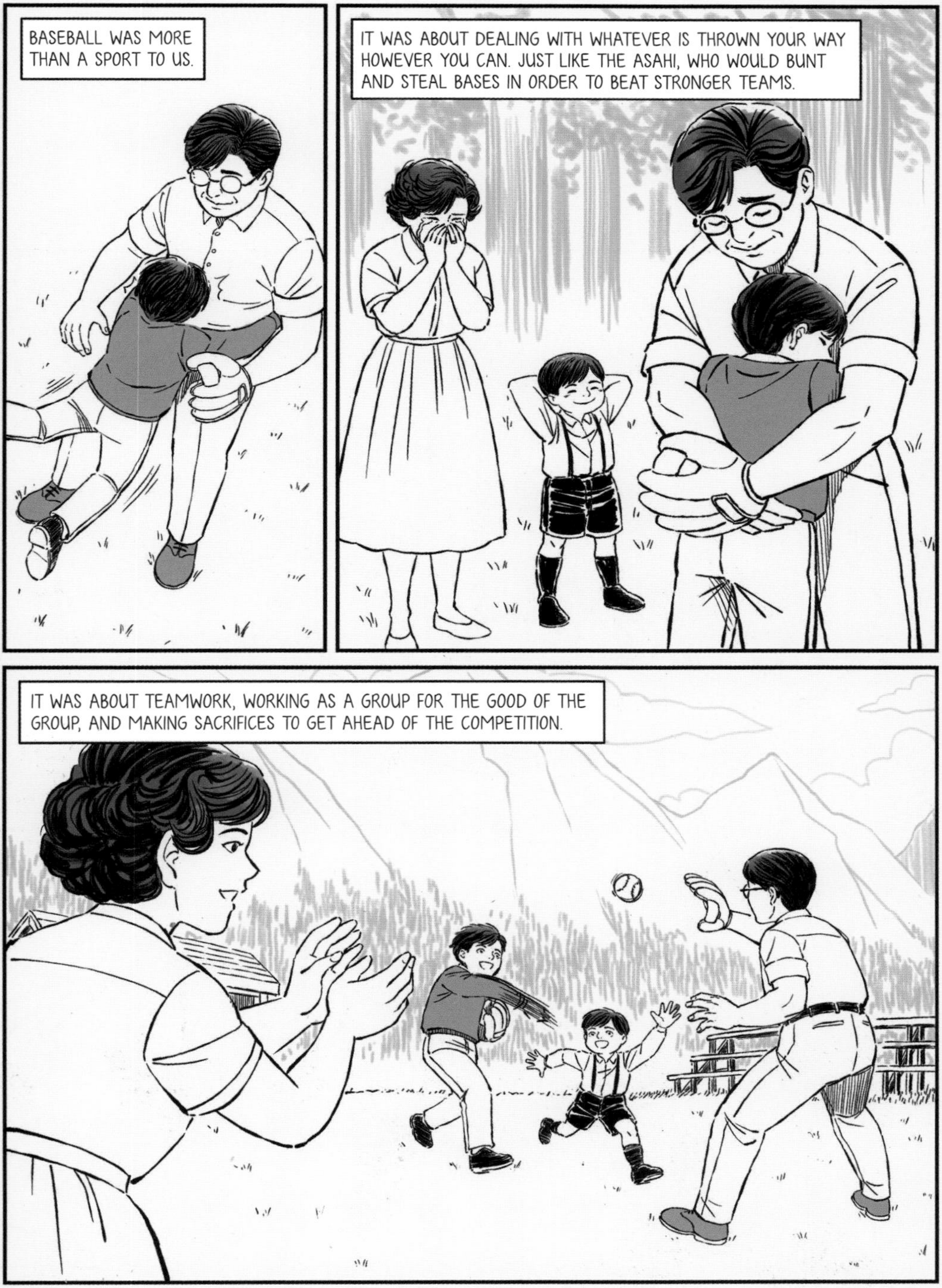
BASEBALL WAS MORE THAN A SPORT TO US.
IT WAS ABOUT DEALING WITH WHATEVER IS THROWN YOUR WAY HOWEVER YOU CAN. JUST LIKE THE ASAHI, WHO WOULD BUNT AND STEAL BASES IN ORDER TO BEAT STRONGER TEAMS.
IT WAS ABOUT TEAMWORK, WORKING AS A GROUP FOR THE GOOD OF THE GROUP, AND MAKING SACRIFICES TO GET AHEAD OF THE COMPETITION.

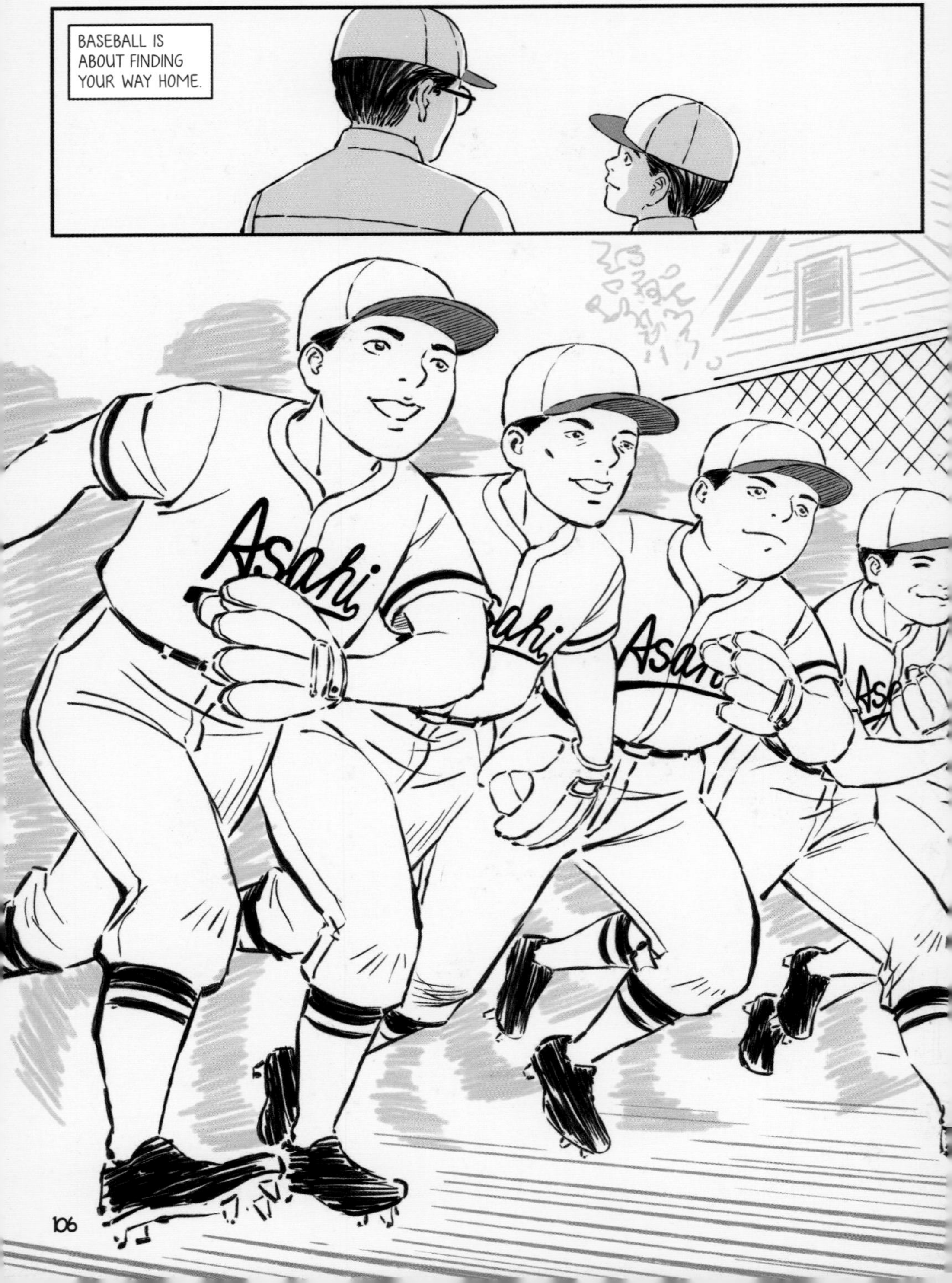
BASEBALL IS ABOUT FINDING YOUR WAY HOME.
Asahi
Asahi
Asahi

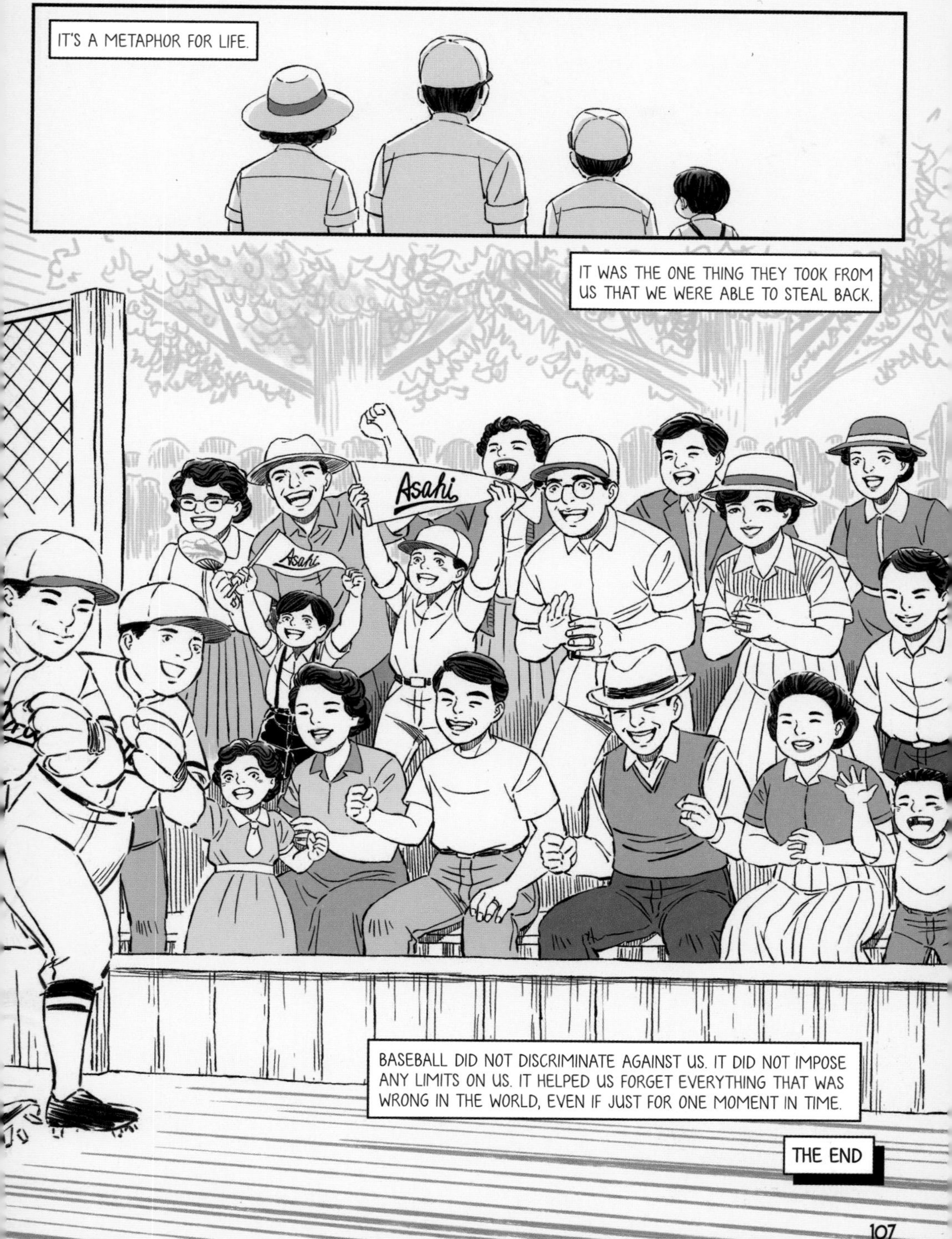
IT'S A METAPHOR FOR LIFE.
IT WAS THE ONE THING THEY TOOK FROM US THAT WE WERE ABLE TO STEAL BACK.
Asahi
Asahi
BASEBALL DID NOT DISCRIMINATE AGAINST US. IT DID NOT IMPOSE ANY LIMITS ON US. IT HELPED US FORGET EVERYTHING THAT WAS WRONG IN THE WORLD, EVEN IF JUST FOR ONE MOMENT IN TIME.
THE END

AFTERWORD

By Susan Aihoshi

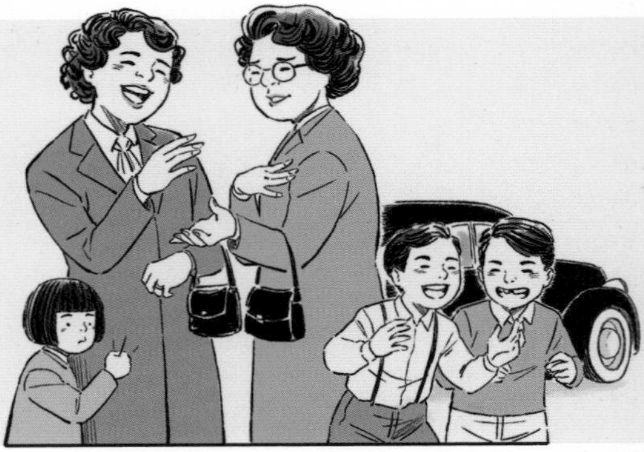

A Personal Story

History is more than a series of past events when your own family experiences them. My grandparents, mother, father and every one of my aunts and uncles living in British Columbia in 1942 were forced to leave their homes, solely because of their Japanese ancestry. They eventually moved to Toronto, Ontario, where I was born. I will never overlook what they endured.

A Racist Attitude

Immigration from Asian countries to North America began during the late 1800s due to poor social, political and economic conditions at home. Hoping for better futures, the newcomers arrived in western coastal areas of the United States and Canada where jobs were plentiful. Asian immigrants worked hard and for less pay than white workers, who resented the competition.

Because Asians were easily identified, they became targets of discrimination even after they received citizenship, had children who were citizens, and established farms or businesses in their new homes. In 1907, anti-Asian feelings led to a riot that damaged shops and property in Vancouver's Chinese and Japanese neighborhoods. The violence eventually stopped but hostility against Asians continued.

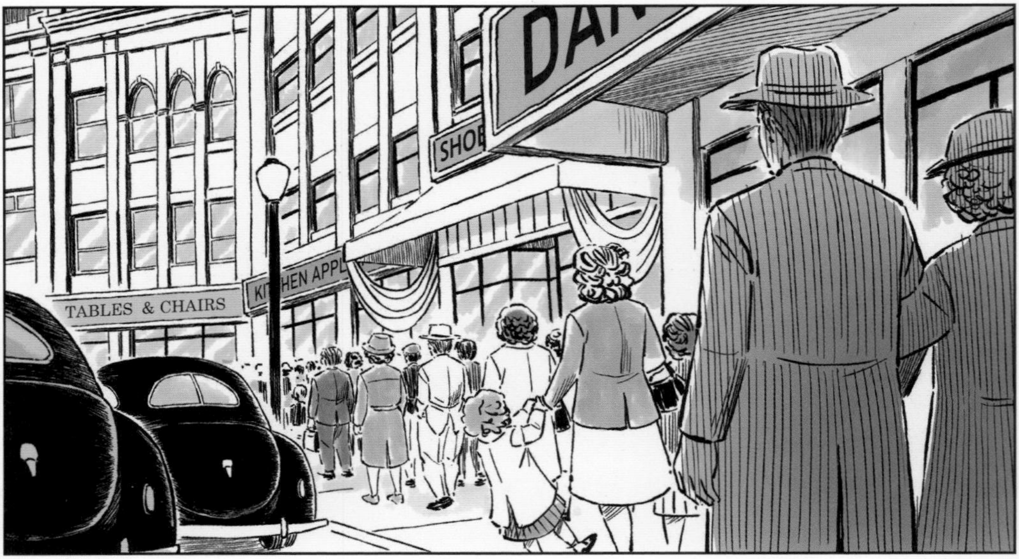
TABLES & CHAIRS

The Attack at Pearl Harbor

On December 7, 1941, Japan launched a surprise attack on the American naval base at Hawaii's Pearl Harbor, triggering the United States' immediate entry into WWII. The raid became the excuse for the eventual uprooting, imprisonment and community destruction of people of Japanese ancestry living on North America's west coast. These disgraceful actions occurred in both Canada and the United States under the justification of threats to national security — without any evidence to support those fears. Labeled as "enemy aliens," the lives of thousands of people of Japanese origin, the majority of whom were Canadian or American citizens, would be forever changed.

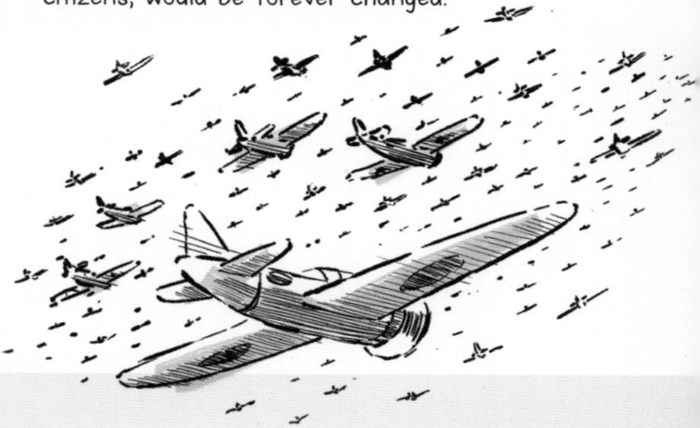

Forced Removal and Confinement

In February of 1942, President Franklin D. Roosevelt gave the military sweeping powers over anyone of Japanese heritage on America's west coast. Over 110 000 people had their activities limited and were put under strict curfews. Soon after, Japanese Americans in these areas had to register themselves and their families and report to control stations. Then they were sent to "relocation centers" that were really prison camps. With little warning, thousands of people had to abandon their homes, businesses, farms and property and live in crowded, makeshift barracks in remote sites surrounded by barbed wire and armed guards.

After Pearl Harbor, the Canadian government immediately seized all Japanese-owned fishing boats on the Pacific coast and closed Japanese schools and newspapers. Approximately 22 000 people began to be uprooted from their homes along British Columbia's coast after Prime Minster William Lyon Mackenzie King declared it a "protected area" in January of 1942. A dusk-to-dawn curfew was imposed, mail was censored and cars, cameras and radios owned by Japanese Canadians had to be turned in to the Custodian of Enemy Alien Property. This government agency was supposed to keep goods and properties for eventual return to their owners but sold them at reduced prices without the owners' consent, using the money to pay for the owners' detention.

Like Japanese Americans, Japanese Canadians often had little warning of their removal and could only bring a limited amount of personal belongings. Men were separated from their families and sent to road camps in the Rockies to perform forced labor. Hastings Park in Vancouver became a clearing center where women, children and older men were kept in livestock buildings. These people were then shipped to "internment camps" — abandoned mining centers in isolated areas of British Columbia's interior known as "ghost towns" or else hastily built shacks without electricity or running water.

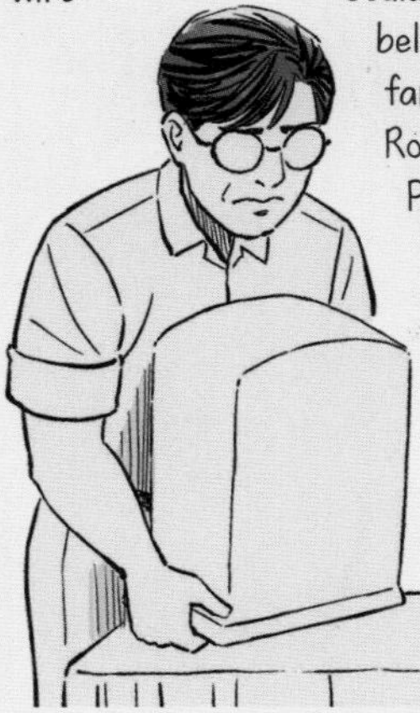

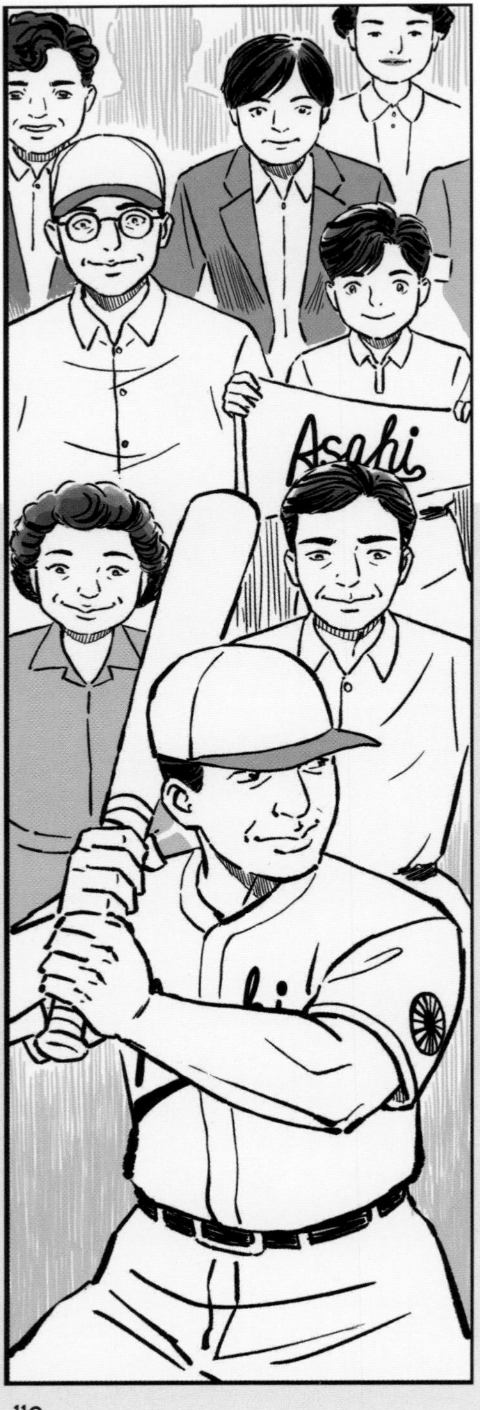
Asahi

Baseball in the Camps

Respected as "America's game," baseball played an important role in the restricted lives of people of Japanese heritage during their confinement. Before Pearl Harbor, the sport was so popular that numerous teams in eight different cities formed the Japanese Pacific Coast Baseball League. Those teams formed the basis of many camp teams in both Canada and the United States. Playing baseball was more than just recreation for the captives, it was one way to show loyalty to their country even while enduring injustice by that same country.

Baseball also helped to encourage morale and inspire those confined in the camps.

The Vancouver Asahi

Until Pearl Harbor, the Japanese Canadian community celebrated Vancouver's Asahi baseball team. Winning ten city championship titles from 1919 to 1940, the Asahi used a style of play that emphasized speed and teamwork to score runs over their bigger and stronger opponents. Even the white population admired their talents. All that ended in 1941, when the Asahi ominously failed to make the Burrard League finals. The team would never play together again.

In 1942, uprooted Asahi members ended up in various British Columbia detention camps. There, baseball teams took shape around a few core Asahi players. In 1943, the Lemon Creek All-Stars won the Slocan Valley Camp Championship in typical Asahi fashion with a squeeze play. "Baseball helped get us through the internment," said Asahi third baseman Kaye Kaminishi.

The Vancouver Asahi team was inducted into the Canadian Baseball Hall of Fame in 2003 and the British Columbia Sports Hall of Fame in 2005.

Life After the Camps

In the decades after their incarceration, Japanese Canadians and Japanese Americans went on to reestablish their shattered lives, with many achieving remarkable success. In 1988, both the American and the Canadian national governments offered formal apologies and financial redress to their citizens of Japanese ancestry who had endured grave wrongs during WWII and after.

My dad loved baseball and I now share his love of the game. I like to think the Asahi was the team that first inspired him.

These links feature the team:

www.historicacanada.ca/content/heritage-minutes/vancouver-asahi
www.virtualmuseum.ca/sgc-cms/expositions-exhibitions/asahi/

Further Resources

Books
Aihoshi, Susan M. *Torn Apart: The Internment Diary of Mary Kobayashi.*
    Scholastic Canada, 2012.
Takei George, Justin Eisinger and Steven Scott. *They Called Us Enemy.*
    Illustrated by Harmony Becker. Top Shelf Productions, 2019.
Walters, Eric. *Caged Eagles.* Orca Book Publishers, 2001.

Films
Obachan's Garden. Directed by Linda Ohama. National Film Board of Canada, 2001.
Sleeping Tigers: The Asahi Baseball Story. Directed by Jari Osborne. National
    Film Board of Canada, 2003.

Video Game
East of the Rockies. Joy Kogawa. National Film Board of Canada, 2019.

To those who didn't know, but now do, and vow never to forget — J.T.

To Mom, Dad, Ruth and Mark. Thanks for all the love, and support. — D.N.

We would like to acknowledge some of the incredible individuals and institutions that helped us with our research and helped shape this book: Our thanks to Susan Aihoshi, Momoko Ito and Karen Lesnik (formerly of the Nikkei Internment Memorial Center); Mika Fukuma (formerly of the Nikkei Voice); the Nikkei National Museum and Cultural Centre; the Japanese Canadian Cultural Centre; Karen Li; everyone at Kids Can Press, especially our dedicated designer Barb Kelly and our editor extraordinaire Jennifer Stokes. And to anyone we may have unintentionally omitted, please know that you are in our hearts and we thank you, too!

— J.T. and D.N.

Text © 2021 J. Torres
Illustrations © 2021 David Namisato

All rights reserved. No part of this publication may be reproduced, stored in a retrieval system or transmitted, in any form or by any means, without the prior written permission of Kids Can Press Ltd. or, in case of photocopying or other reprographic copying, a license from The Canadian Copyright Licensing Agency (Access Copyright). For an Access Copyright license, visit www.accesscopyright.ca or call toll free to 1-800-893-5777.

The poster on p. 23 is based on the original Japanese Canadian relocation notice, which first appeared in the Vancouver Sun and Vancouver Province newspapers on June 19, 1942. An image of the original notice can be found in Vancouver Public Library's Historical Photograph collection, which can be accessed at www.vpl.ca/historicalphotos using VPL accession number 12851.

Published in Canada and the U.S. by Kids Can Press Ltd.
25 Dockside Drive, Toronto, ON M5A 0B5

Kids Can Press is a Corus Entertainment Inc. company
www.kidscanpress.com

The artwork in this book was rendered digitally.
The text is set in Fall for You.

Edited by Jennifer Stokes
Designed by Barb Kelly

Printed and bound in
Shenzhen, China, in 1/2022
by Asia Pacific Offset

CM 21 0 9 8 7 6 5 4 3 2

FSC
www.fsc.org
MIX
Paper from
responsible sources
FSC® C012521

Library and Archives Canada Cataloguing in Publication

Title: Stealing home / J. Torres ; David Namisato.
Names: Torres, J., 1969 – author. | Namisato, David, 1977– artist.
Identifiers: Canadiana 20200389831 | ISBN 9781525303340 (hardcover)
Subjects: CSH: Japanese Canadians — Evacuation and relocation, 1942–1945 — Comic books, strips, etc. | CSH: Japanese Canadians — Evacuation and relocation, 1942–1945—Juvenile fiction. | CSH: Japanese Canadians — Social conditions — 20th century — Comic books, strips, etc. | CSH: Japanese Canadians — Social conditions — 20th century — Juvenile fiction. | LCGFT: Historical comics. | LCGFT: Graphic novels.
Classification: LCC PN6733.T67 S74 2021 | DDC j741.5/971 — dc23

Kids Can Press gratefully acknowledges that the land on which our office is located is the traditional territory of many nations, including the Mississaugas of the Credit, the Anishnabeg, the Chippewa, the Haudenosaunee and the Wendat peoples, and is now home to many diverse First Nations, Inuit and Métis peoples.

We thank the Government of Ontario, through Ontario Creates; the Ontario Arts Council; the Canada Council for the Arts; and the Government of Canada for supporting our publishing activity.

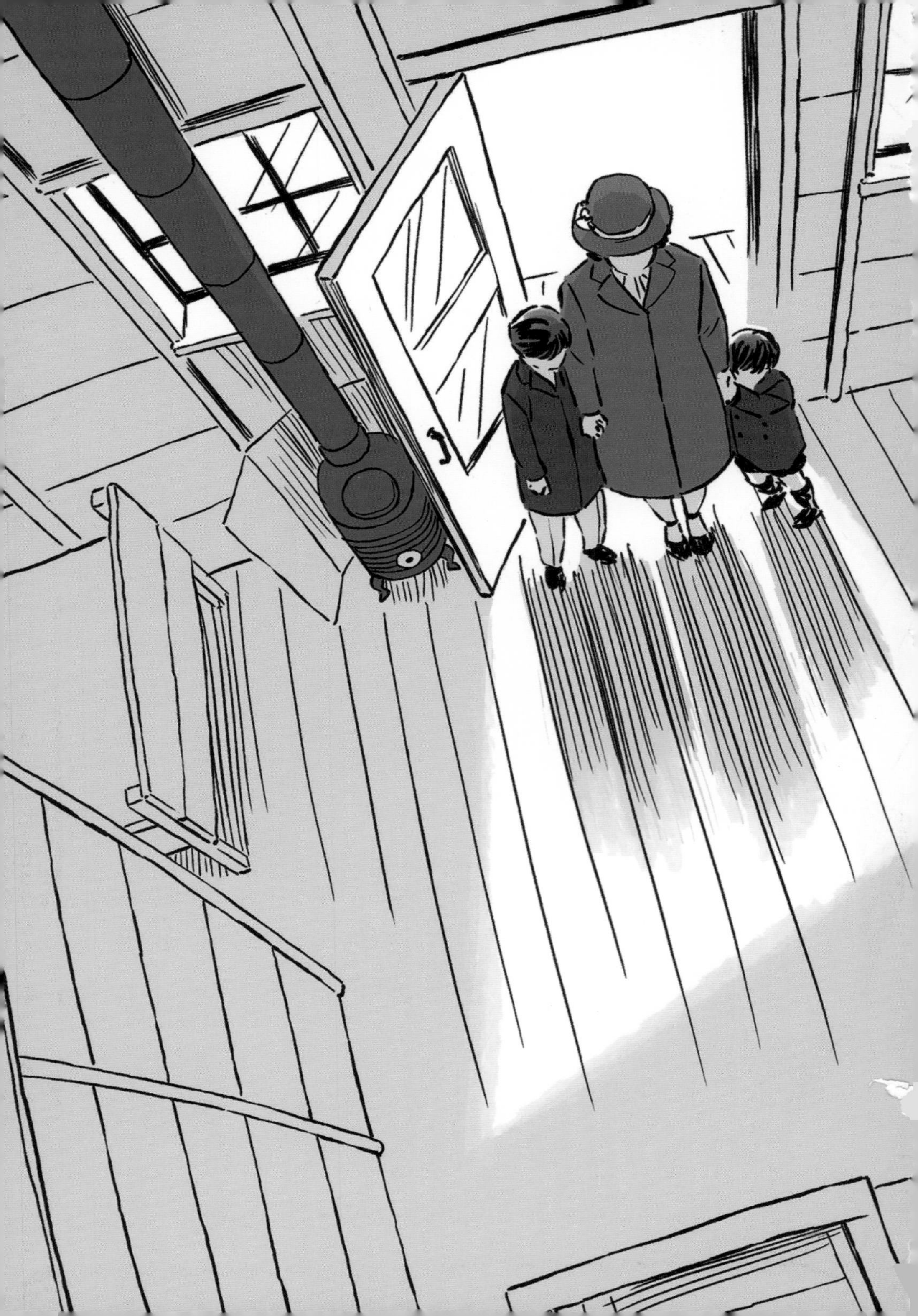